PRAISE

"What a relief it is to see an adolescent song that does not partake of sensational rhetorical exceptionalism of some sort—speak like Twain, Salinger's Holden's Tourette's—for its effect. A crime common if not endemic to the form, of which I am guilty. *Venice Beach* portrays a sad tough boyhood, not reaching for cuddly surrealism. The story is compelling for what in it feels completely true, and not pushed or forced."

—Padgett Powell, author of *Edisto, The Interrogative Mood*, and *Indigo*

"Heartbreak, passion and mystery abound in this powerfully moving coming-of-age story that captures the crazy, vibrant essence of pre-gentrified Venice, a place that pulsed with creative energy. *Venice Beach* in 1968 proves to be the perfect place for a troubled young runaway to discover who he is and what his life is all about; a transformative personal journey that is powerful, heartbreaking, and ultimately hopeful."

—John O'Kane, author of *Venice, CA: A City State of Mind, A Venice Quintet*, and *Jukebox Confessionals*

"Despite the sadness that marks Moon's journey—or perhaps because of it—this book is a true delight to read. Moon's story is in many ways timeless, for it brings to life not only the joys and struggles many young people experienced in the late 1960s, but the joys and struggles they continue to experience today."

—Sebastian Barajas, Department of Childhood Studies, Rutgers University

"After he runs from his secret-wracked and violent family, this searchingly honest novel takes a young teenage boy — and us with him — through urban homelessness, emergency youth care, drug addiction and finally the precarious, risky chance at a cobbled-together but genuine family. You won't forget *Venice Beach*."

—Doug Wilhelm, author of
Street of Storytellers and *The Revealers*

"*Venice Beach* is written with easy, unpretentious prose that lets shine through the authenticity of the young narrator's voice, a teen runaway who, in an attempt to reclaim and redefine his present from his brutal past, has renamed himself after his favorite celestial body. As the moon in the night sky allows us to hold the light when we are in the dark, Moon, the boy, reminds us, as he navigates the unpredictable, and often malevolent impulses of humanity, of the indomitable resilience and essential life-giving power of holding onto hope."

—Ian Chorão, author of *Bruiser*

"*Venice Beach* explores the intense emotions and experiences of a runaway teenage boy trying to understand and overcome a tragic family life as he makes his way into an early adulthood. In a narrative that is at times sad, at times funny, at times scary, and always interesting, Moon takes us on a rich and realistic coming-of-age journey that keeps us simultaneously wanting to know what comes next and hoping the story doesn't come to an end."

—Solange Ribeiro, Chief Academic Officer and Dean,
Adler Graduate School of Psychology

VENICE BEACH

VENICE
BEACH
A Novel

William Mark Habeeb

Rootstock Publishing
Montpelier, VT

First Printing: 2021

Venice Beach Copyright © 2021 William Mark Habeeb

All Rights Reserved.

Release Date: August 17, 2021
Softcover ISBN:978-1-57869-061-9
eBook ISBN: 978-1-57869-062-6

LCCN: 2021907131

Published by Rootstock Publishing
an imprint of Multicultural Media, Inc.
27 Main Street, Suite 6
Montpelier, VT 05602 USA

www.rootstockpublishing.com

info@rootstockpublishing.com

For permissions or to schedule an author interview, contact the author at whabeeb@hotmail.com.

Interior and Cover design by Eddie Vincent ENC Graphic Services (ed.vincent@encirclepub.com)

Cover art by Robert L. Huffstutter

Author Photograph by Noah E. Habeeb

Printed in the USA

"Every human existence is a life in search of a narrative."
–Richard Kearney, *On Stories*

THEN

I DECIDED MY NEW NAME WOULD be Moon.

When I left home, I also left the name I was called for the first thirteen years of my life and had no intention of choosing a new one. My old name was a label attached to a person I no longer wanted to be, a person stuck in a life I no longer could bear, a person who had been labeled all sorts of things by the people around me.

Loser, faggot, pussy, weirdo. My name was just another label I grew to detest, and I didn't feel the need for a new one. A nameless existence would be easier, I thought. One less label.

Renata changed my mind.

Having a name makes it easier to engage with other people, she said. I would like to be able to call you something when we have our sessions. And you can choose whatever new name you want.

Engaging with other people never had made my list of favorites, but I wanted to make Renata happy.

The moon and I had a lot in common: Bullied by meteors and space junk, the moon carried scars and bruises, and people said stupid and mean things about the moon—that it was made of cheese, and cows could jump over it, and it turned people into werewolves. But the moon wasn't affected by its tormentors; it just kept cycling through its phases, reflecting the sun's light and shining it back down on us.

Without the sun's light the moon would be invisible, but that didn't make me think less of the moon. In fact, I envied it. The moon had

1

something that shone light on it, allowing it to be seen. There was no light shining on me, a moon without a sun, invisible, drifting in darkness.

I would sit in the backyard and stare at the moon for hours, even when it was just a sliver, even on frigid winter nights. If I stared at the moon long enough my mind would go quiet and I would stop thinking all those things I was usually thinking. It's a good thing to stop thinking every now and then. Thinking is a highly overrated human function. It causes lots of problems.

I was horrified when I learned that NASA planned to send astronauts to the moon and infect it with members of our species.

What do you want? For the goddamned commies to get there first? my father said when I declared my opposition to NASA's plans. They'll get all the minerals and stuff and before long we'll all be speaking Russian, he said. Is that what you want?

Well, no, I didn't want communists walking around on the moon and I didn't want to learn Russian. I just wanted everybody to leave the moon alone.

My name wasn't the only thing I wanted to shed when I left home. My life to that point was like a cassette tape filled with grating music. I wanted to erase that tape, that life, and make a new recording. It would be my recording, my life's music. I envied amnesiacs. They don't have to work at erasing their tapes and forgetting their miserable lives.

Mind you, I wanted to erase the first thirteen years of my life, not do away with my biological organism, the way Jimmy Hollingsworth did when he atomized his head with his stepfather's twelve-gauge shotgun. The principal called a school assembly and announced that Jimmy had died in a terrible accident, as if you could accidentally stick a shotgun barrel in your mouth and then accidently pull the trigger with your big toe.

Kids aren't stupid; we all knew what really happened.

Like me, Jimmy Hollingsworth was a small boy. He was buck-toothed, jittery, had a high-pitched giggly laugh, and chewed his nails so the tips of his fingers looked raw. Jimmy never talked to anyone at school except me, probably because I also didn't have any friends. I would rather draw or read books about outer space and the oceans, or sit by the creek watching the water gurgle by, than play sports or make-believe war.

Jimmy wanted to be my friend. He would sit with me in the cafeteria every day and always invited me to come over to his house after school. The two of us, sitting alone, were an irresistible target for the other boys, who would walk by and say, Hi, girls! and then spit in our food.

We both were bullied for sport by the bigger boys, but I had an ignitable temper and after a point would fight back—and got the bloody noses to prove it. Jimmy cowered at being bullied and would slink down the hallways from class to class.

I would have preferred if Jimmy had sat elsewhere. We didn't have much in common and Jimmy wasn't very bright. But we both liked superhero comic books, and he always asked to see the pictures I drew.

I spent many hours drawing, usually during class. I would draw real and imagined celestial objects, rocket ships, deep sea creatures and space aliens, and I invented comic book characters. Jimmy especially liked Racoon Man and his sidekick Tadpole Boy. I didn't write stories about them, I just drew them doing various things like punching bad guys, most of whom resembled my father or Uncle Arnie.

I could turn anybody into a cartoon by distorting their features. Most people were pretty funny looking to begin with, and even more so if you distorted their features. It made scary people less scary if I turned them into cartoons, so I drew cartoons of my father and my older brother Jake and the bullies at school and Uncle Arnie and the old woman who lived next door and glared at me even when I was in my own yard.

When I was little, Jake told me she was a witch and he threatened to sell me to her so she could cook me for dinner. I believed him because she did look the part. He told me that she had nabbed and eaten the McCuthers kids, which is why they had disappeared from our neighborhood. Jake described in detail how she had cooked each of them. The McCuthers in fact had moved to Texas, but I didn't learn this until years later.

When my father heard that Jimmy had shot himself, he shook his head and mumbled, What a loser.

My mother said, Hush, Larry. What an awful thing to say. Think what his poor mother's going through. She took another sip from the glass of vodka that over the past several years had become virtually glued to her hand.

Well, she shouldn't have raised a loser, my father retorted with a self-congratulatory snort, the way he did after making what he thought was a clever or witty observation.

Jake made the sound of a shotgun blast—kapow!—and then he and my father snickered. Jake said, I heard Hollingsworth was a fucking faggot.

In that case, no great loss, one less faggot in the world, my father said. Mom refilled her glass with shaky hands. I went into the backyard with my dog Sirius and sat under the sycamore tree waiting for the evening glow to fade out and the night sky to appear.

Jimmy was the only kid at school who talked to me and wanted to be my friend, so I felt a eulogy was in order. I looked up at the infinite universe and said, See ya later, Jimmy. But I didn't really believe anyone would ever see him again.

I'm sorry, Jimmy, I added, and a few tears coursed down my face. Sirius licked my hand and rested his head on my lap. He always understood what I was feeling even before I did.

Sirius was a mutt, a dog stew with maybe a dash of wolf thrown in for flavor. He was small enough to share my bed but not so small that he couldn't bare his teeth and stare down bigger dogs. This made Sirius more of a hero to me than a pet. I would've given anything to have his intimidating growl.

I talked to him more than I talked to any human being and I'm pretty sure he understood every word I said. He was a damn smart dog and my only true friend. No one else in the house had paid Sirius much attention so he became my dog. This doomed his relationship with Jake, who hated Sirius as much as he hated me.

My father didn't like small creatures of any type and grumbled about how much it cost to feed Sirius, as if a can of dog food and some table scraps were going to bankrupt us. I never heard my father complain about the cost of feeding me, but I wouldn't have been surprised if he did. Sirius would growl and bark whenever my father hit me.

My mother had once loved Sirius. When he was a puppy, she would help me bathe him in the metal tub in the backyard; we'd laugh when he splashed soapy water all over us. But when I was eight years old my mother abruptly changed into a different person and no longer seemed to care about much of anything so long as there was booze in the cabinet and a pack of cigarettes on the counter.

She still looked like my mother on the outside but there was a different person inside. I didn't know what had happened or where my old mother had gone, but I missed her terribly. By the time I turned thirteen, I knew she never was coming back and I never would find my sun as long as I lived in that house, in that family, in that life.

When my dad murdered Sirius, he killed all the love that was left in my life.

So, on a drizzly spring day in 1968, I fled. I sat by the window of the Greyhound bus as it pulled out of town, holding my rucksack tightly in my arms, but in my imagination, I was on a spaceship tearing free of Earth's gravity to begin a voyage in search of a sun.

When kids run away from home, people try to find them and send them back. It apparently never occurs to them that kids run away for a reason, and because running away is difficult and scary that reason must be a damn good one.

I don't know, maybe some kids who run away do want to go back home after making a point like scaring their parents or crying out for help or whatever. But I wasn't trying to make a point or cry for help. And if no one knew my old name or where I was from, they couldn't send me back.

When I got to California I revealed nothing about my origins, to the immense frustration of the police officer at the hospital who grilled me as if I were a suspected serial killer instead of a thirteen-year-old escaping from hell.

He promised that he wouldn't force me to go home if I gave him my parents' telephone number. I just want to call them and let them know that you're okay, he said.

Well, I may have been young and inexperienced with the ways of the world, but I wasn't an idiot, so I just shook my head.

He then started threatening me with juvenile prison and reform school and other horrors. I stared at the tile floor and thought how the policeman looked a lot like Curly from the Three Stooges, and how could anyone take Curly seriously? I tried hard not to laugh.

When the policeman finally gave up and dumped me at the youth shelter in Venice, I figured they too would try and send me back home. But then I met Renata, and she seemed to easily understand why I had discarded my old name and why creating a new life was a very different thing from simply fleeing an old life.

And that's why I came to love her.

I didn't encounter the policeman or arrive at the shelter right away. I spent several weeks living on the streets of Los Angeles, after sitting on buses for three days and spending four hours in the St. Louis bus depot waiting for a connection, during which time my bladder nearly exploded before I gathered the courage to enter the men's restroom, which was inhabited by seedy characters and smelled like raw sewage mixed with cigarette smoke. I never pissed so fast in my life.

I decided to go to California because it was far away from my home and on television shows it seemed like people always were happy there and the days permanently sunny. It seemed like a good place to find a sun, and it had an ocean, too. But sometimes I think that there were other things luring me there, and to Venice in particular, things I could not have known at the time. Things that may not even be knowable.

I didn't know what to do when I got to California. I had planned only the running away part—which I did quite well, thank you very much—and hadn't thought about what would happen when I emerged from that Greyhound spaceship.

I'm going to go to California and start my life over, I said to myself, as if there would be a huge banner at the bus station in Los Angeles saying, Welcome to California! Free Food and Housing for All Runaways!

The more unbearable my life had become, the more desperate became my urge to flee. If I really had thought about being all alone in a huge city, I might have scared myself out of running away. So, in order for me to carry out the first step, my mind prevented me from thinking about the consequences. Which shows that you can't really trust your mind because you never know what it's up to. The mind is a sneaky little bastard.

Even had I thought about it, I never would have been prepared for what I saw on the streets of Los Angeles, which I never would have seen on the streets of my hometown: lots of people who were not white, lots of hippies, lots of bums, and lots of aimless teenagers, especially along Hollywood and Sunset Boulevards. I don't remember how I found my way to that part of town; it was like a magnet for the adrift and bereft.

No one bothered me much, not even the other teenagers, which was a great relief after middle school. But middle school is a holding pen for pubescent kids not ready to be unleashed into the real world. The kids on Hollywood and Sunset were already in the real world; they didn't need to mess with me.

I still would get nervous if I saw a group of boys together—predatory teens travel in packs—and I would often duck inside a store before they saw me.

Most of the bums were so drunk or insane that they posed no danger, although I did get into a tussle with a scruffy man of indeterminate age who tried to pull my rucksack off my back. He was stumbling drunkenly but was strong, and I had to keep twisting in spirals to free myself. Passersby kept passing by.

The hippies were harmless. They would ask me for money—can you share some bread, little cat?—but I had no bread to share, and they weren't persistent. I did share their fear of the police.

I had thought dodging the police would be a challenge because they always taught us in school the police were there to help you and take you by the hand and lead you home if you got lost, the last thing I wanted. But the police didn't seem to care about us kids. Maybe they knew we weren't lost.

Or maybe they had more fun harassing hippies and older teenagers; they sometimes rounded them up for no apparent reason and stuffed them into police vans. I was too young, with hair too short to draw attention; I could walk right past a police officer and he wouldn't even look at me.

I usually liked being alone—away from my father and Jake and the bullies at school and the empty vessel that my mother had become—but those weeks in Los Angeles were a different kind of alone. I wasn't alone in my room or the backyard or down by the creek. I was alone in the universe, a vastly bigger stage.

No one at home knew where I was; and no one in Los Angeles knew who I was. And after the first week, I too began to wonder where and who I was.

There wasn't much to think about other than primal needs: food, water, shelter, safety. I was becoming feral. During the days I roamed side streets, sat on bus stop benches and watched people go by, camped out in playgrounds or parks and drew pictures, nursed soft drinks in fast food restaurants. I read every free pamphlet or newspaper I could get my hands on and spent hours in the safe confines of the public library on Sunset trying to look like a schoolboy doing homework.

I spent an entire day in a cemetery sitting under a shade tree between two tombstones reading a long book on Hindu gods that had been handed to me by some bald guys in orange robes who were chanting and dancing on the sidewalk.

I talked to Sirius—or rather, to his ghost; I could see him even though I knew no one else could. He always was with me at night, when the sidewalks teemed with drunks and bums, and police cars whizzed by with sirens screaming. Sometimes people would stare at me as I talked to my dead dog. They probably wondered how someone so young could already be so crazy.

Those people eventually looked away. No one wants to deal with crazy people, even if they're crazy kids. We're all just a few steps away from the nut house and we don't like to be reminded of that.

Finding a place to sleep at night was my biggest challenge. With a 10:00 pm curfew for young people, I had to be out of sight. The cemetery would have been perfect except the idea of being alone in there all night creeped me. Because I was small, I could squeeze into tight places and stay out of sight, but these were usually disgusting places—between dumpsters, in the alley doorways of abandoned buildings, places like that.

By day I could relieve myself in fast food restaurants or gas stations, but if the urge struck at night I had to go alfresco. One night I had a bout of diarrhea but of course no toilet paper, so I wiped my ass with my only pair of socks and left them in the tall weeds behind a liquor store.

My life those first weeks was a series of random motions with no plot or meaning, other than responding to primal needs. I lost track of sunrises and sunsets, which were the only markers of time. I was unsure whether I actually existed or was just an observer of existence; whether I was dreaming or was being dreamt. I sliced my arm one night with a shard from a broken bottle just to make sure I bled, to make sure I was still alive, to make sure I could still feel something.

It bled all right, but I didn't feel much. I lay on my side under the loading dock behind a grocery store, my bleeding arm outstretched, my rucksack under my head, and saw a weed that was growing between a tight crack in the asphalt. It sported a perfect little blue flower. It seemed happy, that flower, even though it lived in a crack in the asphalt under a loading dock.

9

I wondered how it survived, why it survived, why it felt compelled to live and be beautiful in such an ugly situation. I stared at the weed and its little flower and cried. I fell asleep right there, dried blood covering my arm and hand. I awoke near dawn to see a humongous rat about twelve inches from my nose right next to the little weed. He was devouring a piece of rotting lettuce while side-eying me, suspicious. I lay perfectly still, frozen by horror and fascination, and watched him eat.

I wouldn't have found my way to the shelter, and to Renata, had it not been for Max, so I suppose I owe him a debt of gratitude. I was sitting on a bus stop bench on Hollywood, watching cars go by and contemplating whether I ever could become like that weed with its little blue flower. I didn't notice the man sitting at the other end of the bench until he spoke.

What's up today, little fellow?

I ignored him. I had not conversed with another human since I left home—nor had anyone spoken to me, other than a few drunks and crazy people, but they may have been speaking to their hallucinations.

The man sidled a bit closer, but I kept ignoring him. I wanted to walk away but it felt too good to be off my blistered feet, made worse by going sockless in sneakers that were falling apart. The little toe on my left foot poked through my shoe. I hoped the man's bus would arrive soon.

You hungry? he asked, after several failed conversation-starters about the weather and the traffic. Now he was raising the ante.

My cash—the money I had taken from under Jake's mattress, my father's underwear drawer, and the not-so-secret stash in the kitchen pantry—had depleted. All I had eaten the day before was an anemic square-shaped hamburger, a candy bar I pilfered from a convenience store, and an orange I found on the sidewalk. That rat I'd awakened to had eaten better.

Well, I'm starved, the man said. Ever eat at this place? He pointed over his shoulder to a diner behind the bus stop. They got some good breakfast deals—pancakes, bacon, sausages and eggs.

My mouth started watering.

Tell you what, why don't you and me go in there and get something to eat? C'mon, aren't you hungry? And it's on me. I'm Max, by the way. He extended his hand, which I didn't take. But I did look at him for the first time.

He was tall and solid. His wavy black hair was combed straight back. He was clean-shaven and wore wire-rimmed glasses with dark clip-ons that he had flipped up so I could see his brown eyes. His blue seersucker jacket sported a few coffee stains, and the top two buttons of his white shirt were unbuttoned; a large gold cross hung around his neck, nestled in his black chest hair.

His gray pants descended only to mid-shin, exposing his brown loafers and white athletic socks. He looked like a lot of the men back home looked when they wanted to dress up.

Hey, how often do you get an offer for a free breakfast? C'mon, I hate to eat alone—you gonna join me? Max said. He had a warm smile and straight white teeth and his eyes looked friendly, and I was famished.

We sat at a two-person booth near the window. A waitress emptied the dirty ashtray, slapped a damp cloth across the table, and handed us menus.

So, you been living on the streets for long? Max asked.

I didn't like that he had so easily pegged my status. I hid behind the big floppy menu. Don't worry, he said, I ain't a cop or nothing. I lived on the streets myself when I was young, so I recognize a fellow traveler.

Max ordered scrambled eggs and a beer. I ordered pancakes, uttering my first words. Give him some bacon and sausage too, honey, Max said to the waitress. He needs some meat on those skinny bones.

Max lit a cigarette, gazed out the window for a moment, then leaned forward and looked at me as if he were about to share an important secret.

So, how you doing for money, kid? Got enough to get by out there? Got a safe place to sleep at night?

I've got money, I said, referring to the six dollars and change in my pants pocket, which was all I had left.

Look, little buddy, Max said, I'm only asking because my church might be able help you out—no questions asked, we don't pry into your circumstances. And we don't work with the police—we answer to a higher authority.

He fingered the cross around his neck.

We run a program called Luke 18:16—that's the verse where Jesus says, Let the children come to me. And that's what we do. We get you some work and some money, a place to sleep and take a hot shower. We've helped lots of kids out there. It's not easy to survive in this town, believe you me. But you know, we just follow Jesus's example.

Our food arrived and I plowed into my pancakes while Max fiddled with his eggs. After a few minutes he tried again: So, what do you say? Want some work, a place to sleep, some hot meals?

I wiped pancake syrup from my lips. What kind of work? I asked, trying to sound nonchalant, as if I were weighing multiple job offers.

Just some chores around our church. Keeping the grounds looking nice, cleaning the sanctuary, doing some touch-up painting and stuff. There's always something needs doing. And we'll put you up in a dormitory we have not far from here where you can shower and sleep. Look, kid, no one else is going help you out there. God's the only one who really cares. And Jesus.

I did need money. I was filthy and had not slept indoors in weeks. I wasn't into God but if a church was willing to help me, why should I refuse? Grandma used to come by the house every Sunday and take me to church, which was deathly boring, and sitting on those hard pews for an hour made my ass ache.

She never took Jake, but he was older so maybe he refused to go. Afterwards she would buy me ice cream and say things like, my grandson is such a good Christian boy, and Jesus must be so proud of my grandson. Always in the third person as if I weren't there.

Maybe God now was rewarding me for all those boring Sundays with Grandma. Max's offer was the first thing that had happened to me that might halt my steady descent into whatever it was I was descending toward—insanity, dying in my sleep next to a dumpster, being devoured by a huge rat; my mind had come up with many possibilities.

Max paid the check and we left the diner. He chattered the whole time as we walked along Hollywood Boulevard—about Jesus and the church and the dangers of living on the streets and all the kids he had saved. I didn't say much but it was kind of nice to have company. But, for some reason I started thinking about Uncle Arnie.

Not really thoughts, exactly, more like images, like flashbacks.

We turned off Hollywood and after several blocks came to an old brick building with a few broken windows, rusted metal fire escape stairs, and a windowless green metal front door. The faint sound of a radio was coming from somewhere inside. It did not look very church-like. Next door was an auto repair shop.

This is where the church keeps rooms for the kids we help, Max said. I'll take you to the church later but let's get you settled first. He flashed his nice warm smile again, a stark contrast to the surroundings.

My encounter with Max had not felt completely right to me from the beginning, but as he talked during breakfast the ratio of right feeling to wrong feeling had shifted slightly toward right. But now Max wanted me to enter a derelict building with him. The ratio was shifting rapidly to wrong. Images of Uncle Arnie lingered; my body tensed.

Um . . . you know, maybe I'll just try living on my own a little bit longer, I said, and took a few steps away from Max.

He reached over and gripped my arm tightly, clearly with no intention of letting go. Look kiddo, he said softly, I know you're confused, but trust me—I'm going to help you. Now come on inside, there's some people I want you to meet.

Max's grip tightened, but with his other hand he patted my shoulder affectionately. My heart pounded as if it were trying to break out of my chest and escape.

Max guided me toward the door. It seemed that the nation's second largest city had suddenly become empty, and if I yelled no one would hear me except Max. I couldn't break his grip and run for it. Max opened the green metal door with a key and pulled me in; the door clanged shut behind us.

Max slightly eased his grip on my arm and still rested his other hand gently on my shoulder. He led me up three flights of stairs and down the length of a dimly lit hallway that smelled of rotting garbage. Behind one door I heard two men arguing in a foreign language and behind another the hard splatter of a shower. Max opened the last door at the end of the hall.

Bright sunlight streamed in like spotlights through two small windows and I had to shield my eyes to see what was there. It wasn't much: two mattresses on the floor, a wooden table holding a television set, a small fan under the table that was oscillating slowly, a few T-shirts and empty pizza boxes scattered on the floor, and two teenage boys in their underwear.

They were sitting cross-legged next to each other on one of the mattresses, watching a game show on the television, which was fluctuating between a wiggly picture and pure snow. A large open bag of potato chips lay between them.

You said you were going to fix the TV, Max, one of the boys said as soon as we walked in; he had a husky voice, I guessed he was at least sixteen. And who's the dwarf?

I assumed he was referring to me.

This is your new roommate . . . what's your name, buddy? Max asked me.

I didn't reply.

OK, maybe he'll tell you guys his name, Max said. But he's a good kid and he's going to be staying here, so make room. And kid, why don't you take a shower, he said to me. We like cleanliness around here. It's next to godliness.

What about the TV, Max? said the second boy.

I'll take care of it, I told you already. I've got to run. I'll be back in a while. Keep an eye on your new friend, Max said as he closed the door behind him.

The older boy had a case of volcanic acne; he was smoking a small, hand-rolled cigarette. The other boy, who was smaller and younger but was trying to get a mustache going, grabbed a fistful of chips, half of which fell onto the mattress as he stuffed them in his mouth.

I took off my rucksack and stepped into the bathroom. The tub was badly stained, the enamel cracked. The toilet was missing its seat and the sides of the bowl were caked with dried shit. The bathroom door had no doorknob and kept drifting open. I peed and flushed but there didn't appear to be much water in the tank.

Aren't you going to shower? the older boy asked.

Maybe later, I said, and sat down on the unoccupied mattress. It sagged even under my light weight.

What's your name, kid? the younger boy asked.

I shrugged.

You don't know your own name? Are you a retard or something?

So, what are these jobs we're supposed to do? I said. And how much do they pay us?

The ratio now had shifted so far toward wrong that I'm not sure why I even asked that question, why I still accepted Max's line, why I thought that two guys in their underwear smoking and swearing were somehow involved in a church youth program. Hope dies hard.

They looked at each other and started laughing. Hope died.

Are you kidding me, man? The jobs? Did Max pull that Jesus stuff on you? That's fucking hilarious, said the older boy.

Yeah, coughed the younger boy, trying to clear his airway of chips. The only jobs you'll be doing are blow jobs. And as for your pay, see the roof over your head? Consider yourself paid.

And the food, the older boy added, stuffing some chips into his mouth. You get food. And dope. And a place to shit. But hey, it's better than sleeping on the street. Trust me.

I fell back on the mattress and stared at the roof over my head. In the middle of the ceiling was a dome light with a weak lightbulb. The bottom of the frosted glass dome was filled with bug carcasses. They had managed to get inside, perhaps in search of their sun, but then were trapped and couldn't get out. I felt bad for them; they must have been scared, if bugs can feel fear.

The last decision I'd made in my life was to run away from home. Since I had arrived in Los Angeles nothing in my life had been the result of my decisions. Things just happened or they didn't happen, I had nothing to do with it. Was this just another thing happening? And was it a good thing? I was essentially out of money and I had not showered or slept indoors in weeks. And whatever things these guys had to do to survive, it was obvious that they had, indeed, survived.

I stood up and faced the door, rucksack on my back.

The older boy rose from the mattress and stood between me and the door. He was a good five inches taller than me and much more muscular. Look, he said, don't be an idiot, kid. You're not going to survive out there. You can run back home if you want, wherever the hell your home is. I guess it depends on how bad your home is. Personally, I'd rather be here. Shit, I'd rather be dead. Look, if you get really stoned first, it's not so bad. There are some perverted fuckers out there, but we'll look out for you, and Max will deal with anybody who, like, really hurts you.

I slowly sat back down on the mattress and he returned to his perch in front of the television. Give me a toke, he said to the other boy, and took a drag on what was left of the cigarette.

Uncle Arnie, my father's brother, would stay with us whenever his wife kicked him out of the house, which was frequently. He was supposed to sleep in the basement but around the time I turned ten he started coming to my bedroom during the night, the stench of beer and tobacco on his breath as he squeezed next to me. He would start rubbing my stomach with his calloused hands and then moved farther south.

I would close my eyes tightly and try to will myself back to sleep, so my memories were mostly sensations—of his weight on top of me, of his fingers groping and probing, of my arms and legs being moved and twisted like I was a rag doll. Sometimes he put his hand over my mouth, but he didn't need to because I was silent, my whole being reduced to a single moot point in space. In the morning he was gone, but I was sore and sometimes there was blood on the sheets.

I never told my mother about it, but she had checked out of life by the time it all started, and I didn't believe she would do anything. I didn't dare say anything to my father; I couldn't imagine him defending me against a pack of rabid wolves, much less against his brother.

Sometimes when Uncle Arnie came over, I would sneak a few swigs from my mother's vodka bottle before bedtime—it made her numb, I thought, maybe it would work for me. It helped a few times but only because I drank so much that as soon as Uncle Arnie lay on top of me, I threw up and I guess vomit was a turn-off for him because he swore and crawled off me.

So I had more job experience than those boys imagined. I knew how not to scream, how to focus my mind on anything other than what was being done to me, how not to tell anyone about it.

I had left home in order to find my sun, I thought, and this is where my search would end. I felt like the punch line of a cosmic joke.

It was still better than being a punching bag for my father and watching my mother slowly decompose in front of my eyes. And I wouldn't be alone anymore, there would be some people in my life—even if they were Max and the two boys on the other mattress. The older boy, at least, didn't seem too bad, and Max certainly wouldn't want to send me back home or call my parents.

And I was so tired.

I pulled my sketchbook and pen out of the rucksack and started drawing, even though my hands were shaking. I filled a page with various geometric shapes—circles and triangles and rectangles, eternal shapes, things in perfect symmetry, things that were complete in themselves. After about fifteen minutes I stood up.

What are you doing, said the older boy. He rose unsteadily. They had been smoking so much, the room was as hazy as the rest of Los Angeles.

I'm going to take a shower, I said without making eye contact.

Good idea—no offense, but you stink to high heaven, said the younger boy. When you're clean, you can come out here and audition your job skills, he added. He slipped off his jockeys and threw them in my direction then lay back naked on the mattress.

The older boy punched him hard in the shoulder and said, Leave the kid alone, I'm sure he's been through enough shit already. He lit another cigarette and inhaled deeply. Go on, kid, he said to me. Take a long shower, I'm sure it's been a while.

I went into the bathroom and closed the door as much as it would close. I turned the shower on all the way; it sputtered and spit but eventually came out full force. The pipes groaned. As I started to undress, I caught my image in the mirror above the sink. The mirror was stained and corroded and had so many cracks, my face looked shattered, almost unrecognizable.

Steam from the shower began condensing on the mirror and I watched as my face slowly disappeared. I stopped undressing. This journey, this last-gasp attempt at life, was about finding my sun so that I could see myself and be seen. I knew that wouldn't happen in this apartment. I also knew it wouldn't happen back on the streets. But if I was going to end the journey, I thought, I would rather end it Jimmy's way, quickly and on my terms.

I peeked through the hole where the doorknob had been; both boys were on their backs, passing the cigarette back and forth. I put my shirt back on, slipped on my rucksack and slowly opened the bathroom door hoping that its squeaky hinges would be drowned out by the shower. I took a deep breath, then charged to the apartment door. I flung it open and took off down the hall faster than I ever had run before, my rucksack flopping up and down on my back.

Hey! Come back here! one of the boys yelled. I could hear two sets of feet coming after me down the hall, but I had a good head start. I entered the stairwell and hurtled down, two steps at a time.

The boys stopped their chase. The older one yelled down the stairwell, You're going to die on the streets, kid. You're making a big mistake.

I reached the ground floor, turned out of the stairwell toward the front door, and ran smack into Max. He cursed and grunted and we both fell. We looked at each other for a split second, then I jumped up and ran out the door.

Hold on! Max yelled.

I ran toward Hollywood Boulevard where there would be people and traffic. I could hear Max behind me. It was several blocks to Hollywood and there was no way I could outrun him. He had much longer legs and, despite my initial head start, he was closing in. I caught a glimpse of a large black crow on the edge of the sidewalk, raising its wings to take off as I raced by.

Shit! Fucking bird! Max yelled.

I looked over my shoulder; the crow had flown right into Max's head. Max was shielding his face with his arms. He stumbled and fell to the sidewalk. I reached the corner of Hollywood and just kept running, right into the busy intersection. I was running not just from Max but from everything.

I had no goal, no destination, no purpose. It was pure flight. And I would have kept running had I not collided at full speed into the side of a car driving across my path. I bounced off like a rubber ball and landed on my back. Cars screeched to a stop to keep from running over me. I couldn't breathe. As I blacked out, I was pretty sure I was dying. But I wasn't frightened; I felt a sense of relief, like a bad movie finally had come to an end.

When I came to, faces were peering at me from above. I tried to sit up, but someone gently pushed my shoulders back down and said, you need to lie still, sonny.

I have to go, I whispered with difficulty; my chest hurt too much to speak normally. Every breath felt like I was inhaling a cinderblock.

Calm down, sonny, you need to stay still.

I twisted my head around and saw Max standing on the sidewalk, doubled over to catch his breath. I looked at the person who was holding me down. It was a policeman. I had collided with a police car; its lights were flashing.

I looked back, but Max had disappeared. Sirius's ghost licked my hand and face.

I was taken by ambulance to a hospital where I was poked and X-rayed and declared unhurt except for bruised ribs, which felt like crushed ribs, but who was I to argue with doctors.

I wouldn't give the hospital my name or address or any other information, so they called in the police and I was grilled by that officer who looked like Curly. Before saying a word to me he rifled through my rucksack looking for drugs. When he finally accepted that I wasn't going to tell him anything despite his threats, he checked me out of the hospital and put me in the back of his car.

He drove to a police station where I assumed I would be tortured until I revealed my name and origins. I tried to steel myself for the ordeal, but I was so exhausted and in such pain, I feared I would break. But all they did was take my fingerprints and order me to sit on a wooden bench in a hallway, where for several hours I tried to breathe as shallowly as possible. Every few minutes I would impulsively take a deep breath which caused such pain that I moaned loudly on the exhale.

I watched officers escort handcuffed men and a few women down the hall and through a set of double doors. One of the men, a young guy with shoulder-length hair and no shirt or shoes, looked at me and yelled, Fuck the Man, little dude. Fuck the Man.

Around midnight an officer walked up to me, snapped his fingers and said, Up, right now. He took me by the arm, and we walked back through the station and out the front door. He pulled me along at such a rapid pace, it was like being dragged; I had to take short, staccato breaths but it still hurt. He put me in the back of a patrol car and we drove off. He didn't utter a word to me, but his radio crackled the whole time.

We stopped in front of a two-story white building in a neighborhood of small run-down houses. The officer led me up the front steps; I wondered why there were no bars on the windows of this jail. It was dark inside except for one dimly lit room near the front door. A small sign on the door said Venice Beach Youth Crisis Center.

The officer rang the bell and a few minutes later a Black man with a large Afro opened the door. He yawned, rubbed his eyes, and scratched his chest through his unbuttoned denim shirt.

Got one for you, if you've got room, said the officer. No drugs but he's uncooperative. He was hanging out on Hollywood, got into some kind of ruckus. That's all I know. They're getting younger and younger out there.

I was scared of Black people and had never actually spoken to one. Everyone in my neighborhood back home was white. My father said that all Black men were would-be killers and rapists and were too lazy to work, although my dad worked a steady job only when money got low, and then only until he got fired, laid-off, or quit. My father pontificated about lots of things he didn't know much about. Not that I did know about them, but I knew he sure didn't.

My father was like the planet Jupiter, which is composed mostly of hot gasses with only a small solid core. I once drew a cartoon character that had my father's head—complete with his crew cut and the scary Fu Manchu mustache he wore at the time—and a fat round body that looked like Jupiter, complete with Jupiter's big oval red spot. I left it on the kitchen table and my father saw it.

I'm sure he knew it was him because of the crew cut and mustache, but he acted like he didn't. What the fuck is this trash, he said, and wadded it up and threw it on the floor. Later that night, well into his second six-pack, he looked at me and slurred, You're a useless little pecker-head.

I don't think he liked the drawing.

So I didn't believe what my father said about Black people or anything else. Still, there I was face-to-face with a Black man with a large Afro just like the Black men I had seen on the television news who always seemed angry about things.

You need a place to sleep? the Black man asked through a yawn. I nodded. He leaned against the open door and motioned me in. You mighty small to be out there at this time of night. How old are you? He closed and locked the door.

Fifteen, I said.

Un-huh, he said. And I'm Snow fucking White. Now cut the bullshit—how old?

Thirteen, I confessed. I didn't want to admit to being so young, so naïve, so small and weak and helpless. But after that day, who was I fooling?

I had made two decisions that day—to go to Max's apartment, and to run from Max's apartment. I was now back in the realm where things just happened to me. I hoped this would not be a bad thing.

Well, the beds are full-up tonight, but we never turn anyone away, the Black man said. You can grab some sleep on a couch in the common room. The counselors will be here at seven and they'll sort you out.

He led me into a room with a large table surrounded with folding chairs, several sagging couches, a television set with rabbit-ear antennae, a ping pong table without a net, and some threadbare chairs. I selected a couch, took off my rucksack and sat down.

You hungry? Thirsty?

I shook my head, even though I was starving.

He started to walk out, then turned around. What's your name? he asked.

I don't have a name anymore, I replied, declaring my label-less existence.

He took it in stride: Well, I do—Maurice. I'll be in the office all night. Get some sleep if you can.

I couldn't fall asleep, despite being exhausted. My feet ached, my stomach growled, my mind raced. The large front window had a sill deep enough for me to fit in, if I sat sideways, so I jumped up, pulled my knees to my aching chest, and leaned against the glass pane. I felt snug and safe, like a roly-poly bug all balled up. Outside the window a flickering streetlight encircled in flying insects cast an erratic glow. The street was quiet, but I could hear the muffled hum of freeway traffic.

I looked off in the distance in hopes I might see the Pacific Ocean. If this place was called Venice Beach, I thought, the ocean must be nearby. But all I could see were small houses and low-rise buildings receding into the darkness. After all this time in Los Angeles, I still had not managed to stumble upon the largest body of water in the world.

Outer space and the oceans were my two obsessions, I suppose because they were the two worlds farthest removed from my world. By the time I was eight, I had read all the books on astronomy and oceanography in the public library, including the ones for adults, and by the time I was ten I had reread them. But until I ran away, I never had been more than fifty miles from home, so I knew about oceans only from books.

My favorite book, which I smuggled out of the library and kept under my mattress, had color photographs of the creatures that live in the ocean's greatest depths, under the greatest pressure. Viperfish with huge mouths and saber-like teeth, Vampire Squid from Hell that generate their own light, Stalked Toads with antennae and spiky scales, snake-like Gulper Eel that slither along the ocean bed and swallow their dinner whole.

I had no interest in the more beautiful fish in the ocean's shallower warm waters, the plump little fish with rainbow colors and silly little clown faces who dart about in their schools without a care in the world. I loved the ugly misfits who lived in the cold dark waters near the ocean's bottom.

They weren't really misfits: they fit in perfectly where they lived. They knew how to live in darkness. I was the misfit, stuck in a life that made no sense to me.

Fascinated with oceans, I was terrified of water. I didn't know how to swim, I never got in a swimming pool, and I panicked at the thought of having my head under water, even in the safe confines of the bathtub. I had nightmares about being under water. It wasn't so much a fear of drowning—I was capable of holding my breath—it was more a fear of being entombed in water.

Still, I longed to see the ocean, to feel it lapping at my feet, to wade out a wee bit and stand in the same water that was home to all those creatures living in darkness.

You can't spend hours reading about outer space and the oceans without becoming aware of your own insignificance, which was terrifying but also had an upside: If my life was insignificant, I figured, then so too were the lives of my father, my brother, Uncle Arnie, the bullies who tormented me at school, gym teachers, and all the others. At least I didn't suffer from delusions of significance.

I was talking in a quiet voice to Sirius, whose ghost was curled on the floor beneath the window, and I must have dozed off because suddenly it was morning and I heard voices coming from upstairs and creaking pipes and showers. The world was awake. I yawned and shifted my position to ease my throbbing ribs, but stayed up there in the windowsill where I could observe the world around me without being part of it, the way I liked.

The room soon filled with teenage boys and girls sitting in little clusters, eating donuts and drinking orange juice. None looked fully awake yet and none seemed to notice me. I was hungry but I didn't want to climb down from the windowsill. I searched again for the Pacific, now that it was light outside.

Good morning, she said.

The woman was thin, all arms and legs. She had reddish-brown hair that fell straight onto her shoulders. She was dressed casually— jeans, sandals, and a black T-shirt—so I didn't think she was a police officer or a doctor. She wasn't smiling but there was something gentle and kind in her expression. Freckled, she had green eyes, which I never had seen before, except on a neighbor's cat that Sirius had devoted his life to liquidating.

I normally avoided eye contact with people but the two emeralds above her nose were mesmerizing. She smelled like sweet berries, no doubt from the soap or shampoo she used. It was the nicest thing

I had smelled in a long time. She looked about the same age as my mother. I could see from her furrowed brow that she was assessing the situation. Of me. It felt good to be the object of her attention.

Maurice told me you arrived very late last night. Did you sleep?

I shook my head.

I'm Renata. What's your name?

Is the Pacific Ocean near here? I asked.

Yeah, it's about a mile away, but you can't see it from this window. You're facing north and it's due west. So, what's your name?

I don't have a name.

Renata pulled up a chair and sat down. Do you mean you can't recall your name?

No, that's not what I said. I know what my name used to be, but it's not my name anymore. I don't want a name. I don't need a name.

My ribs ached and I was exhausted. I didn't feel like talking.

I understand, Renata said, and nodded her head. But I didn't think she did.

Will you tell me where you're from?

No, I won't.

How old are you?

Thirteen or so, I said. I pried my eyes from hers and looked out the window again.

Why don't you want a name? I'd like to know about that.

Maybe I was loopy from lack of sleep, but it seemed to me at that moment this woman, Renata, really did want to know. For the past five years I had been pretty much mute—not on the inside, mind you, where I talked a lot, but my mother had been the only one on the outside who ever cared what I had to say or felt. And then she'd stopped caring.

Because I want to erase my old life and start over, I said, still looking out the window. I can't start a new life with my old name. I don't want to be the person who had that name. And I don't need a name, anyway. I've gotten by okay without one. I know you probably don't understand.

I had not spoken so many words to a single human being in a long time.

I understand better than you think, Renata said.

We both were silent for a few minutes. The room had grown louder and a guy with a clipboard was trying to announce something over the din, but no one was listening.

What is this place? I asked. Is it some kind of jail for kids?

No, Renata said and smiled for the first time. It's not a jail for anybody. We'll talk about this place, she said, and I'll sign you in. Come with me.

I climbed down from the windowsill and Renata led me across the room, resting one hand softly on my shoulder. I had no idea where I was or who Renata was; I once again was putting trust in an adult I didn't know, letting things happen. I grabbed two donuts as I walked past the large table.

Renata's windowless little office contained a desk and, across from it, a small couch. Sit down, she said, pointing to the couch. I'll be right back—I have to go get the intake paperwork.

I scarfed down the donuts and put my head back. I was out cold in seconds, only to be jolted awake by the distressed howls of a girl in the room next door; I could hear Renata's voice through the wall. I caught myself drooling, and my brain felt encased in a dense fog. I sat up and scratched my itchy head, watching dandruff flakes float to the floor like snow flurries. I looked for Sirius's ghost, but he wasn't there.

The fog lifted, and the prior day came back, disconnected pieces of memory slowly rearranging themselves into the correct sequence. My eyelids were heavy, my head nodding and bouncing off my chest.

Renata walked in mid-bounce and sat on the couch next to me. Her nice smell made me self-conscious about my stench, but she seemed not to mind. I suppose she was used to stinky kids. She asked if I needed to see a nurse—I shook my head—and then she explained what a shelter was and told me the rules: no drugs, no alcohol, no sex, no weapons, no fighting, front door locked at 8:00 pm, lights out at

11:00, breakfast at 7:00 am, two group and one individual counseling sessions every day, tutoring for those who need it, three community chores each day.

Do you agree to those rules? she asked.

Are you going to try and send me back home? That's what this place is all about, isn't it?

We're going to try and do what's best for you.

Well, I can tell you that going back home is not what's best for me.

We won't force you to do anything.

All right then, I said.

Good. I'll show you the showers and we'll find you a bed. We don't normally allow sleeping during the day, but I'll make an exception. You've yawned about a dozen times in the past few minutes.

The upstairs boys' dorm was a large room with a badly-scuffed wooden floor, buzzing florescent lights, and peeling paint. It smelled of cigarettes, sweat, and dirty socks, and contained four rows of army surplus cots and a large utility sink in one corner.

That one's free; he never came back last night. Renata pointed to a cot under a window. Grab it and it's yours. Join us downstairs when you've rested up, okay?

I lay down on the squishy foam mattress and closed my eyes. I thought I would fall asleep quickly but as I started to drift off, my mind came untethered, strange images erupted through the mental mush. My left leg suddenly jerked violently. I heard my mother's voice as clear as if she were there next to me; my eyes popped open and I gasped.

I rolled over and curled up into a ball, pulling my rucksack with its few possessions close to my chest. I reached down for Sirius, but he wasn't there, even his ghost dead now. I buried my face in the foam pillow. It smelled faintly of vomit.

I slept like a dead man and woke late in the afternoon. All the other kids were in counseling sessions or in the common room with tutors. The boys' shower room was empty, so for the first time since leaving home I felt warm water flow over me. I soaped up at least four times. Several coats of grime dissolved into the drain.

I had forgotten how nice it was to be naked. In the summer I would sneak outside in the middle of the night, take off my pajamas and lie naked in the weedy backyard with Sirius at my side, the soft summer breeze dancing over my body without so much as a thin layer of cotton between me and the infinite universe.

I once fell asleep like that and awoke at sunrise, exposed to the neighborhood, my father at the backdoor yelling, Get inside this house, you fucking pervert! He slapped me across the face hard enough to leave a handprint, and later that morning I heard him telling my mom, That faggot kid of yours ain't normal.

After my shower I went downstairs where they were serving dinner, bowls of macaroni scattered with meat-like debris, and slices of white bread stacked high on plates. We all sat at one long table. I found a seat and focused on my plate to avoid making eye contact. All the other boys were older, bigger, and tougher-looking than me.

A girl sat next to me and started talking nonstop, hardly pausing for air. At first I thought she was talking to herself, like a crazy person, but no, she was talking to me. She said that when she got pregnant her parents kicked her out of the house and her boyfriend was a jerk who bolted town and she heard he was in Fresno.

I felt bad for her; at least I had left home voluntarily, all she did was get pregnant. It's not like she killed somebody. I tried to engage her in conversation, something I wasn't very good at, but she was pretty much stuck on broadcast and didn't respond much except to tell me that her name was Luanne. She called me honey bun, which was kind of nice, and during a five-minute span asked me three times how old I was. So the fourth time she asked I said, seventy-two, but she just kept on talking.

Luanne had curly blond hair and a round bulge below her stomach, the bulge that was the source of her problems, the bulge that got her booted out of her home, the bulge that soon would be launched into this unhappy world. She offered me a cigarette, which I put in my pants pocket.

I helped clear the dishes after dinner, and some of the boys started arguing loudly over what to put on the television. A few kids sat on couches and stared into space or mumbled to themselves. Two counselors cruised around the room keeping order. I still wasn't sure what this place was all about or if I wanted to stay but at least I wasn't on the street and it seemed like a better arrangement than Max had offered.

I wandered down the hallway. Maurice's office door was open, but I didn't enter—that Afro still scared me. I had seen him talking and laughing with the white counselors so I thought maybe in California Black people and white people talk to each other.

I watched from the hallway as he ate tuna fish out of a can while reading a newspaper that lay flat on an otherwise bare desk.

Come on in, why don't you, he said without looking up from his newspaper. I hope you ain't one of them kids who wants to sleep all day and lurk around all night—are you? We don't go for that. He pushed his newspaper aside and looked at me for the first time. I slowly crossed the threshold.

I was just really tired today, I said. I usually sleep at night.

So what you been up to on the streets?

Not much. Just living.

Maurice chuckled. Just living, huh? Well, that's what I've been doing too, since day number one. Where you from? I bet you're one of them Orange County kids—can't take the family scene no more, hitchhikes to the city, finds out it's a living hell. Is that it?

What's Orange County?

You know—Disneyland, lawn sprinklers, shopping malls, white folks.

Oh. No, I've never been to Disneyland.

Maurice looked at me and squinted. You aren't from around here? From LA?

No. I'm from pretty far away. It took me three days on busses to get here.

Shit, I'm impressed, little dude. Man, you must've really wanted to get away from something to make you come all the way out to this crazy city. What you plan to do now?

That was an excellent question, but one for which I had no answer, so I shrugged and sat down on the floor against the wall opposite Maurice's desk. The room smelled like tuna fish. Maurice's Afro wasn't so scary now.

Maurice tossed the empty tuna can into the trash. Listen man, he said, I'm just the nighttime security guard. But let me tell you something: whatever it was that made you run must've been some bad shit. Running takes balls but running doesn't solve problems. Sometimes you've got to run so you can see things clearly and sort things out.

I don't want to sort things. I want to start over.

Maurice looked out the window and scratched his chin. That may work for you, and I hope it does, he said. I try to forget my past, but it sure doesn't forget me. It keeps popping up when I least expect. But I got more past than you do, and a meaner past, I suspect. But maybe you can do it.

We sat in comfortable silence. Eventually, Maurice leaned across the desk toward me. Let me tell you something, he said. Most of the kids who come through this place go right back on the streets or right back to their pimp or their dealer or the daddy who's beating them or screwing them or whatever it is they ran from. That's the hard-ass truth. You've got to really want something different, and then make it happen.

He got up from his chair and stretched—a long, luxurious, full-body stretch. I've got to walk around now and make sure everything's cool. I'll see you tomorrow if tonight's dinner doesn't kill you first.

I lay on my cot and tried to be invisible as the other boys filed into the bunk room, cursing and barking at each other. Once the lights were out, I rolled onto my back and stared at the ceiling. I thought of Sirius and hugged the foam pillow just as I would hug Sirius in my bed at home, but it was a poor substitute for his soft fur and doggy smell, his tongue licking my chin as I fell asleep.

I thought of my mother and how she would tuck me into bed every night when I was little, and tell me wonderful stories she made up about an explorer named Simon the Adventurer who sailed around the world, travelling to jungles and deserts and exotic cities. She told me these were our special stories, she didn't tell them to Jake, and that I shouldn't tell anyone else about them.

Then she would kiss my head and say, sweet dreams, Sweet Pea.

I would fall asleep thinking about Simon the Adventurer and wishing that my mother and I could join him in his travels. But that was years ago, before she started collapsing every night on the couch in a half-crocked stupor, often before the sun went down. At first, I would sit on the floor next to her, watching her breathe and holding her hand. I often fell asleep on the floor next to the couch until my father came out and kicked me awake and told me to go to my room. Eventually I gave up and learned to put myself to bed.

I missed my old mother. But I had missed her for years. She left me long before I left her. I had once been her beloved and it didn't matter then what my father or Jake or the rest of the damn world thought of me. So what if I was a misfit—I was beloved.

I didn't trust my memory of the past few weeks: Had I really travelled for three days on buses, sleeping fitfully as we rumbled in and out of small towns? Was Max real or a nightmare? I didn't even trust that present moment: What if it all were a dream and I awoke in my old room to another day of my father's rage and my mother's glassy-eyed indifference?

Or in a mental hospital, strapped to a bed while doctors in white coats looked at my chart and murmured to each other? What if I were dead and was now in Purgatory prior to my descent into Hell? Maybe

I had died on the way to California, or maybe my father had murdered me like he had Sirius, or maybe I had put a shotgun barrel in my mouth and pulled the trigger with my big toe like Jimmy Hollingsworth did, and what I thought was me running away was just my soul flying out of the house.

I put the pillow over my head to block the avalanche of thoughts, as if they were coming from outside my head instead of from deep inside it.

I fell asleep and right into my recurring nightmare: I am in the middle of the vast ocean on a cloudless sunny day and although I can't swim I am miraculously staying afloat and feel no fear. The ocean is holding me up, its waters warm and comforting. Seagulls dance overhead, their call a musical score. I am happy. It is bliss. Like nothing I ever felt in waking life.

Then in an instant the sky turns dark, a sudden solar eclipse. The waves grow big and sinister as if they are conscious beings instead of swells of sea water. They toss me up and down and rise so high around me, I no longer can see the horizon. I am all alone in this angry ocean turned against me. Beneath me is cold dark water where those creatures with sharp teeth who had never seen sunlight live.

I scream but no sound comes out of my mouth. The ocean no longer holds me up and I begin to kick and flail and sink. I take one desperate breath before my head descends into the darkness beneath the waves.

I burst awake, as always, with a loud gasp; I had swallowed the wrong way; I was drowning in spit.

What the fuck? I'm trying to sleep, asshole!

For a second I thought it was Jake but then I remembered where I was. My pillow was on the floor. My heart was pounding. I hated that dream. It always made me swallow the wrong way.

I'm sorry, I whispered, and tried not to cough.

I groped my way to the door, careful not to bump into a cot and disturb another of my dormmates. I went into the bathroom and splashed cold water over my face. I looked at the scruffy kid in the mirror: water dripping from his chin, circles under his eyes, brown disheveled hair matted down on one side, oversized ears poking through strands of hair like early spring buds.

I shared features with my mother—the high cheekbones and brown eyes and small frame, but I didn't see much of my father. My lips were fuller than anyone else's in the family and my nose was bigger. Not longer, but bigger, as if it were intended for someone with a gigantic head.

I felt profoundly ugly.

Jake had constantly reminded me of my nose and ears. He would come up behind me and pull hard on my ears and say, Let's fly away, Dumbo, or he would elbow me in the nose—sometimes hard enough to cause a nosebleed—and say, Sorry, your nose was blocking my way.

After my mother checked out of life, Jake became more brazen because there was no one to defend me. My father either ignored him or laughed along with him.

Jake and I shared only our parents. I never saw him reading a book, and God knows he never was moved to look at the night sky. He was five years older than me and would graduate from high school that year. His interests were, in no particular order: skipping school to drink and smoke with his friends; looking at magazines with pictures of cars, guns, or naked women; watching sports on TV; and belching. He also liked to go hunting and fishing with my father. Their all-day trips were vacation days for me.

I looked down my shorts. I had lots of fuzz that I didn't believe officially qualified as pubes, but my balls had dropped so things were happening down there. I knew the process, because one week of seventh grade science class was devoted to sex education. We watched an animated filmstrip about Mr. Sperm and Miss Egg, which the boys laughed through and the girls giggled through, and the teacher, Miss Hambrick, kept saying, Shhh! Pay attention! She seemed very ill at ease. She probably had not been visited by Mr. Sperm in many years.

But my real sex education had come thanks to Jake and his friends, who would sit around after school smoking cigarettes and drinking beer. I would eavesdrop while pretending to draw or read. They would talk about the girls at school that they wanted to do and how they would go about doing it. After I discovered Jake's stash of porn magazines, one day when he was on a hunting trip, I saw what doing it entailed and where in the girl you do it.

And that evening, the evening of the day when I put it all together, I looked at my father as he drank beer and picked at the corn on his foot while watching a baseball game on television, and I thought about what he had done to my mother to make his Mr. Sperm and my mother's Miss Egg combine to form me. I looked down at my body—at my hands and my arms and my feet and my flesh—and was both amazed and repulsed that I had been created by my father's Mr. Sperm rocketing out of his pecker to join Miss Egg inside my mother.

I started to feel nauseated. My father belched loudly. I went into the backyard with Sirius and sat under the sycamore tree and tried not to vomit. I looked back at the house and wished that a stork had brought me there, or better yet, to a different house.

Now I stepped back and took in my entire reflected self: My image in the mirror certainly resembled a whole boy, with limbs and hair and a face and a covering of skin that defined my boundaries with the world. But I didn't feel like the image, like a whole person. I felt more like one of those modern paintings where it's hard to make out what's what, where a nose juts out from the side of the face and an eye is floating above the head and you can't tell where the person ends, and the background begins.

I went into the hallway and sat at the top of the stairs. I listened to the jazz music wafting up from Maurice's radio and rubbed my feet, which had spent the day in shoes at least one size too small. My ribs still ached. I thought about how cool it would be to visit Proxima Centauri, the closest star to our sun, and to look back at the sun, which would be a small twinkling speck in the night sky.

And I thought about the fact that I was on a small planet circling a small twinkling speck in the night sky of Proxima Centauri. I felt so insignificant. And it felt wonderful.

I didn't step outside the shelter for over a week. I had so little money to spend, and after my time on the streets there was little enticement, other than the ocean, which I knew must be somewhere nearby. I performed my mandated chores, drew in my sketchbook, and read every single one of the books the shelter possessed—westerns, Hardy Boys mysteries, biographies of presidents and athletes, pamphlets about drugs and venereal diseases.

When I got through those, I borrowed books from the counselors' offices, books with titles like *Adolescent Psychology* and *Crises of Adolescence.* None helped me understand my life but they did help me diagnose a few of my fellow inmates.

The shelter was something of a cross between a mental asylum and a warehouse for juvenile refuse. Some of the kids were intimidating, and I did my best to avoid them. Fighting was grounds for expulsion; that didn't prevent threatening looks and errant elbows, but the counselors generally kept things under control. I hated kitchen duty the most because of too many knives in the same confined space as too many disturbed teenagers.

But, for the most part the shelter was like a space station in the dark and unfeeling void. I sat on the front steps at night to check on the moon and spend a little time without thinking. I hung out with Maurice in his office every night. He told me about the jazz and blues music we listened to on his radio, and how white musicians stole a lot of ideas from Black guys with crazy names like Leadbelly and Fats Domino and Professor Longhair.

He told me about Louisiana, where he grew up, and how his father was lynched by three white guys who never got arrested, and about prison, where he had spent eleven years and had three stab wounds to show for it, and how when he was a teenager he was very angry but he now practiced Zen, which I had never heard of but sounded like what I do when I stare at the moon. He said it helped him to be more at peace.

I met every day for a counseling session with Renata, who Maurice told me had insisted on being the counselor assigned to me. Renata listened to me, and no one had listened to me since my mother faded away. She never again asked for my name or where I was from. She encouraged me to talk about the crazy thoughts and feelings that raced around inside my head like Indy cars, and assured me that crazy thoughts didn't mean I was a crazy person.

I had my doubts about that and didn't want to end up in a straitjacket, so I didn't tell her all of my crazy thoughts. Nothing I said seemed to shock her, though, and I found myself telling her things no one else had ever heard, about feeling shattered in pieces like a modern art painting and even about Uncle Arnie.

Talking about the past was not what I had wanted to do. I wanted to be free of my past—not just the events of my past, but from the feelings. I had thought it would be easy to erase the first thirteen years of my life, but I was finding it hard now that someone wanted to listen.

Maybe Maurice was right, and the past doesn't forget you. It's like a long tail that extends behind you, stretching back out of sight, and no matter how fast you run or how suddenly you turn, it's still connected to your ass. To this day I still don't know whether I'm pulling that tail or whether that tail is pushing me to wherever it wants me to go.

It was at one of my sessions with Renata that she persuaded me to choose a new name. I already had started to wonder whether my past would go away if I chose a new name. Maybe being nameless was not such a good idea. It would make Renata happy to know that I had done something she suggested.

So I became Moon.

I didn't know how to recognize happiness, never having been around happy people. My father didn't live along a spectrum of happy to sad. He lived drunk and angry or sober and irritable, yelling or mumbling, employed or not employed, hungry or flatulently full, awake or snoring.

After a while, I figured out how these combined. Angry went with not employed, yelling with hungry, snoring with full—which helped me avoid getting smacked and punched more.

For the first eight years of my life, my mother laughed at television shows and cooked dinner and watched me draw pictures at the kitchen table and stayed home and read books to me when I was sick. I often faked being sick so that she would stay home, and we could read books together. But then she melted away like the ice cubes in her glass. She and my father always had argued, but after my father hit her, she would disappear for several days and I was left alone.

But I remembered this: In the weeks right before her sudden descent, my mother was happy in a way I never had seen a person; not giddy, not bubbly, but joyfully at peace. I guess it was like a flaring candle flame right before it dies out. I was young, but I remembered.

Those weeks living in the shelter were the first time I had experienced something akin to happiness—or at least the absence of unhappiness. There were things I didn't like about the shelter: the open-stall showers and the fights that broke out among the older boys, and the screams and moans that echoed through the building when one of the kids was having a breakdown, or when a new arrival showed up in the throes of a drug overdose, or the police would come arrest somebody who was using the shelter as a hideout.

I didn't like those twice-daily group sessions, where the counselors tried to get us to Open up and Express your hurt and Talk it out. I soon figured out that saying, I'm not ready to share, was an acceptable answer as long as you sounded sincere.

If it was happiness I felt, it was mostly because of Renata and Maurice. And Luanne, who always offered me cigarettes, so before long I had a stash of Kool Menthols under my foam mattress. Luanne came to see me at least once a day in tears and she'd say, Me and my baby need a hug, and I would try to oblige, but her baby-bulge made it hard to get my arms around her, so then I would draw funny pictures until she started to laugh through her tears.

And Diego, a Mexican kid who was barely taller than me but had facial hair and talked to me all the time, probably because I was the only other person at his eye level. He didn't speak English well, so I didn't always understand him. We would look through magazines and I would point to the pictures and teach him how to say the words in English, and he would tell me how to say them in Spanish. Diego showed me the scars on his wrist where he had tried *suicidio* with a broken light bulb.

● ☽ ☽) ○ ((☾ ●

I thought I had found an agreeable space station in the void. Until:

Moon, it's time to discuss where things are going from here, Renata said at the beginning of our session.

Where what's going?

What I mean is, we need to finalize a plan for you and determine where you're going.

I'm not going back home. I've told you that already. I thought you understood.

I do understand. I'm not suggesting you return to your home. But we can only house you here for thirty days. This is a crisis facility, not a long-term residence. I explained that to you when you arrived.

Maybe she had, maybe she hadn't, but it was news to me. Devastating news.

So what am I supposed to do? I said. Go back and live on the streets?

No, that's not going to happen, Renata said. She leaned over and squeezed my shoulder gently. We're going to figure this out. Don't worry.

She explained the two options: A juvenile home run by Los Angeles County, which sounded kind of like a prison with a school attached, or a foster family who would get paid by the county to take me in.

A juvenile home is not the kind of place for someone like you, Renata said. I believe a foster family is the better option.

You mean go live with some strange family like a stray dog from the pound?

No Moon, foster families are carefully chosen. We work hard to find a situation that is right for the individual child. We'll make it a good solution. I promise you.

Solution for who? I said. Actually, I kind of yelled it. I was now one of those distraught howling shelter kids. Have you listened to anything I've been telling you? I yelled. This is a solution for you, not for me.

I was standing up now and hyperventilating, and I think Renata was afraid that I was going to pass out and maybe have a stroke right there in her office because she reached out like she wanted to catch me if I collapsed, and at that moment I wanted nothing more than to collapse right into her, to be enveloped and protected by her, to be loved and wanted by her. I shook my head vigorously.

I'm not going to go live with a family, I said. I just ran away from a family. Why can't I stay here? I'll do more chores, so I don't cost you anything. I'll prepare dinner and clean up every day. I'll be useful.

My hands are tied, Renata said. I can't change the shelter's policy. She spoke in that calm voice she used with the kids who were having breakdowns, but she seemed upset; her calm tone was a poor act. I know this isn't what you want, she said in a near-whisper, as if she were violating official rules by saying it.

I walked out and sat in the common room. A game show was on the television. A contestant was deliriously jumping up and down because she had just won a washing machine, and I thought how wonderful life would be if a washing machine could make me as happy.

In the short time since I had fled home, I'd lived on the streets, burned through most of my money, been briefly held captive by a pimp, and found a refuge where I met some nice people. And now I was being expelled to go live with a family I didn't know. My old life, my sunless life, had led me to this huge, smoggy, bewildering city where I thought I was going to start anew, where maybe I wouldn't be a misfit, as if a change in geography would change my life. But it hadn't changed.

A scream came from down the hall: Gus, a husky boy of about sixteen with greasy hair, who slept on the cot next to me and talked loudly in his sleep, was holding a kitchen knife and swinging it wildly. The counselors had encircled him and were trying to persuade him to put the knife down. One of the counselors, Melanie, was sitting on the floor against the wall sobbing, her right arm covered in blood, her left hand covering her eyes.

Renata was part of the circle cautiously closing in on Gus. I joined the other kids watching the drama. Gus was still swinging at all comers, but his grip on the knife seemed tenuous. He was frightened. Tears were streaming down his face. I could see that it would end with his being overpowered or surrendering.

I had seen enough.

Renata's office door was open; I walked in and sat in her chair behind the desk. I imagined her saying, Of course you can live here, Moon, for as long as you want, forever if you want. There were some papers on the desk, on County of Los Angeles letterhead, but none of them looked interesting. Her purse was on the floor next to the chair and a magazine was sticking partially out. I pulled it out and looked at the address label; I repeated the address to myself several times and then stuck the magazine back in her purse.

A framed photo of a teenage boy sat on the desk; it was facing Renata's chair so I'd never noticed it before. It was a school photo. The boy had shoulder-length dark hair parted right down the middle, light-colored eyes—the photo was black and white so I couldn't see colors—and a dimpled smile. It was a real smile, like he was thinking of something funny, not a forced school-photo smile.

It didn't seem to bother him that some of his teeth were crooked. His face was smooth except for sideburns that faded out about an inch down. He looked kind of like a boob-less girl with sideburns.

What are you doing in here?

Standing in the door was the boob-less girl with sideburns, minus the smile. He had a bunch of pimples that didn't show up in the school photo. His voice was deep. He was skinny and his long arms and legs made him appear taller than he was.

I'm just sitting here while all that gets worked out, I said, nodding toward the hallway where Gus now was crying loudly and blubbering a medley of obscenities. I just had my session with Renata, I said. But that didn't explain why I was sitting in her chair.

Well maybe you better come sit on this side of the desk, he said. It was an order, not a suggestion. I walked around and sat on the small couch. He crossed his arms and looked down at me.

You look pretty young to be in this place.

Yeah, I said, but it's where I am. Are you Renata's . . .

Son. Do I look like my picture?

Yeah . . . I mean, I can tell it's you.

Three policemen ran past the door. Renata's son turned his head to watch, but I couldn't see anything. Mom, step back, he said, and walked out of sight.

There were scuffling sounds and more obscenities from Gus that quickly transformed into sobs. It's under control now, people, everybody step back, one of the policemen said.

Renata's son came back to the door. So where's your family? he asked.

I don't have a family.

Oh, sorry, man. You're an orphan? What happened?

No, they're still alive. I guess. They live pretty far from here. Things weren't working out there, so I ran away and came out here. They don't know where I am. I'm never going back.

You came out here by yourself? Shit, that's pretty heavy, he said.

Yeah, I guess it is. Do you and your mom live near here?

Not too far.

Near the ocean?

Everywhere here is near the ocean, kid. That's why they call it Venice Beach, he laughed.

I've never seen the ocean.

You're shitting me. How could you have missed it? Half the planet is ocean. And you're in Venice Beach, for God's sake.

I felt foolish, so to make myself feel better I corrected him: Actually, seventy percent of the planet is ocean, I said. I just haven't managed to see it yet.

Well, maybe I'll take you to the beach sometime. You know, when you're not being counseled, he said, and nodded toward Renata's desk.

Really? That would be cool.

My mom doesn't like me to hang out with the shelter kids. No offense, but some of you guys are royally fucked-up, and I think she's afraid they'll find my dismembered body parts in a ravine somewhere. But I'm seventeen, I can take care of myself. Anyway, you don't seem too homicidal.

He laughed and I smiled weakly.

Renata walked in the room with blood on her hands and shirt.

You okay, Mom? the boy asked.

Yeah, the blood is from Melanie. She'll be fine, it wasn't a deep slash, just a long one. She saw me: Moon, what's up?

Nothing. I just came in here while all that was going on.

Is your name really Moon? Renata's son asked. That's wild, man. I love that.

Ben, will you go help Jackson with that stopped-up sink in the girl's bathroom? And then we've got to go home.

Right, boss-lady, Ben said. Catch you later, Moon, he said as he left the room.

Renata crouched down so we were eye-to-eye. Moon, we're going to work this out, she said, sounding like a doctor who had earlier delivered a terminal diagnosis. We'll find a good foster situation for you. Trust me. Work with me. Okay?

I nodded slightly but I didn't say okay. That would've been lying.

I lay on my cot that night watching the dancing shadows on the ceiling made by the flickering streetlights outside. To Renata I was just another runaway, another shelter kid like the hundreds that had preceded me and the hundreds that would follow me. I had started to think that she felt differently about me, that I was special to her the way she had become special to me. I had told her so much and now she was just passing me down the assembly line.

But why would I be special to her? I thought. She had a son and probably a husband and other children. A family. I was just a runaway fleeing his hell, to be processed and moved out to make room for other runaways fleeing their hells. Those fleeing hell were in no position to demand special treatment. It was enough that we get a cot and free meals for thirty days.

I thought of Ben. I had never encountered a nonthreatening older boy, but then most of my encounters had been with Jake and his friends and the older boys at school for whom I was a walking bull's-eye. But I doubted Ben was serious about going to the beach with me. He probably had forgotten about it already.

I decided I would have to run away again, be on my own, fend for myself. The fact that I had failed at it the first go-round was not encouraging. I was mad at Renata for drawing me in to feel close to her, which really meant I was mad at her for being who she was, so I should have been mad at myself for allowing her to complicate my emotions. I was just beginning my new life and already I had to start erasing Renata, which meant erasing something that made me feel good.

I listened to the snores, took in the stench, and adjusted my shorts to accommodate my hard-on—which coincidentally had arisen when I was thinking about Renata—and wished that tomorrow would never come. I was tired of tomorrows. I suppose Jimmy Hollingsworth had grown tired of his tomorrows. But eventually I fell asleep and tomorrow came.

After a breakfast of powdered orange drink and stale pastries, I sat at an empty table in the common room, opened my sketchbook and turned to a blank page. But I didn't know what to draw. I thought about the blank page of my life. I decided to leave the shelter, head down to the ocean and then start walking down the beach until I found a secluded spot where I could live, just me and the moon and the stars and the ocean, and wait for something to happen. I didn't have much money, so I'd either steal food or starve and die.

A hard tap on my shoulder. I jumped.

Whoa, didn't mean to scare you, man. You must've been in orbit or something.

It was Ben. He was in shorts and flip-flops. His sudden appearance was like a counterpoint to my ruminations, and left me speechless.

Well, are we going to the beach or is your schedule full? he said.

Yeah, I said. I didn't think you were serious. I mean, sure, let's go. I just have to be back in time for my session with your . . . with Renata.

I grabbed my rucksack, signed out in the office, and followed Ben out the door, feeling the sun on my face for the first time in two weeks. We walked through neighborhoods of small bungalows and down a busy street of junky little shops, bars, and liquor stores. Some of the storefronts were boarded up. Venice was scruffier and even dirtier than Hollywood, but felt less feverish, more like a rundown small town.

Welcome to the Slum by the Sea, Ben said as he saw me taking it in. How'd you make your way to Venice, anyway? he asked.

We walked side by side; Ben had a casual gait, as if he didn't know where he was going and didn't care.

When I got to Los Angeles, I didn't know anyone or where to go or anything, I said. It wasn't so great, especially at night. I just waited for something to happen—good, bad, whatever. But I was running out of money. And then I got mixed up with this creepy guy. I got away from him—it's a long story—but that's how I ended up at the shelter. The police took me there.

So, where'd you run away from? Where's your home—or, your old home?

I didn't feel comfortable sharing any identifying information. It's three days away by bus, I said. A long trip.

I've often thought about striking out and leaving home, Ben said. But that would be just too weird, wouldn't it? My mom runs a youth shelter, and her own kid runs away, he laughed. But I'll be eighteen next year and then it's no longer called running away.

Why would you want to run away?

Ben ignored my question but he stopped and grabbed my arm. Hey man, you can't swim in jeans, he said.

Swim. The very word produced fear. All I wanted was to stand in the ocean and feel the waves lap my feet.

I'll just role up my pants, I said.

Not cool, Ben said. You'll look like a hick.

We turned down a commercial street for a few blocks and stopped at a store called Zodiac. A woman was setting up a rack of tie-dyed T-shirts on the sidewalk. She looked like an older version of the hippies I had seen on Hollywood and Sunset: she had long, curly blond hair and a bright red headband to keep it out of her face. She was wearing red cat-eye sunglasses and a long white dress, more like a huge shirt, with flowers sewn all over it. From the way she moved, the way she was setting things up, I presumed she was the store owner, not an employee.

Hey, baby, I didn't expect to see you today. She hugged Ben.

Ben and I went into the store—he seemed to know it very well— and found a pair of cutoff jeans in my size. I changed into them and stuffed my pants into my rucksack. We walked out without paying. I get a family discount, Ben said.

We walked a few more blocks, then turned at the corner. Directly in front of me was the ocean, partially hidden by a small grove of towering oil derricks along the beach. The sunlight sparkled on the water's surface. Waves broke on the shore in a lazy rhythm. My eyes followed the coastline north, where mountains jutted into the sea.

I looked at the far horizon; it was hard to tell where the blue ocean ended, and the blue sky began. I was at the end of the Earth. And the sound. Oceans are loud, something you can't tell from photographs. My senses demanded my full energy and my pace slowed until I ground to a complete stop.

Nothing I had learned from books—the photographs, the facts, the details—approached the reality; it was beyond words and images. I wanted to take it all in without thought, with my senses alone. I wanted time to stop. Ben turned to see me standing mesmerized, twenty feet behind him.

C'mon, he yelled.

I ran to catch up. We crossed a busy street against the light and then took off along the beach, the sand kicked up by Ben's feet stinging my face. We got to the water's edge, and while I kicked off my shoes and peeled off my shirt, Ben splashed ahead into the waves, then dove forward and disappeared under the surf. He emerged a few seconds later, shaking his head and running his hands through his long hair.

I walked slowly in the wet sand until the remnants of a breaking wave rolled over my feet up to my ankles, the chilly water a sharp contrast to the hot sun beating on my back. I waded farther out, to knee-level, gathered some water in my cupped hands and tasted its saltiness. I continued, to where the waves were breaking, and forged on until the waves were bumping against my stomach, then my chest, the deepest water I ever had been in.

I had walked far enough out that I no longer could see the beach without turning my head: there was only ocean. I imagined the downward slope of the sea bottom and realized there was nothing but water between me and the deepest and darkest place on Earth, the Mariana Trench, 36,000 feet below the Pacific. I imagined being pulled out to sea until I was alone in the middle of the ocean, just like in my nightmare.

Fear began winning out over ecstasy. I turned and started to retreat back to shallower water.

Something under the water grabbed my ankles. Tentacles. An octopus. It tightened its grip and pulled, drawing me out to sea toward the Trench, I thought. I briefly saw the sky as I fell backwards into the water. I squeezed my eyes shut as the ocean rushed over me and roared in my ears. I was pushed down by a wave. I tried to get up, but another wave pushed me down again. I couldn't hold my breath much longer.

Just as I was certain that these were my last seconds alive, that I was going to drown in three feet of Pacific Ocean water, I felt the sand under my feet. I stood up, emerging from the depths, gasping for breath, grateful to be alive.

Ben was laughing. He wasn't an octopus.

Fuck you! I screamed. I can't swim. I could've drowned! My fists were clinched. At that moment, had I been armed, I would have shot Ben stone-cold dead.

Sorry, man, just horsing around, Ben said. He looked shocked; my anger had startled him. But he kept smiling and his laughter kept arising in little spasms.

I can't swim, I repeated a bit more calmly. I can't stand having my head under water.

My temper was out of all proportion to my ability to inflict damage. Jake and kids at school knew this and thrived on igniting me, always to my detriment. I would take hapless swings at kids twice my size, knowing full well their retaliatory strike would be on target. Armed with a fork, I once chased Daryl O'Connor around the cafeteria after he stuck his fat fingers in my chocolate pudding and then rubbed them in my hair. I intended to fork his eyes out.

Miss Ferguson, the girl's gym teacher, wrested the fork from my hand and dragged me to the principal's office, which provoked howls of laughter. The thing is, I never knew for sure when my temper would erupt. I would put up with a lot of shit and then suddenly—kaboom!—I would explode.

Except with my father; I knew better than to explode with him.

Sorry, Ben said. For real. I assumed you could swim and liked water since you were so gaga about seeing the ocean. I was just goofing around, ace.

I tried to exorcise my rage.

Ben reached out his hand in apology and I slowly took it. I couldn't begin explaining to Ben the invisible tripwires that crisscrossed my life. Now I felt bad because he seemed genuinely remorseful. He was just doing what normal guys do. I was the misfit, not him.

C'mon, let's walk up the beach, Ben said. We walked in shin-deep water, where the waves sloshed back and forth. A long pier extended into the ocean about a mile or so ahead. People on the beach were playing volleyball and throwing Frisbees. I had finally arrived in the television version of California, although on television they must have taken care not to film the oil derricks.

After a while we walked out of the water and plopped down in the sand. I asked Ben if he had any brothers or sisters.

Nope, it's just me and my mom.

Where's your dad?

He lives in Iowa. But I've never seen him. At least, not since I was old enough to remember things.

Why don't you see him?

It's complicated. Fucked up. My mom was afraid he would try and get a judge to take me away from her. Which could've happened. See, it's kind of a weird situation—I mean, the reason why they split and all. But he's never tried to find me as far as I know. He's got another family now. I've seen his picture, an old one, but I don't know him, so it doesn't bother me that he's not around. It's just the way things are. Nothing I can do about it.

Ben picked up a handful of sand and released it slowly, like the sand in an hourglass. So what's the story with your family, he asked. Why'd you run away?

I gave Ben the condensed answer: My father and my brother hated me, I said. Always did, as far as I can remember. My mother was okay—I mean, I think she loved me and all—but then she started drinking a lot and sometimes she would go away, and I never knew if she was coming back. And even when she was there, she was like, I don't know, not there. I think she wants to die. Maybe I did something wrong. I can't figure it out and I gave up trying.

Then my father murdered my dog, so there was no point in staying.

48

That sounds pretty awful, man, he said. But it still must've taken iron balls to run away at your age. I guess you had no choice.

Your mom wants me to go live with a foster family, I said. They can't be worse people than my family but that's not what I want. I think it's a threat. I think she's saying that so I'll break down and tell her where I'm from so they can send me back home. That's what everybody wants, isn't it? Send all the strange and fucked-up kids back to where they came from? Get them out of sight and out of mind?

Look, man, my mom is strange too, Ben said. Trust me. That's why she moved us out here, to Venice. This is the world capital of strange. When she left my dad, she left everything she had except for me. She even changed her name so they couldn't track her down. Her parents and brother disowned her—so I don't even have grandparents or an uncle. She paid a big price for being strange. She's not playing games with you. There's nothing phony about her.

Then she should know why I don't want to live with a foster family.

C'mon, you're what—thirteen? How're you going to survive on your own?

I didn't tell Ben my fantasy of living alone on an isolated beach until I starved to death.

When I was little, my mom and I lived on a commune up near Ojai, Ben said. It was like a family but we weren't related to anybody. We still go visit up there. Sometimes I wish we'd stayed, but my mom wanted to do something more than grow vegetables.

She liked to write poetry, still does, and she knew some poets and writers who were hanging out down here and putting out a magazine. So we moved here and lived with them in this cool old house that was falling apart. It was right on a canal and just a few blocks from the beach. There was an oil derrick in the backyard, and every night that pumping sound would put me to sleep. My mom worked on the magazine and I was like the official house kid, because nobody else had a kid.

It was crazy, but a good kind of crazy, at least for a little kid. But as I got older my mom decided that she needed a better job, more stability, you know? She went to school at night and got her counseling degree, and then she got a job and we moved to our own place and, voila, here we are.

We sat in silence, each having revealed as much as we were willing to. It felt good, though, like undoing just a few buttons on your coat and letting fresh, cool air inside.

Let's get some food, Ben said. Anything you want, it's on me. But I don't eat meat, nothing that's been killed. No burgers or fried chicken.

Jake and my father would count down the days to the opening of deer season. The year I turned eleven they took me along, though I can't imagine why. We left the house before sunrise, all three of us sitting in the front seat of the pickup. The windows were rolled up and the smoke from my father's cigarettes clouded the cab. I kept nodding off, and Jake would jab me awake with an elbow when my head lolled against his shoulder.

We pulled over on the side of a dirt road and walked through the woods for a good thirty minutes. It was wonderful being in the woods at sunrise, gentle light filtering through the trees, the musty smell of fallen leaves, a chorus of chirping birds. Only Jake and my father carried guns. I was along for the male bonding, I suppose. The three of us squeezed into a two-person ground blind and quietly waited as the forest awoke.

My dad spotted the first deer, a doe, and nudged Jake. I watched as it crept cautiously in the brush toward us, ending up about fifty feet away, nibbling on leaves and raising her head nervously. She and I made eye contact; she tilted her head slightly, as if trying to understand why two eyes were peering back at her from the branches. Her black nose twitched; her ears stood erect, vigilant.

I wanted to hug her neck, caress her soft, delicate face, and scratch her ears like I did with Sirius. She was beautiful.

I jumped at the crack of Jake's gun; the doe stumbled, fell on its front legs, then collapsed on its side. My father and Jake whooped and hollered; it was Jake's first kill. I was horrified. Tears rolled down my face and I tried to keep Jake and my father from seeing them.

When we got home that evening, I wanted to tell my mother about the deer and about how it had died, collapsing on the ground, its dead eyes, the same eyes that just moments before had peered into mine, and how I touched its warm blood, blood that soon dried and caked on my fingers. I didn't want to wash it off.

But Mom was on the couch in her usual benumbed state, so I crawled into bed, Sirius curled next to me, my fingers stained with the deer's blood.

But I still ate things that had been killed.

Ben and I shared a cheese pizza, and when someone put a song on the jukebox we discovered that we both loved The Doors. The first time I heard the song *People Are Strange* on the radio, I knew that at least one other person, Jim Morrison, knew how I felt. I bought the album, but Jake forbade me to touch his stereo, so I could only play it when he wasn't around, and even then at a very low volume in case he walked into the house.

Ben told me that The Doors lived in Venice, and that he'd once seen Morrison on the street, and how John Densmore, The Doors' drummer, once went into Zodiac to buy some T-shirts. He said the fact that I loved The Doors and ended up in Venice must be the result of karma.

I didn't know what karma was, but it sounded like a good thing. And I told Ben about outer space and how I hated the space program and Ben said he thought it was all just part of the military-industrial complex and he agreed that we shouldn't be going to the moon any more than we should be fighting in Vietnam.

I'll have to register for the draft soon, he said. I may be in Vietnam before I even get laid. The army should let you get laid first. There's this girl in my class I really like, and she flirts with me, but every guy in class wants to go out with her. I'm trying to nerve-up and ask her out.

I didn't have anything to contribute to a conversation about girls. I found the topic scary. But the fact that he was talking to me about it made me feel like one of the guys.

Your parents must have been a little bit cool to name you Moon, Ben said. I explained that I had changed my name because I wanted to do away with the old me.

Just like my mom did, Ben said. But for some reason she kept my name. I'm named after her father, my grandfather who I've never even seen. I should change my name, too. Why should I go around with his name?

We spent the next twenty minutes trying to come up with a new name for Ben. I want something strange and cool, like yours, Ben said. Before long we were laughing hysterically at the possibilities. We finally settled on Orgasm. I had not laughed so hard in, well, ever.

The sound of my own uncontrollable laugh was new to me and much higher pitched than I would have liked. The owner of the pizza parlor came over and said, Are you boys done eating now? I think he really was asking us to leave.

After lunch we spent an hour in a record store's listening room, playing The Doors and other albums that we had no intention of buying. We were standing close in that small listening room and Ben smelled like perspiration and pizza and wet clothes, and someone alive and vital. I liked it.

We emerged from the store squinting in the bright afternoon sun and walked down to the Venice Beach boardwalk.

A large group of people had gathered on the beach listening to someone speaking through a megaphone from a makeshift stage. Pot smoke was wafting everywhere. I wondered if it would get me high and if so, how I would recognize being high? I inhaled deeply.

The man speaking through the megaphone was wearing a green army jacket with an upside-down American flag sewn over his heart, a red bandana, and torn jeans. His left leg was missing. He leaned on a crutch while his empty pant leg fluttered in the wind like he was doing a one-legged jig.

We're sending our boys thousands of miles from their homes, from their families, to kill innocent Vietnamese people who never did a goddamned thing to a single one of us, he said. We have lost our country. The crowd cheered and started chanting something I couldn't make out.

This war isn't about us, he said. It's about the bankers and industrialists who rule this country. This is Lyndon Johnson's war and I'll be goddamned if I'm going to die for that fucker.

I didn't know anything about Vietnam. Outer space and the oceans seemed more relevant to my life. But I had seen anti-war protesters on the TV news, and my father would shout things like, Look at those pinko faggots. Goddamned cowards—they should be over there killing as many commie gooks as they can.

I concluded that if my father supported the war, it must be a bad thing. But beyond that I didn't have a strong opinion.

We sat down in the sand. After a few minutes a guy in a dirty yellow T-shirt, with the words Peace, Love, Dope emblazoned in green across the front, came over and squeezed in right between us, even though there really wasn't enough room. He had a white-man's Afro and pock marks on his face. He looked to be a few years older than Ben.

Hello, my friend, he said to Ben in a kind of sing-song voice. They clearly were acquainted. Interested in scoring some weed today? I'm taking orders.

Not today, man, Ben said, and nodded slightly toward me as if to say the topic was inappropriate in my presence, which I found offensive as I had been actively inhaling fumes for the past thirty minutes.

It's the usual good stuff. Homegrown. Venice's finest. No additives. Nice, mellow high.

That's okay, man. Not today, Ben said.

Well, you know where to find me. He turned to me. Just ask anybody in town for Skip. I'm world famous, at least in Venice Beach. He winked at me and sauntered away.

Oh shit, Ben said, looking at his watch. I've got to get to work. I'm bagging groceries on the late shift today. Worst summer job I've ever had. Crabby old ladies stand there and count their change as if I can't do arithmetic. Can you find your way back to shelter-world?

He gave me general directions, said, See you later, Moon-man, then suddenly his arms were wrapped around me in a hug—a masculine hug, the kind football players give each other.

My arms remained limp at my sides. Not counting Uncle Arnie, it was my first full-body human-to-human physical contact, the first time there was no empty space between me and another person, in years. He held the hug for a few seconds, then turned and trotted away.

I walked at a slow pace back to the shelter, the sound of the ocean gradually fading away.

I didn't say much during my session with Renata that afternoon. I wanted to ask her about her, about why she had left her husband and her home and changed her name, what she was searching for. Now that I knew more about her life, I wanted to ask her how she possibly could think I would be happy in a foster family. I was angry at her for not letting me know how much she understood. I gave curt answers to her questions.

It was two o'clock in the morning and I still couldn't find my mind's off switch. I sat cross-legged on my cot, in the dark, in a room filled with other lost and desperate souls, and I thought: The moment I arrived in Los Angeles marked the end of certainty. The day I ran away, I was certain that I was slowly dying, certain my mother never would be who she was before, certain my father always would hate me, certain school was a prison with me at the bottom of the social order, certain if I didn't flee, the only option left would be to pull a trigger with my big toe. I had no doubts.

But the moment I stepped off that bus, I was certain of nothing:

not where I would sleep, not where I would find food, not even where the ocean was. And now I was more uncertain.

I squeezed my eyes shut but images flashed before me: Renata, Mom, Jimmy Hollingsworth, Sirius, Max, the ocean, Ben, the Greyhound bus . . . over and over, rapid-fire, like a slide show run amok. I saw my imagined foster family: a nicely dressed church-going clan, like the families on television shows, and then I appeared in the picture, a stray from the runaway kid pound, with a big nose and big ears and unkempt hair, brought in and given warm milk and a little doggy bed to sleep on until he could be coerced into returning to his real family, the family he had fled, the family that murdered its dogs. Well fuck that, I thought, which was the only certainty that arose from all those images.

And then I saw Ben's image again, and it froze on my mind's screen, and I remembered how he smelled and how easy it was talking to him and how nice it felt when his arms were wrapped around me, and remembering that physical contact with Ben made me ache to have it again.

My eyes popped open. Oh shit, I said out loud. After years of being called faggot and homo and queer, now I was thinking about a guy and missing him, his smell, his touch, his hug. I needed desperately to go outside and look at the moon, to shut off my unstrung mind.

I crept downstairs, toward the reassuring sound of Maurice's radio. I stood at his door; he was slouched in his chair dozing, or maybe he just had his eyes closed because his fingers were keeping a barely perceptible beat with the music.

I coughed.

He opened his eyes, blinked a few times and looked at his watch.

Can I come in, I said. He scratched his head and sat up straighter. I took that as a yes and sat down on the floor across from his desk.

Well, a white boy in boxer shorts. At 2:15 am. To what do I owe this honor?

I'm confused, I said. I don't know what to do.

And then, to my mortification, I started sobbing. It was more like a spasm, a convulsion, an emotional seismic event beyond my control.

Even in the worst of times, even when my father or Jake would hit me, or kids at school would slam me into the lockers, even when Uncle Arnie was manhandling me, I managed to hold back tears. I wouldn't give them the pleasure of seeing my pain. I reserved tears for my pillow or for Sirius's soft furry back.

Maurice reached in his drawer and handed me a wad of tissues.

Everyone in this damn building is confused, Moon. That's why they're here. And I don't just mean you kids, but the counselors too. You kids are just the honest ones. You kids are out there screaming, I'm fucked up! I'm confused! while the rest of us pretend to have it all together. But we don't. No one does. If they say they do, they're lying.

Thanks, I said, but that's not the least bit reassuring. I blew my nose in the tissues.

I can only tell you how I see it.

Renata wants to send me to a foster family. I can't do that. What should I do?

I can't tell you what to do. No one can do that except you, little man. I can listen, I can give you tissues, but I can't tell you what to do.

Can I live with you?

Say what?

I was dead serious. Maurice leaned back in his chair and put his hands behind his head.

Moon, my man, I'm flattered. But first of all, your white face wouldn't last thirty seconds in my neighborhood. And second, that wouldn't solve your problems, it would only relocate them.

After a few minutes of silence, I said, I know it's after 11:00, but can I go outside, just on the front steps, and look at the moon?

The moon was a waning crescent, almost straight overhead. I sat on the steps and stared at it, and before long I stopped thinking and my eyes got heavy. I went back inside, and Maurice locked the door. I went upstairs and found someone on my cot, sound asleep, and then I saw that he was there because he had puked all over his own cot, so I went back downstairs and curled up on a couch in the common room.

I awoke to the sound of voices, early risers coming down for breakfast, and there I was on the couch in my boxer shorts and a T-shirt.

Hey, honey bun. Luanne plopped down next to me. Want a smoke, she asked.

I took the cigarette, planning to add it to my collection, only this time she also extended her lighter, so I lit up, my first ever smoke. I coughed but, by God, I smoked it. I instantly felt several years older.

Guess what? she said. I'm going home. My counselor and I met with my parents yesterday, and we talked and cried and hugged and now everything is okay. The baby is going to be adopted, and then I'll finish high school. Isn't that great?

She would go to a hospital in Nevada where she would have her baby, give it to someone else, then go home and be normal again. I was happy for her. I wished my problems could just pop out of me and be given to someone else to deal with.

I tried to flick the ash from my cigarette, but it wasn't as easy as it looks in the movies and I ended up flicking the entire cigarette across the room, where it smoldered under a table.

I would have to flee, once again: I had made the decision as I sat on the shelter steps after the moon cleared my mind.

The decision to run away the first time was difficult, as first times always are. I had planned it for months, in great detail, even before Sirius's murder. I figured out the bus schedules and prices, searched the house for stashes of money, and studied the calendar for the perfect date to make my move, as if I were planning D-Day.

But even after Sirius's murder I kept postponing; fear is powerful. It was an all-too-routine event that was the final straw in a life full of straws.

I had come home from school after a visit to the public library, followed by a meander along the creek, anything to delay my return to the shabby house with the weedy front yard, warped aluminum siding and sagging gutters, a sad house that never had been much of a home. I found my mother slumped in a chair at the kitchen table, her head resting on her folded arms, a puddle of vomit on the floor. A cigarette had fallen from her hand and burned itself out on the table, leaving a scorch mark.

I checked to make sure she was breathing, then sat on the couch in the front room with my library book. It was on the planet Mercury; I looked at the photos but couldn't concentrate enough to read the text; I kept listening for the sound of my mother's breathing.

I heard my father drive up to the house. He walked in without saying a word to me and went into the kitchen. He came out with a beer.

Clean up that shit, he said.

Jake never cleaned up after her. Make Jake do it, I said. My dad had murdered Sirius just two weeks before. I despised him.

Jake works after school, he said. He's good for something. You just sit around like a pussy, reading books and drawing stupid pictures. He then kicked the book out of my hands and across the room, his steel-toed work boot barely missing my hand.

I flinched, but otherwise remained still, staring at the space in front of me where the book had been, continuing to read imagined words now ten feet away.

You clean it up, like I told you. He slammed the screen door behind him, got in his truck and drove off.

I'd been hungry but cleaning up vomit is a real appetite killer. I tried to rouse my mother, but she just mumbled something incomprehensible and then groaned. I went outside and sat by the grave I had dug for Sirius and marked with a smooth stone I'd found at the bottom of the creek. I'd carved his name into the stone with a nail. The sky was darkening and the window to the universe was about to open.

I searched for Sirius, the Dog Star, the brightest star in Earth's sky, just as my Sirius had been the brightest thing in my life. Most people spend their days walking around our little dust speck of a planet thinking they are important, that their lives matter, but they never bother to look up at night. The infinite universe doesn't care diddly-squat about us or anything we do. I bet they're scared to look. I never have been.

As I waited for infinity that night, I had a moment of sudden clarity: If I don't escape, I will see my mother dead; and then I will die.

I carried out my plan the next day.

The second time I decided to run away, from the shelter, was different. I was wiser by a few months. I knew the world was a cold place where it wasn't easy to survive. I knew a foster family would offer a roof, a bed, hot food—but I was searching for my sun, and wouldn't find it there. I was certain they would end up hating me, finding me weird, maybe returning me and demanding a refund.

It would take the county a few days to finalize my foster family arrangement, so I figured I would stay at the shelter and take advantage of the free meals as long as I could. Renata could have stopped our counseling sessions because my case had been settled and a plan was in place. She could have moved on to the next runaway. But she wanted to keep meeting and I wanted to keep being with her, even though I was angry at her and knew seeing her would only make it harder to erase her after I left.

Our sessions often lasted longer than the allotted time. We talked about my nightmares, about Sirius, about my fascination with space and oceans. At what would be our last session, Renata asked, Do you miss anyone from your past? Isn't there anyone you would like to talk to again, to see again?

I felt like she wanted me to admit that there was somebody I missed and longed for, to prove I was a normal kid who would break down and cry for my mommy. But the only ones I missed were Sirius and the old mother, and neither were coming back. I never would be a normal kid.

I turned the tables: What about you? Do you miss your family in Iowa?

Renata sat back in her chair, folded her arms and cleared her throat a few times as she tried to rebalance the counselor-patient relationship.

I know you and Ben spent a day together, she said. I guess he told you some things about me.

I nodded and smiled.

Yeah, she said, I do miss them. But I didn't reject them, they rejected me. They rejected who I was. It's a complicated story. But my story isn't relevant to helping you, and that's what I'm here for.

Well, my family rejected me, too, I said. They left me no choice but to run away. So, we have the same story. And it's really not that complicated. Sometimes you have to go away.

Was I trying to give her a hint, an official warning that things weren't going to go as she planned? Maybe I felt guilty about misleading her and wanted her to catch me in that deception. But even so, what could she have done?

It troubled me when I couldn't make my feelings about Renata and Ben go away. They were uncontrollable, like wild animals running around inside my head, pouncing whenever I let my guard down. It was the first time I realized a good feeling could be worse than a bad feeling, because with the good feeling came a longing, a yearning for something I would never have.

I dreamed about Jimmy Hollingsworth that night and I woke up wondering. What was the last thought Jimmy had in his head before he blew it off? What happened to Jimmy's last thought? Did it get splattered on the wall with his brains? Or was it still there, in another dimension, his disembodied thought—probably something along the lines of, Life Sucks—floating in space along with millions of other disembodied last thoughts? Maybe there's a ring of last thoughts, circling the Earth.

At lunch I stowed some extra sandwiches in my rucksack, then signed out in the office and walked out the door.

Much easier than the first time I ran away, when I cut out of school, quietly snuck into the house—I counted on my mother being asleep— packed some clothes and food and grabbed as much cash as I could. I'd peeked into my mother's bedroom and sure enough, she was asleep on the bed. I watched her chest rise and fall but turned away when I felt tears welling up. I rode my bike to the Greyhound station, showed the clerk a phony letter from my parents I had typed, saying I had permission to travel alone to California to visit my dying grandmother.

I didn't breathe a sigh of relief until I was fifty miles out of town and there was nothing but cornfields out the window. I was excited. I finally had escaped and started my journey to find a sun. Things could only get better—or so I had thought.

I wasn't so hopeful the second time I ran away. Sure, I was free. No one could force me to live with a foster family or send me back home. But a fine line separates freedom and a free fall. I wasn't sure which side of that line I was on.

I retraced the route Ben and I had taken to the beach. When I walked past Zodiac, I saw Ben's friend inside, behind the cash register, but she didn't see me and probably would not have remembered me if she had.

The boardwalk was crowded with all kinds of people—old people with canes, young people on skateboards, hippies and panhandlers. An old woman dressed in gaudy rags—it was hard to describe them as clothes—offered to read my palm and predict my future, but I feared what she might say. Street musicians were competing with the jukebox music blasting out of bars, creating a cacophony with a background beat of rhythmically pumping oil wells. The breeze coming off the ocean was warm, and the sound of the waves was calming. I started to feel better—perhaps because I was among my people, the misfits.

A few policemen strolled along in pairs, so I tried to walk with purpose, even though I had no purpose. It was a Saturday and there were lots of other teenagers around. I walked south until the boardwalk ended, where a canal entered the ocean. The beach was almost deserted, except for a few older people in beach chairs.

I'll just keep walking south, I thought, until I get to an empty beach, even if I have to go all the way to Mexico to find one. But I would have to go back inland and cross the canal and I wasn't going to worry about that until the next day. At that moment I was content to take in the ocean and wait for the sun to set.

I put my rucksack under my head and stretched out in the sand. My mood had curiously improved. I was on my own again, but I found comfort in that, a certain emotional safety in being all alone. A heart cannot break by itself.

When it started to get dark, I snuggled into a narrow space bounded by two large rocks, near where the canal entered the ocean. I tried to make drawings of the ocean, but it was hard to capture the breaking waves. I drew an oil derrick pretty well, just crisscrossing steel bars, but the seagull I tried to draw didn't turn out so good, even though he landed not ten feet from me and then stood there as if he were posing—I just wasn't good at drawing reality. I never could draw Sirius well. I was much better at drawing things and people the way I saw them in my mind.

It soon got too dark to draw, but it was a clear night and the canvas of stars over the Pacific was glorious. I fell asleep to the sound of the surf.

I awoke, to a milky dawn sky, covered in sand but otherwise in one piece. I was hungry and thirsty. The beach was dotted with other people who had spent the night on the sand. I assumed, like me, they had nowhere else to go. I looked north up the boardwalk; it was quiet so early on a Sunday morning, but a few shops were open and some early risers were milling about.

The comfort and safety I'd felt the night before had vanished, as if my mind had reassessed things as I slept. I was the same person, in the same location, facing the same facts, but I now felt untethered. Like I was hurtling through space and could see the beauty of the stars and the galaxies as I flew past them, but couldn't share this beauty with anyone else, and it was cold and dark, and the Earth was getting smaller and smaller.

I walked back to the boardwalk and bought a donut and a grape soda, a transaction that reminded me how little money I had left. I sat on a bench facing the ocean and watched the gulls swoop low over the beach. I chose one gull and watched its every move, trying to get inside its head and imagine its intent, its purpose. Gulls were majestic in flight, riding the air currents effortlessly, even joyfully. But on the sand, they chased each other around the beach on their spindly legs and became comical. Masters of the air, misfits on land.

I must have been sitting there for at least an hour, judging by the expanding sunlight, when I sensed someone behind me peering over my shoulder.

Well, I thought I recognized you.

Skip, the pot dealer, was wearing the same Peace, Love, Dope shirt. He sat next to me on the bench, lit a cigarette and scratched his crotch. So, my little friend, you're out early. Where's your brother?

He's not my brother.

Skip looked at my rucksack. He reached over and tousled my hair; I pulled away as sand flew from my head.

You sleeping on the beach? That's not a good idea. Every few weeks the pigs round up all the people sleeping on the beach and throw them in the slammer. I've been there. It ain't fun. He took a long drag on his cigarette.

I'll be okay. I'm not staying around here much longer.

That so? Too bad, because Venice is a good place to be, especially for somebody who's not tied down by family or relations. But don't sleep on the beach. It's better if you find somewhere to crash, you know what I mean?

I knew exactly what he meant, but the only place I had found to crash had ordered me to leave.

Where you headed? he said.

I don't know for sure. Down the beach. Maybe to Mexico.

Jesus. Good luck, man. I been down there. Crazy scene. Tijuana, Baja. Good dope, but crazy scene. And you'll get the runs like you've never had, like a damn pipe burst in your guts. But they generally leave gringos alone, so that's not a bad plan.

Well, I've got to go, I said, and stood up.

Whoa there, not so fast. What's the rush? Mexico ain't going anywhere. Want a smoke?

I slowly sat back down. Skip offered me a cigarette, which I took and he lighted.

You know, you're going to need some cash money if you're headed to Mexico, Skip said.

I'll get by.

I can fix you up with some work to get some extra *pesos* in that wallet.

I stood up and tossed the cigarette in the sand. I'm not interested in that, I said. And I'll yell if you try anything.

Skip reached up and touched my arm.

Let go! I shouted, which he did quickly and looked over his shoulder to make sure no one heard me.

Hey, hey . . . cool out, man. I'm not a cop or nothing. I just asked if you wanted to make a little cash.

I don't want to do that. I'll make money some other way.

Do *what*, man? I haven't said anything yet.

We looked at each other quizzically.

What did you think I was proposing here, little man? he said.

I didn't answer, but I must have looked as agitated as I felt.

Skip slid closer to me. You think I'm one of those Hollywood Boulevard perverts who wants to pimp you out, don't you?

I nodded slowly.

Oh, man, no way, no way. That ain't my business. Not my cup of tea. I make people happy in the head, not in the nuts.

So what's the work you're talking about, I asked, still wary.

Relax. I'm not going to hurt you—I'm into peace and love, Skip said. He took a long drag on his cigarette. Here's the deal, he said. I take orders from customers, you dig? And these orders got to be delivered. Now, the cops around here, they know me because we've had some interactions in the past. So, it's not smart for me to walk around town carrying the product on my person, you dig? But you—they ain't going to suspect you, you're only a kid. And even if they do nab you, they'd just slap you on the wrist, maybe send you to juvie for a few months. But I'd go to San Quentin and grow old there. Are you putting this together? That's the job—I take orders, you make deliveries and collect payments, and I give you cash money for each delivery. All you need is feet, which you seem to have two of. You dig?

That's how I began my career as a drug-runner in Venice Beach. My first job. My entrée into the business world.

Skip said he would pay me $1.50 per delivery. If I made ten deliveries each day, I would earn more than Jake made at his after-school job; that certainly would thicken my wallet. And if the police hadn't stopped me during all those days on Hollywood Boulevard, why would they now?

I could eat on a few bucks a day but the issue of where to sleep posed a problem. Skip scratched his head and lit another cigarette. Tell you what, you can crash at my pad for a while. It gets crowded sometimes with my other business associates, but there's usually a free couch and lots of floor space. There's a roof on top so you won't get rained on. And it's rent-free. Sound like a deal?

Yeah, sounds okay, I said. It was better than waking up covered with sand. My mood lifted. I felt relieved that my bold plans of the day before would not happen, at least not yet, relieved to still be in Venice Beach. Somewhere deep inside my sneaky little mind I remembered that Skip knew Ben.

Skip's pad was a one-story clapboard bungalow about a mile from the beach, along the same canal that entered the ocean near where I'd slept. It had a small front yard of dirt, weeds, and an anemic tree. The front room contained an assortment of mismatched furniture, including three threadbare couches, a few beanbag chairs, a record player, and a television set. White bed sheets covered the windows. A coffee table— made from an old wooden door straddling cinder blocks—was covered with empty beer cans and full ashtrays.

I accepted Skip's offer to take a shower. The water was hot but there was no shower curtain, no soap, and no towels. I dried myself with my shirt, hung it up on the towel rack, put my pants on, and went into the kitchen. Skip and two other guys were sitting at an aluminum picnic table filling little plastic bags with marijuana. I sat down and watched them work.

Skip introduced me to Wallace and Jorge. Meet the Man in the Moon, our new delivery boy, he said. Jorge was a short, stocky Mexican of about twenty. He asked me if I wanted a beer, I said no thanks, but he handed me one anyway. Wallace was tall and bony, almost skeletal. His dark hair was in a ponytail and he had long, thick sideburns that nearly touched each other under his chin. At first glance you might have thought he was a teenager, but on closer look his face was too chiseled and his teeth were so yellow, he must have been smoking for at least twenty years.

Wallace didn't say much, but Jorge and Skip talked about stuff in a jargon that made little sense to me. Jorge would periodically break into a Spanish song.

I picked up a handful of the dried marijuana. It was greenish-brown and smelled earthy and kind of sweet, different from the smell of burning marijuana. It's Acapulco Gold, Jorge said. The best shit there is, the only thing we sell.

The breeze from outside caused the sheets covering the open kitchen window to flap like the wings of a wounded bird. The beer tasted bitter but was easier to swallow than the swigs of vodka I'd nipped from my mother's bottles. I drank the whole can, accepted Jorge's offer for a second and drank it too as I watched them fill the bags. The breeze felt nice on my bare chest and my eyes got heavy. I rose and belched loudly, walked dizzily into the front room, and collapsed on a couch.

I abruptly woke when Penny and her boyfriend, Lance—two more of Skip's business associates—burst into the house and announced it was time to party. It was early afternoon. Lance was short, thick, muscular, and totally bald except for a bushy mustache. He was wearing cowboy boots, cutoff jeans and a sleeveless white T-shirt. A Chinese dragon was tattooed on his upper left arm. His broad toothy smile seemed permanently affixed to his face, or maybe he was just happy all the time.

Penny was petite, no taller than me. She chain-smoked and swore about every other word, and had a loud, deep rumbling laugh that sounded funny coming from someone so tiny. She was wearing cowboy boots that went to her knees; it was more like she was standing in them than wearing them. When Skip introduced us, she said, Hey there, Baby, you're a cutie. She always called me Baby from then on.

Lance lit a misshapen little green cigar and took a deep draw. Skip put a Frank Zappa album on the record player. Lance handed the cigar to Penny, who took a deep inhale and passed it to me. It's a Thai stick, Baby, said Penny as she exhaled. It's the best. We're trying to get Skippy to add it to his product line.

I held the little cigar for a second, watching the smoke curling up, knowing that I was about to take a significant life step, like kissing a girl for the first time or jumping off the high dive. Things were moving fast on this summer day.

Come on, Man in the Moon, it's going to burn away, Skip said.

I put the little cigar to my lips and inhaled deeply, as Lance and Penny had done. It felt like hot lava pouring into my lungs. I was in agony but held my breath because I was afraid it would burn as much going out as it had going in. Then my lungs exploded. I barked like a sea lion and erupted into a cascade of coughs. Everyone was staring at me.

First time, *amigo?* Jorge asked.

I nodded then sneezed three times in quick succession.

You did fucking great, Baby, Penny said and took the cigar from my hand. It came around two more times. When it was finished, I lay back on the couch and closed my eyes. All I felt was lung pain and an exceedingly dry mouth. I wanted something to drink but couldn't translate the urge into physical movement. I fell asleep and had my recurrent ocean nightmare, only it was less scary than usual, and for the first time I knew what was going to happen before it happened.

And then I saw Renata and Ben waving to me from across a busy street, but there was a circus parade with elephants and clowns going down the street that made it impossible to cross. I wanted desperately to get to them. I felt a tingly feeling in my groin, like someone opened a soda can inside my scrotum and the little bubbles rose up to my chest. It reminded me of when I would put my face over a freshly poured glass of ginger ale and feel those sweet-smelling little bubbles dancing on my skin, only this time they were dancing inside my balls and they felt really good.

And then Hunter Posey, a bully from school I loathed with biblical passion, suddenly appeared. You goddamned faggot, Posey said, as he often did. I wanted Renata and Ben to cross the street and protect me, but they couldn't because of the parade and Posey started chasing me down the street. My legs were so heavy I could barely run, but fortunately I could fly. I lifted off and soared away with a flock of seagulls, the sun's gentle rays caressing my back.

I opened my eyes; someone was lightly rubbing my bare back, the way my mother used to do at night while she told me Simon the Adventurer stories. It was Penny. Jorge was dancing by himself to the music. I heard Skip's animated voice from the kitchen. I saw my mother standing next to him and wondered how she had found me. She was smiling, like she hadn't done in years, but then her face started to melt like candle wax and drip down onto her clothes until there was nothing left but a skeletal head, still smiling, ghoul-like.

I gasped and the image disappeared.

You okay, Baby? Penny said. I nodded yes but I wasn't sure. My mom melted, I said, but Penny wasn't listening.

What'd you say? Jorge asked me. Whose melting? He had stopped dancing and was sitting on the floor in front of me, smoking a cigarette and drinking a beer. I was so thirsty that I lunged for the beer but only managed to knock over an ashtray. Jorge put the beer can in my hand but I forgot to wrap my fingers around it so it fell to the floor. He picked it up and held it to my lips, like a zookeeper feeding a baby animal.

I took a long swig, much of which dribbled down my chin and onto my stomach. Then I belched. I had to pee so bad it hurt, but it took several attempts before I succeeded in standing up. I walked down the hall toward the bathroom, but I couldn't feel anything below my eyes; it was like I was watching a movie of somebody going down a hallway.

I pushed the bathroom door open and closed it behind me; it was pitch dark inside. I groped along the wall for the light switch. My head kept hitting the metal bar that ran across the room and little metal wires that hung from the bar kept hitting me in the face. I groped about, but I couldn't find the toilet. Pee was about to rush out of me like a mighty river. I was afraid it would rip right through my pants.

Someone rapped on the door.

In a minute. I've got to pee, I yelled.

The door opened. It was Lance. You're in the closet, man, he said.

Yeah, right. The closet, man, I repeated. A wire coat hanger dangled next to my face. The dragon tattoo on Lance's arm was laughing at me.

Lance took me by the arm and directed me across the hall to the bathroom. I closed the door and stumbled to the toilet. I fumbled briefly with my zipper but then gave up and squeezed my pants down to my knees the way little kids do when they pee. I peed for what seemed like an hour, my eyes closing and opening slowly, rhythmically. I listened to the musical sound of the pee hitting the water: At first it was a deep strong base, then gradually became a tenor and ended in little driblets that sounded like tingly xylophone notes.

When I was done, I slouched against the wall until a knock on the door brought me back. Hey Baby, I need to get in there and change a tampon. It's a fucking emergency.

I'm done, I yelled, much louder than I needed to but that's the way it came out. I flushed the toilet and turned to the door but my pants were still at my knees, so I fell like timber. My face was buried in a shag bathroom carpet that smelled of urine and mold. I grabbed hold of the sink, pulled myself up, and opened the door. Penny looked down and said, Baby, you need to fix your pants.

I was wobbling precariously and holding onto the sink for dear life.

69

Penny leaned down and pulled my pants up and kissed me on the nose. Lance, would you come help him, she said.

I don't recall much else about that day.

I slept that night on a beanbag chair, curled up like a cat. The next morning Skip jostled me awake and sat me down at the kitchen table. I had a throbbing headache, and my throat was scratchy. He gave me a beer, which appeared to be the only beverage in the house. He said it would cure the headache, but after a few sips I switched to tap water.

We ate frosted Pop Tarts right out of the package. He unfolded a map of Venice Beach and Santa Monica. Most of my clients live somewhere on this here map, Skip said. We're right here—he made an X on the map—I'll give you a list of addresses, how much to deliver to each, and how much they owe. Make sure you get back here with the bread before dark. And remember: no cash, no dope. I don't do credit.

It seemed easy enough. The list had eight addresses on it and it only took me about thirty minutes to plot the best route. I looked up one more address: the one that was on the magazine in Renata's office, which I had memorized. It was not far from the shelter, which I also found on the map, and just a few blocks off the route that Ben and I had taken to the beach.

I figured out how I could walk there from Skip's—not that I had any intention of doing so. I reminded myself that they now were part of my past.

Skip and I stuffed the baggies into my rucksack, and I got up to leave. Wait a sec, Skip said. There's one more thing you got to know: If you get stopped by the pigs, you do not, under any circumstances, lead them back to this house. You dig?

Okay. But what do I do if they stop me?

Make up some shit, man. Say you got the grass from a Mexican in East LA, or from some Black guy at the bus station, or you found it in a public restroom, or just point to some guy on the street and say you got it from him. I don't care what you say, just don't lead them here no matter what.

He grasped my shoulders and looked me in the eyes. Look man, this is a risky business, and we're all in it together until the heat's on, then we're all in it alone, you dig?

Yeah, I dig.

Good. Now get out there and do your job. You'll be twelve bucks richer tonight.

Skip gave me a blue LA Dodgers baseball cap and a pair of sunglasses that were large for my face but fit snugly behind my ears. He tucked my shaggy hair under the hat. It's a good idea to look a little different when you're working the streets, he said. It makes it harder for anyone to identify you later if you get busted.

I hit the streets to play Santa Claus to Skip's clients. The interactions were easy: Customers were happy to get their pot, and I had no trouble collecting payment. When I got back to Skip's he handed me $12 and over the next five days I made $82.50, more money than I'd ever had in my life. I bought a new pair of sneakers, a full size-and-a-half larger than the old ones, and some new sketchbooks.

Skip's house was abuzz. People came and went throughout the day and night, making it hard to sleep for more than two or three hours at a stretch. Lance and Penny usually showed up after midnight and before long all the lights were on, music was playing, and pot smoke filled the air.

I got a slew of new characters to turn into cartoons. Most of them were halfway to cartoonhood to begin with. I filled an entire sketchbook, which I labeled Casa Skip.

Most of Skip's associates were either friendly or ignored me. Clyde, a burly ex-con, was the only one I didn't like. He had a big skull-and-crossbones tattoo on one arm, a long dark beard balancing his buzz cut, and steely gray eyes. He talked to himself, carried a gun in his waistband, and never smiled.

Clyde was Skip's enforcer, which explained why most people paid up without question. When Clyde got stoned, he would sometimes punch at the empty space in front of him as if he were in a fight. I avoided him and never stood near him when he was stoned. I didn't make a cartoon character of him because I feared he might find it.

One night I was sitting on the floor eating Chinese food from a carry-out carton, when Tony sat down next to me. Tony was slight, almost wispy, and had the mannerisms and long wavy hair of a girl. He was the first guy I'd ever seen with earrings, and sometimes I could see traces of lipstick and nail polish. Tony would have been big-time Prey at my old school.

He's my sales rep to the faggot community, Skip later told me. They are great customers.

Tony was very friendly and told me about how he had come to Los Angeles from Texas after his parents kicked him out of the house and, like me, he had no intention of ever returning. He said he had gotten drafted by the army but was rejected. They don't like people who are into loving men and not killing them, he said. And thank God for that because I would've gone AWOL the first day.

I told him how I'd been kicked out of the shelter, so I kind of knew what he had gone through.

I noticed that Clyde was glaring at us as we talked; it reminded me of sitting with Jimmy Hollingsworth in the cafeteria at school. Later that night Clyde cornered me in the hallway outside the bathroom door, pushed me up against the wall with one hand around my neck, and said, One fucking faggot around here is already one too many.

I still talked to Tony when he came over, even if Clyde was there. I figured Skip wouldn't let Clyde do anything too bad. Tony knew what it was like to be Prey and he and I shared a lot of experiences, including violent fathers and drunken mothers. Tony ignored Clyde, but once whispered to me: Clyde needs to get fucked, like most macho guys, but I sure as hell don't want to be the one to do it—he's not my type.

A young woman named Samantha showed up one night and never left; I wasn't really sure why she was there. She slept on the kitchen floor in a sleeping bag. She said she was between gigs, but never said what her gigs were. One morning she came into the kitchen after a shower and was wearing nothing but very tight shorts. She sat right across from me cradling a coffee cup in one hand and massaging her temple with the other. I couldn't help staring at her breasts, although I pretended to be doing other things, like opening a box of Pop Tarts and studying my street map. I had never seen a real, live girl's breasts before.

Looking at Samantha and her breasts made that soda can in my scrotum pop open and those little tingly bubbles start rising up. My pants started to feel tighter at the crotch. I was thinking about how strange it was that something the eyes see could generate bubbles in the scrotum—perhaps there's a long nerve connecting the eyes and the scrotum?—when Skip walked into the kitchen.

Nice vista, huh Moon?

I was staring, an unwrapped Pop Tart suspended from my hand, my eyes focused right on those two cherry-topped scoops on Samantha's chest, while the bubbles rose. I quickly looked down at the map.

Skip laughed. Don't embarrass him, Skippy, Samantha said. She came over to me, leaned down, tilted my head up by the chin and kissed me on the lips. Her breasts dangled just inches away. The bubbles now were reaching my throat. Moon likes the female body, she said. That's healthy and normal.

I was happy to discover this. I had not been sure if I liked the female body and now a girl was declaring that I did. I had always felt strange when other guys talked about girls—girls at school, girls on TV, each other's sisters, or whatever—and about how they would love to fuck them. I didn't feel that urge. The girls at school were scary and mean, at least the pretty ones were. Most were taller than me and liked to hang with the cool boys and the athletic boys. I was terrified at the thought of just speaking to one of those girls.

Posey and his gang once dragged Jimmy Hollingsworth from the showers after gym class, shoved him buck naked into the girls' locker room, and held the door shut. The girls laughed and threw their gym shoes at Jimmy.

I was terrified for weeks that they would do the same thing to me, so I started skipping gym class and ended up making an F, perhaps the first recorded F in gym class history. My father, who normally took no interest in my schoolwork, said, How in fuck do you make an F in gym? And for once, I don't think he was being mean; I think he genuinely was curious.

But now a girl had kissed me, while exposing her breasts no less, and I was awash in bubbles. I imagined returning back to my old school with Samantha on my arm, and we would walk down the hall and all the boys would burn with envy, and Samantha would look right at Posey and say, Hi there, little boy, and I'd just laugh, give Posey the finger and say, Who's the faggot now?

It didn't take long for me to develop a pot habit. After a few nights at Skip's, the Pope would have become a pothead. I avoided Thai sticks after that first experience, but regular pot quickly became my mind balm. It amazed me how inhaling a bit of smoke could change my whole perspective on life and cause me to have the most profound observations, none of which I could recall later.

I'd go into the backyard, which was a patch of sandy dirt with a rusted metal toolshed and a high wooden fence separating Skip's house from the neighbors. On one side lived a biker gang that sometimes came over to party; on the other lived an elderly woman who was stone-cold deaf, which is why she never complained about the noise coming from Skip's, and behind us was the canal. I would lie on the ground, smoke the joint slowly and look at the sky.

One relatively smog-free night, when the moon was a mere sliver and the sky was clear and dark, I could make out the Pleiades, the Seven Sisters, the most beautiful star cluster in the sky, part of the constellation Taurus. If you look straight at the Pleiades you can't see them; their light is too weak, and your eye's blind spot blocks them. You have to look at them out of the corner of your eye.

If my father was the planet Jupiter, my mother was the Pleiades. If you looked at her straight on, you saw a pathetic, skin-and-bones drunk. But if you looked out of the corner of your eye, you could see her beauty, but only fleetingly.

So, I smoked a joint and looked at the Pleiades out of the corner of my eye and thought of my mom and how I wanted badly to see her, and for her to see me, the way we had seen each other when I was little. For the past five years I had only seen her out of the corner of my eye, and I don't think she saw me at all. I felt sad and for the first time I smoked a joint all the way down until it was a tiny roach and burned my finger on the last toke.

I was alone in the universe, but it was okay, because the moon and the Pleiades were still in the sky, watching over me. And I fell asleep on the ground in the backyard of Skip's bungalow in Venice, music and laughter wafting from the house.

Skip's house was not a bad space station, despite the round-the-clock activity and a diet that consisted principally of beer and frosted Pop Tarts (Skip angrily sent me back to the store once when I returned with un-frosted Pop Tarts). Skip and his associates were as afraid of the police as I was, so there was no risk that they would turn me in.

On the rare occasions when I was in the house alone, I would play The Doors' new album and sing along like a rock star. Skip told me The Doors were his customers and promised to introduce me to them, but he never did, so I think he was lying.

I walked miles every day making deliveries and got to know my new hometown well. The better I got to know it the more I felt it was the perfect place for a misfit to fit in. Venice Beach was like the terrestrial version of the Mariana Trench, and all around me were human equivalents of those bizarre sea creatures: long-haired hippies who smoked joints right out in the open, tattooed bikers, guitarists on street corners playing for tips, snake-handlers—with real snakes—and palm readers, people of various hues of color, and neatly-dressed tourists taking photographs.

On one section of the beach, the women sunbathed topless—I learned to master the sidelong glance—and not far away was a gathering place for bodybuilders, whose well-oiled, bulging muscles made a distortion of the human shape.

Policemen were around, especially along the boardwalk, but it never was clear what exactly they were policing, other than the periodic fistfight, usually among drunks who were pretty ineffective at hitting each other. As a shaggy-haired teenager in a dirty T-shirt with a rucksack on my back, I was just part of the background. One of the locals.

Skip had all kinds of customers. An elderly man with a stubbly white beard and moist eyes answered his door wearing pajama bottoms and no shirt; his sagging boobs were bigger than Samantha's, but not nearly as nice. A television was blasting in the background and a fat gray cat was making figure eights around the man's feet.

Skip, I said, which was all I usually needed to say.

He looked confused. I was about to excuse myself and leave when he croaked, You from Skip?

We conducted our business. It helps my aches and pains, helps me sleep, he said, as if he needed to justify to me why he was buying an illegal substance. He gave me a $5 tip. Stay safe out there, sonny, it's a mean world. But I already knew that.

A group of UCLA college guys who shared a small house in Santa Monica invited me inside and taught me how to use a bong. One exceedingly drunk middle-aged guy gave me a $20 bill as a tip. A couple of bikers insisted on buying me lunch one day at a biker bar down the street from their house.

While I ate fried chicken and French fries, they entertained me with stories about their cross-country road trips. They told me that I could get a motorcycle license when I turned fifteen and promised to take me on a road trip when I did. You can ride my old Harley, one of them said, if I ever get around to fixing the brakes.

I imagined myself on that Harley, roaring down a California highway with my biker friends, the sun on my back and the wind in my face. For the first time in my entire life, I felt manly.

In a matter of weeks, I had become a cocky little raggedy-haired drug runner, bringing people their highs as I fattened my wallet and got stoned every night; I never thought work could be such fun. I fell in love with Venice Beach and its scruffy craziness. I felt I had become its embodiment.

I wondered whether I had found my sun, whether I could do this job forever, and maybe Samantha and I would get married some day—in fact, we hadn't even talked since that first embarrassing encounter, but having happy fantasies was a new experience for me.

Yet each morning, as I plotted my delivery route on the map, I always noted the little dot I had made where Renata and Ben lived. Sometimes my deliveries took me close to that dot, once only three blocks away, but I never walked down their street to see where they lived. I felt like a moth flying around a lightbulb, too afraid, or too smart, to alight.

Every time I consulted the map to find my next address I noted where I was in relation to that dot. And at night when I fell asleep under the watchful moon and the Pleiades, I knew that dot was there, too, and I knew that Renata and Ben were there. That dot was like a child's blankie, and I was just a tough little man who still slept with a blankie.

Drug running was not the laid-back career it first appeared to be. On an overcast and drizzly morning after I had made my first delivery of the day and was walking to my next one, I took a shortcut through a part of town I hadn't been in yet, an area on the map labeled Oakwood. Venice was a shabby town, but Oakwood took things to a new level: I couldn't tell if the streets were even paved—they were hard and smooth from traffic but looked more like compacted dirt.

The houses were flimsy even by Venice standards and the few people I saw on the streets were various shades of brown. I had become much less anxious about that, but now I didn't see a single soul as pale as me. I consulted my map and found a different route to my next delivery. As I stuck the map in my back pocket, I saw a young Black man, not more than fifteen feet behind me, just standing there and watching me like he was waiting for me to continue onward.

I started walking slowly and sure enough, he followed me. I picked up my pace and he did too, but always stayed about the same distance behind me.

My new route took me to a busier street, but he stayed on my trail. It got to the point where I wasn't even trying to monitor him discreetly, I was looking over my shoulder at him. His blank expression never changed but our eyes met whenever I looked back.

I got to a busy intersection and had to wait for the light to change; traffic was too heavy to try and cross against it. I assumed the guy would stop fifteen feet behind me but before I could react, he was standing right next to me.

Smoke? he said, and pulled a cigarette pack out of his pocket.

I shook my head. He lit one and took a long drag.

The light changed and we started crossing the street, side by side. You V-13? he said as we reached the middle of the crosswalk. Excuse me? I said. I been on you for a week now, he said, don't think you can bullshit me.

When we got to the other side of the street, I considered dashing off, but I didn't know which direction to go and anyway he was bigger than me and looked athletic.

Come here, he said, and with his index finger he signaled me to follow him to a bus stop bench. We sat down; I was reminded of Max, the pimp who claimed to know Jesus, and that other bus stop bench.

So, he said, you V-13?

I had no idea what he was talking about. I . . . I don't know what that means, I said.

He nodded his head a few times as if he was considering what I'd said, trying to determine if I was telling the truth. I honestly don't know what that means, I said, hoping that in this case ignorance of the law was a perfectly fine excuse.

He finished his cigarette, sniffed a few times, then rose and stood over me, looking down. I saw the shape of a gun under his shirt. Well, I suggest you find out what it means, he said. And find out where you should and shouldn't be doing business. And make sure I don't have to talk to you about it again. I'll be watching.

I finished my deliveries quickly, looking constantly over my shoulder, and returned to Skip's. When I told him about the encounter, he made me show him exactly on the map where I first saw the guy and then the exact route we took from there. He rubbed his chin; he looked concerned.

What does V-13 mean? I said.

Look, Man in the Moon, I'm not the big boss of this operation, okay? I'm *your* boss, but there are bigger bosses. We're just a bunch of gringos selling to other gringos, we're just a piece of a bigger pie.

So what does V-13 mean?

V-13 is . . . well, listen, there's things I don't want to say, and you don't need to know. Let's just say that the guy you took a little walk with thought you were in an area where you shouldn't be. And looking at this map, he was right. It's my bad, Moon. Give me that map and I'll mark on it the areas where you shouldn't be, not even cutting through.

$$● ◗ ◗ ◗ ○ ◖ ◖ ◖ ●$$

The whole V-13 business made me feel less confident on the streets, now that it wasn't just the police I had to worry about; at least the police wore uniforms to identify themselves. But I kept at it, being careful to avoid the neighborhoods Skip had marked on the map, and more alert to the people around me.

I would have been content if my arrangement with Skip lasted forever. Alas, summer was coming to an end and school was about to start up again; a teenage boy on the streets during the middle of the day would draw attention, even in Venice Beach, and no disguise could make me look beyond school age.

I suggested making my deliveries in the evening and staying indoors all day, but Skip didn't trust that I would stay out of sight and didn't want to give the police any excuse to come knocking. He was adamant: I was now becoming a risk to him and he wanted me to move out. Loyalty didn't run deep in Skip's world.

So once again, my space station was ordering me to abandon ship. I had a nice wad of cash but wasn't old enough to rent a room. Jorge said that my money would go a lot farther in Mexico and no one would care about my age or whether I was in school. I wouldn't need a passport to enter Mexico and buses went there every day from Los Angeles, so I wouldn't have to walk down the beach to get there.

I didn't know any Spanish other than the words Diego at the shelter had taught me, so Jorge started teaching me useful expressions: hello, please, can I sleep here, fuck you, got any pot? I'll have a beer, she's hot.

Skip grudgingly agreed that I could work a few more weekends after schools had reopened. Don't even think about stepping outside the house on a weekday, he said, and don't stand near a window. I'm taking a big risk here.

I wanted to have $400 before I left, which Jorge said was more than the average Mexican makes in a year. I already had $340 in my secret hiding place in the toolshed and I told Skip to give me as many deliveries as he had. I'd be on the streets all weekend if necessary.

I didn't want to go to Mexico. I didn't want to leave Venice Beach. I didn't want to go so far away from that dot on my map. But I also feared alighting on that dot. Renata and Ben had started appearing in my dreams, more as images and feelings than as actors in a coherent plot, but they were comforting images and nice feelings, feelings that sometimes induced those bubbles.

I kept reminding myself that Renata had wanted me to go to a foster home and if I encountered her again, she probably would turn me over to the police, who would put me in a juvenile home. Kids disappeared from the shelter all the time; she probably had forgotten me, and I didn't see any benefit in reminding her.

But the thought of leaving Venice for Mexico, or anywhere else, became increasingly distressing, a level of distress that even the nightly backyard joint wasn't relieving. I had felt less distressed about leaving my hometown of thirteen years than leaving my home here of several months. I was tired of running.

And then things got complicated: I sat down on a muggy Sunday morning—the last day that I would be working—with a list of fourteen addresses and eighteen baggies of pot. I still didn't know what I was going to do on Monday morning, when Skip wanted me out of the house, but I knew that whatever I did, I had to do it with as much money as possible in my pocket. I got out my map and started marking addresses.

And there it was, the third address on the list: the dot.

I was not completely surprised. I had known Ben was one of Skip's customers from that day on the beach weeks earlier. Somewhere in my mind I knew—I hoped?—that Ben and Renata's address eventually would show up on my list, and when it did, my plan had been to tell Skip that no one was home and let one of his other couriers make the delivery.

Now it finally had showed up, on my last day of work. Skip's notation on the address—Deal only with the young dude—meant that if anyone else answered the door, I was to excuse myself and leave. I left Skip's place feeling feverish. My stomach was roiling even though I hadn't eaten breakfast. The still, muggy air and low clouds blocked the sun.

I made Renata and Ben's dot the last delivery of the day. It gave me that much longer to agonize, to vacillate, to not know what I was going to do. By late afternoon I was standing in front of the next-to-last house. I had not stopped for lunch, but I wasn't feeling hunger or thirst, as if my body had shut down. I had passed on several offers to take a break and share a joint; I was empty, in every sense.

The house in front of me had a rusted-out car parked in the yard and a mean-looking dog chained to a tree, pulling hard to devour me as I skirted past him to the door. A haggard middle-aged woman dressed in a bathrobe came outside before I even knocked. Skip, I said.

She went back inside while the dog snarled at me. She returned with wadded bills, and we made the exchange without a word.

I walked back toward the sidewalk, stopping to ask the dog his opinion about what I should do. He ceased barking and cocked his head when he heard my voice, but then answered me by resuming his ferocious rant.

I wanted someone, even a dog, to tell me what to do, what it all meant. I closed my eyes and tried to invoke Sirius's ghost, but he had moved on to wherever dog ghosts go.

I argued with myself: Renata and Ben were now back in my life, even if it was only through a chance delivery assignment on my last day of work, maybe my last day in Venice. Versus: Renata and Ben were out of my life, and I was out of theirs, regardless of what my delivery list said.

I started walking in the general direction of Skip's house. I was fighting back tears of uncertain origin: grief, nostalgia, longing, fear. I wish tears would announce their origin; as it was, they only added to my confusion.

An hour later, without having made a conscious decision—in fact, contrary to what I thought had been my decision—I was sitting on the curb across the street from the dot that marked Renata's address. It was a small, white brick apartment building. I watched a few people enter and leave through the double glass door. I thought about how Renata had gone there every night after our sessions, while I slept on a foam mattress less than a mile away.

I wondered if she had thought about me since I disappeared or if she just marked it up to another failed case plan, another lost kid. I was hardly the first or the only.

I was wearing my disguise—the baseball cap and sunglasses, and a pale blue T-shirt emblazoned with a green peace sign that I'd found in a pile of dirty clothes at Skip's. I made sure that my hair was stuffed up inside the cap and I tilted the visor down a bit to cover my forehead. I was pretty much concealed except for my mouth and chin. Even if Renata or Ben answered the door, I doubted they would recognize me.

Renata saw dozens of kids every week, and I had only spent one day with Ben, many weeks before. I double-checked the apartment number, adjusted my sunglasses and crossed the street. I steeled myself: This was a job, I couldn't let old history get in the way. I'd just do my business and leave. I needed the cash.

I entered the small lobby, a bank of post boxes to the right, a bulletin board with fraying fliers to the left. I walked up the open staircase to the third-floor landing; apartment 303 was smack in front of me. I heard loud music playing inside so Ben probably was home.

I knocked and waited. I knocked again, harder, and then heard the rustling sounds of someone approaching the door. It opened just a crack.

Yeah?

Skip, I said into the crack. I tried to speak in a lower voice.

Come on in, Ben said. The door opened wide enough for me to enter but Ben stayed behind it, shielding himself from view. I walked in, reached into my pack and pulled out a baggie of the best pot in Venice Beach.

Here you go, man, I said, and kept my head down.

Hold on, let me get my dough.

Ben went down a short hallway and into what must have been his bedroom. I glanced up and tried to take in the room, but he only took a moment so I quickly looked down again. I had not seen his face.

How old are you? he asked as he handed me the bills. I got this question often on my deliveries.

Doesn't matter, I said, trying to use my voice as little as possible.

Skip's corrupting youth now, I guess.

Yeah, guess so. I turned to leave, feeling a confusing mix of relief and distress.

Wait a minute, Ben said. Have you delivered to me before?

I froze, my back to Ben. No, I said. I mean maybe, yeah, I don't know. I don't remember you.

I kept my head down but I didn't keep walking out the door.

Ben suddenly grabbed my arm. Take off your hat, he said.

No, I've got to go, the deal's over, I said.

He didn't let go of my arm. He reached over my head and pushed the door shut.

Look at me, he said. Take off the shades.

I was still facing the door. Sweat dripped down my forehead. I wanted to open the door and run; I also wanted to stay right there, with Ben, in Renata's home.

Time was not standing still: I was straddling a fault line; the crevice was widening and I had to choose which side to jump toward. I turned abruptly, pushed Ben back as hard as I could and lunged for the door.

Ben grabbed my arm again with one hand and pulled off my hat with the other. Holy fuck, he said.

I grabbed the doorknob but Ben pried my hand from it and pulled me back forcefully. I fell over and brought him down with me. Neither of us said a decipherable word, just grunts and gasps, as we wrestled on the floor while music blasted from the stereo.

I struggled mightily but wasn't sure if I wanted to break free, because if I did, I would run for the door and back to Casa Skip and then to Mexico. If I remained in this kicking, punching, writhing, and not altogether unpleasant embrace with Ben, maybe something else would happen, even if I didn't know what.

It was a question of honor, I suppose, and my temper had a life of its own and was now in high gear. Ben punched me hard in the gut and pinned me on my back. I was breathing heavy and my heart was pounding; stinging sweat rolled into my eyes; my sunglasses were askew. Blood from Ben's nose—I'd scored an impressive blow—dripped onto my shirt, which was ripped at the neck.

Get off, I yelled after I caught my breath. I tried to buck him off but he didn't budge. He held me down to make sure I understood who had won.

Fueled by temper, I kept struggling and swearing until my muscles surrendered. I had no choice but to concede.

Please get off me, I said through my teeth.

Ben let go of my wrists but kept sitting on me. I wiped my hand across my face and saw that I too was bleeding; my lower lip was sore and beginning to swell. Ben rose, went to the door, pulled a key out of his pocket and locked the deadbolt from the inside. He apparently had decided which side of the fault line I was to be on.

The baggie of pot had not survived our tussle and marijuana was scattered across the floor, on our clothes and in our hair. Help me clean this shit up, Ben said matter-of-factly, as if we had spent the afternoon hanging out together.

I rose to my knees and started sweeping up the dried leaves with my hands and putting them back in the plastic baggie. Ben did the same. We worked in silence right next to each other. I avoided eye contact and focused on picking up every last bit of pot.

When we had gathered all we could, Ben got a carpet sweeper out of the closet and started rolling it over the rug. I tried to see his expression, but he was leaning over and his long hair fell like a veil over his face. I felt awkward and nervous. I also felt curiously happy. I reached into my pants pocket and found half a joint, lit it, and took a drag.

What the fuck are you doing? Ben had stopped sweeping; I could see his face now: He was angry and blood from his nose covered his chin and made him look wild and dangerous, like a wounded animal.

The same thing you were going do after you bought that ounce, I said.

Ben walked over, plucked the joint from my hand, took it into the kitchen and washed it down the drain. He came back into the room and walked directly toward me. I was still sitting on the floor and raised my arms protectively over my head. He stopped inches from me; I was looking at his knees.

Get up.

I started to, but I guess I wasn't fast enough because Ben grabbed me under my arms, lifted me off the floor, and slammed me onto a couch. I slunk into its corner not knowing what was coming next.

I had dealt with my father's rages and Jake's bullying, but I could usually see those coming and had learned their patterns and how to avoid them. Even if I couldn't, the outcomes were predictable: my father usually smacked me across the face with an open hand. Jake used fists but he wasn't as strong as my father, so it didn't hurt as much. My father also kicked. Usually, Sirius was his target, but once, when I was blocking his view of the television, he kicked me so hard in the chest, I needed X-rays.

I didn't know what to expect from Ben. He seemed furious and I didn't know why, other than his bloody nose. He had started the fight, I was just there to make a delivery. I was about to point this out to him, when he reached down and grabbed my shoulders.

Do you have any fucking idea how upset my mom has been since you ran off? he said. Do you have any fucking idea what you've put her through?

I wasn't expecting questions, neither of which I could answer. Ben was digging into my shoulders so hard they hurt. My lower lip throbbed.

Let go, I said, and tried to push him away.

You reek, Ben said, and let go of my shoulders as if he feared a stink contagion. I had showered only a few times at Skip's and very likely did reek.

Where the hell are you living?

I'm getting by. Why do you care?

Ben sat down next to me and put his hands over his face.

I felt less threatened now. If Renata was upset that I had run away, she probably would be even more upset if Ben murdered me.

I told Renata I didn't want to live in a foster home, I said. I told you, too.

So you had to run away? Bolt out the door? You couldn't think of any other options?

Like what? I said.

Ben didn't answer; he knew I was right, so I rubbed it in.

Go ahead, Ben, tell me, what options? Your mom told me I had to leave. So I got a head start by a few days. What's the difference? Either way I was gone. Wasn't that the goal? Make room for some new fucked-up kids?

Ben stood up and paced for a minute, then sat on the coffee table facing me; our knees were touching. You don't get it, man, he said. Mom wanted what was best for you. She knows you're weird. She was working to find a family that would be right for you, it's all she thought about. She feels this was all her fault. She's been on the phone every day with every police force in southern California. They found this kid's rotting carcass on the side of some deserted road and she was so scared it was you, she made me drive her all the way up to Santa Clarita to the morgue.

Ben went into the kitchen and came back with two bottles of orange soda, still talking. It was the most disgusting thing I've ever seen, that rotted body with bones sticking through the flesh. I almost hurled. But it was too tall to be you.

Can I go pee? I asked.

Down the hall, second door. And don't try to climb out the window. It's three stories down. You'll break your legs, and I'm not going to scrape you off the pavement.

I looked in the bathroom mirror. My lower lip was red and oozing blood, but was not as big as it felt. My hair was in a state of chaos, having been stuck under that baseball cap all day. I hadn't had a haircut since my father had murdered Sirius. I never wanted to cut my hair again. It was now down to my collar. I wanted to be a mass of hair.

Ben was on the couch, his bare feet on the wooden coffee table. He didn't look up when I came back in the room. I sat down on the couch a safe distance from him and took a long swig of orange soda.

I took in the room: It was small, as was the whole apartment, but large double windows let in a stream of light that made it feel open. A long table with dozens of plants and cacti was in front of the windows. The furniture was basic and eclectic, as if each piece had been purchased at a different yard sale.

Lots of art posters hung on the wall and on the side table next to me sat a framed photo of Renata and a woman who looked familiar to me but I couldn't place; they were smiling, their arms around each other. Next to it was a photo of Ben, I guessed around age ten, smiling on the beach. A wooden dining table stood just outside the kitchen, covered with a bright yellow tablecloth; at one end were three placemats, at the other were stacks of books, magazines, and mail.

Ben broke the silence. Are you really working for Skip?

I need to survive, don't I?

Do you have any idea what could've happened to you, dealing with a bunch of drug dealers?

I noted that Ben was speaking in the past tense, as if my career as a drug runner was over. As if he had a plan, or at least an intention.

I'm about to give it up, I said. I've made enough money now. This is my last day. I'm going to Mexico tomorrow.

I said this with great confidence, as if it still were the operative plan, but I knew now that it wasn't going to happen, and I was relieved it wasn't going to happen, even though I didn't know what was going to happen instead.

You're what? Mexico? Oh, man, are you trying to out-stupid yourself? Ben reached over and rested his hand on my shoulder. A shower wouldn't kill you, he said.

I showered until the water turned cold, then changed into one of Ben's T-shirts and a pair of his cutoff jeans that fell to my knees, but he was so skinny the waist fit fine. I left my dirty clothes on the bathroom floor. As if I lived there.

Listen, Ben said when I walked back out, Mom will be home soon. She had to go in to the shelter today. Don't mention why you came here. I mean the dope and all. I'll come up with something to explain it.

I knew your address, I said. I saw it in your mother's office. I could've come here on my own any time.

You mean you've been out there, peddling drugs, and you knew where we were the whole time?

Yeah, I knew. And I also knew Renata wanted me to go live with a foster family, so why would I come here? Now you've locked the door, so I have no choice.

Ben stared at me until I squirmed. Then he stood up, went to the door, unlocked the deadbolt and opened it wide.

Okay, so you've got a choice now, he said. Adios, amigo. If I'm ever in Mexico, I'll look you up.

I stood there in Ben's baggy clothes, barefoot, my hair still damp from the shower. Ben knew I wasn't going anywhere, and so did I. I had been revealed. He knew I was where I wanted to be; he knew it as soon as I told him I had known his address and now he was making me admit it.

Those weeks on the street, collecting pot money and hanging out at Skip's and smoking joints with my biker buddies, had made me feel tough. But I wasn't. I was the pathetic kid lying on the ground in Skip's backyard, getting teary at seeing the Pleiades and missing my dead dog.

I sat down on the floor, leaned my back against the wall and sighed. It was a sigh of surrender. I didn't want Ben to see my face, so I stared at my toes.

I'll die if I go back to my family, I said, but I won't be a charity case for some other family so they can feel good about themselves. I'd probably die one way or the other if I went to Mexico, but at least I'd die fighting. Not like Jimmy. But maybe his way was better. It was quicker, that's for damn sure.

I was kind of talking to myself now. Or to my toes.

Who's Jimmy? Ben said.

It doesn't matter.

Ben gently closed the door and sat down next to me on the floor. He was a gracious victor.

Renata opened the door to see me and Ben, her son, sitting side by side on the floor. The instant I saw her, feelings I had not been consciously aware of engulfed me like water over a crumbling levee. My gut tightened and tears started to collect behind my eyelids; I blinked hard several times to keep them at bay.

See, emotional situations are like supernovas, those stellar explosions that light up entire galaxies but are deadly for anyone who lives nearby. That apartment in Venice became a supernova. Seeing Renata in tears and feeling her embrace caused my levees to completely fail, and even Ben was wiping away tears as he tried to comfort his mother.

Renata's embrace was hard, as if she wanted to confirm I really was there, and angry, as if she really wanted to hit me but settled for a hard embrace. I put my arms around her and muttered, I'm sorry—an apology not for what I had done but for upsetting her.

The supernova cooled a bit and Renata collapsed on the floor next to us, sitting cross-legged, her head in her hands. Ben told her that he'd run into me on the boardwalk and convinced me to come home with him; Renata didn't ask about his bloody nose or my swollen lip.

I told Renata I'd been living on the streets, and she wondered why the police had not found me. I called them every day, she said. Maybe they weren't looking hard, I said, which probably was the truth.

The door opened and the woman from the store where Ben and I had stopped on the way to the beach entered the apartment with two grocery bags, apparently clueless about the dangers of supernovas. She saw Renata's tear-streaked face, then looked at Ben and then me, whom she clearly didn't recognize. But I could see her mind assembling the pieces.

What's going on? Is that the boy who ran away from the shelter?

Bingo, Ben said.

She put the bags on the table, knelt down and kissed Renata on the lips and caressed her hair, something I never had seen two women do, not even on television. My God, she said, you must be relieved, baby.

We sat in silence for a while, the woman cradling Renata in her arms. No one wanted to speak because no one knew what was to happen next; it was like intermission in a play where the actors hadn't yet seen the script for the next act.

The woman Renata called Shirley eventually stood up. I think you all have things to figure out, she said. I'll leave you alone for a while. She went to her bedroom and closed the door.

Is there anything you want or need to tell me about what went on these past weeks? Renata said.

No, I said. I'm okay.

I'm pretty pissed at you, Renata said.

I know. I mean I know now. I assumed that you had just, you know . . .

Forgotten about you?

Yeah.

Now I'm even more pissed, Renata said. She lit a cigarette. But I can understand, given your past, why you would've thought that. It's just sad that you thought I didn't care.

But you did tell me I had to leave, and I did tell you that I didn't want to live with a foster family.

My main goal was to keep you out of juvenile home, out of an institution of any sort, because that's normally what they would have done with you. You were all the things Child Services hates—of unknown origin, uncooperative, underage. Juvenile home material. And I was fighting so hard to prevent that outcome because it would've been such a bad place for you.

She stubbed out her cigarette in an ashtray and lit another one. But I have to tell you the truth, Moon. I was having trouble finding a family that I thought would be good foster parents for you. The county sent me a bunch of profiles, but they all seemed so . . . I don't know, they just didn't seem right.

I told you that—and I didn't even need to see the profiles, I said.

Renata smiled and rubbed her forehead. Yeah, she said, you did. But honestly, I was getting desperate. I didn't know what I was going to do or where you were going to end up. And now, because you ran away from the shelter while this was in progress, you'll be seen by Child Services as a risk. They'll insist on juvenile home.

Why do other people get to decide where I can live? I said. Why even involve Child Services? As far as they're concerned, I'm gone, I don't exist. The police didn't even look for me.

You have to live somewhere safe, Renata said. I can't send you back out on the street.

I looked at Ben for a sign of encouragement, for a sign that he knew what I was thinking, but he was poker-faced.

I thought you listened to me during those sessions we had, I said to Renata. I told you why I left my home and changed my name and everything. I thought you understood me. And when you suggested moving in with some strange family, it was like you didn't hear a word I said.

Renata leaned back and looked toward the ceiling, but her eyes were closed. She took a few more puffs of her cigarette; her exhales sounded like soft breezes.

I did—I do—understand you, she said. I know you're searching for your sun. And I know what that search is like. I really do. But there are limited options, Moon. Why don't you tell me what you want, but it's got to be something that I can actually make happen.

I didn't have the courage to tell her what I wanted to happen. I didn't want to hear her say No. I didn't want to hear Ben say No.

I don't know, I lied, because I'm not sure what you can make happen.

Well, you can come back to the shelter while we figure things out. I can make that happen. You're not going back out on the street.

Let him stay here tonight, Ben said. It's late. You can take him back to shelter-world tomorrow.

Shirley came out of her bedroom and joined us; she took a cigarette from Renata's pack and lit it. I'm happy you're safe, she said to me; but she wasn't smiling. Maybe she was happy I was safe, but she didn't seem happy I was sitting there.

Renata has been so upset about this, Shirley said. In fact, I've been worried about her health. And Ben has been upset—did he tell you that?

Ben looked down, as if he were embarrassed Shirley had revealed this. Yeah, I was worried about Mom, he said.

Shirley scowled when Renata told her I would be staying over that night. Renata ordered pizzas which we ate mostly in silence.

The walls of Ben's bedroom were covered with posters, making the room look gift-wrapped. Band posters and anti-war posters and peace sign posters and on the ceiling a big poster of a marijuana leaf. A donkey piñata was hanging from the light fixture. Renata piled some blankets on the floor and put Ben's sleeping bag on top to make a bed for me, then she and Shirley went to their room. Apparently they shared a bed.

Ben sat cross-legged on his bed, his back against the wall. OK, man, it's just me and you now, he said, like our day at the beach. Tell me what you want. I know what you don't want. Tell me what you do want. I know you've got something in mind so go ahead and blurt it out.

I was laying on top of the sleeping bag staring at the marijuana leaf poster on the ceiling. I always had concealed my wants because they never mattered to anyone else so there was no need to reveal them. Would my mother have stopped drinking and returned to her old self if I had told her that was what I wanted? Would my father have stopped hitting me? Would Uncle Arnie have been banned from our house?

I couldn't see Ben, which made it easier to answer because I was speaking to the ceiling, to a marijuana leaf. Alright, I said, I'll tell you.

I realized as soon as I said that, I had put myself in a position to be rejected, to be hurt. I should've gone to Mexico, I thought. I steeled myself for rejection. I just hoped Ben wouldn't laugh.

Alright, I repeated. I want to stay here. With you and Renata. Why can't this be my foster family?

I sat up and looked at Ben; he would have to reject me to my face.

Yeah, he said, I kind of figured that's what you were plotting. But this isn't a normal family, foster or otherwise. My mom left my dad because she doesn't like men. I mean, she doesn't want to sleep with men. She likes women. Her parents and her brother think she's a pervert who's going to burn in lesbian hell, so they cut off completely from her—and from me, even though I was just a baby and had nothing to do with anything, except being born, which wasn't my idea in the first place.

My father and her family, they don't know where we are. And I guess my dad's happy to be rid of me since I'm the residue of their empty marriage. My mom and Shirley are like a married couple, except that . . . well, you know. So, we've had to live a lie. Venice Beach is a pretty cool town, but it still isn't cool to be lesbians with a kid in the house.

The Child Services people, people my mother works with every day, they could've tried to take me away if they'd known. That's why I can't invite friends over and I have to tell people my mom dates guys and my father died when I was young and all this other horseshit. I've gotten good at making up horseshit. It would've been nice to be in a normal family, but this isn't one. If Mom wanted to foster you, she'd have to apply to Child Services. They'd investigate and find out this isn't a normal family.

We were silent for a few minutes. I knew that Ben had just told me things he rarely if ever shared.

Look, I'd be totally cool with you living here, Ben said. Really, I would. I'd like to have someone around. I think you're kind of nuts, but that would make it a better fit. You'd be just another nut in the nut dish. But I don't see how Mom can foster you.

So why can't I live here without doing all the official foster family stuff? I said.

I think that's called kidnapping.

Not if I want to be here. And no one knows who I am. I don't officially exist. It's perfect. I can live here, and no one will know.

Whoa, dude, slow down, Ben laughed. He stretched out on his bed and put his hands behind his head.

After a few minutes he said, Okay, man, I'll talk to Mom tomorrow morning and try to persuade her. We're already living a bunch of lies, but this one would be big. I don't know what would happen if we got caught. It's probably a crime. I turn eighteen next year, so they wouldn't bother with taking me away, but Mom would lose her job for sure. I know from how upset she's been she cares about you and doesn't want you to get hurt, but this is a lot to ask. Shirley will have a say, too, and I'm pretty sure she won't like it, but it's my mom's apartment. I'll do my best.

I wanted to hug Ben, not just out of gratitude but to feel his arms around me again. But instead, I awkwardly extended my hand, and we shook as if it were a business deal and not about my life.

The morning light seeping in through the blinds woke me. I stood up and stretched. I looked at Ben; he had taken his shirt off during the night and I watched his bare chest gently expand and contract as he breathed. He jerked suddenly and his eyes flickered open and saw me standing next to his bed. He propped up on his elbows and patted the mattress indicating for me to sit down. Have you been awake all night long staring at me? he said.

No, I woke up a few minutes ago.

Good. Because that would've been really creepy, he said, and yawned loudly. I smell coffee, she's up. Stay here and I'll go talk to her.

I felt like a defendant waiting to hear my sentence. All I was guilty of was being lost, of wanting a home in the void, where I could find my sun. Surely the jury would understand that.

I sat at the card table that served as Ben's homework desk, tore some paper out of one of his school notebooks and tried to draw my mother's face but it didn't look like her. I was having difficulty picturing her in my mind. So I drew Sirius's profile with his ears perked up the way they did when I would talk to him, and then crumpled up the paper.

I lay down on Ben's bed and before long nodded off. I awoke about forty-five minutes later with a headache. My nap had been fitful and anxious, and I tried to assemble the dream images in my head, but they eluded me, except for my mother; I could see her more clearly in my dreams. I got up and opened the window to let in some air. No screen blocked me from leaning out, with my folded arms resting on the sill. A crow was perched on a telephone wire about ten feet away.

I suddenly had a preposterous thought. Is that you? I said. It might be the same crow that had flown into Max and saved me from recapture.

The crow cocked its head.

If it is, thanks, I said. I owe you one.

Who are you talking to? Renata was standing at the bedroom door.

A bird, I said. I didn't hear you come in.

She closed the door behind her and joined me at the window. That crow? she said. Those guys wake me up most mornings, cawing at each other like crazy.

We watched the crow for a few minutes. He spread his wings and cawed but didn't fly away. Renata sat down on the bed, but I remained at the window and waited.

Moon, you are asking me to do the stupidest thing I've ever done in my life. And that's saying a boatload. If we get caught, I'd lose my job and possibly face criminal charges, and you'd go straight to juvenile detention, maybe even a state psychiatric institution. Do you understand that?

You can say no, I said. I don't want to put you at risk. I swear I don't.

Can I really say no? You're not actually giving me a choice, are you? I know you'll run away again otherwise—am I right?

I nodded. But that's not your responsibility, I said.

Cut the shit, Moon. You're making it my responsibility. You were lucky this time. I have no idea how you survived out there and why they couldn't find you, but don't expect that luck to happen again. So my choice is either to agree to what you want, and what Ben wants, or to send you to . . . I don't know, to your death maybe. I feel like a hostage.

I don't want you to feel like that, I said. But you and Ben are the only people I feel safe around.

I knew that a foster family would probably be a physically a safe place, but what I was trying to tell Renata is that with her and Ben, I felt safe in my head; I just didn't know how to say that.

I turned and leaned out the window to cool the emotional heat that was rising in my chest and making it hard to take a deep breath. A tear slipped from my eye and dropped three flights down. The crow was still perched on the wire, head atilt, eavesdropping on this very private scene in apartment 303. Shoo, I yelled, then immediately felt bad for doing so.

I felt Renata's hand, first on my shoulder then gently squeezing the back of my neck. I pulled my head back inside but continued to look out the window.

Ben was five when we moved here from the commune up near Ojai, Renata said. God, it seems so long ago. There was a community here— poets and writers and artists —and they were in rebellion against all those things that everyone was telling us were the normal things to do, like get married, have a family, buy a house, make lots of money and consume things you don't really need, and to only fall in love with the opposite sex.

We didn't march and protest and stuff like that, like what's going on today with the war in Nam and all. We were in rebellion in the way we lived, the poems we wrote, our art. I thought it was such a cool thing because I knew I wasn't normal—not by the standard definition— and never could be unless I faked my entire life. And that would've been a life of misery. Venice Beach was a safe place to be abnormal, at least safer than anywhere else. And you could almost live on air here, everything was so cheap, and we all helped each other.

Are those people still here? I asked.

Some of them, but the community kind of dissolved. Things like that don't last long. There are too many people who want to crush it. Ideas are dangerous. As for me, I wasn't really a poet—not a good one, anyway. But I do have an affinity for young people who are lost and in pain. I know what you guys are going through. And when I started getting to know you in our sessions . . . it's like you'd been part of that Venice community and didn't even know it. You got here on your own.

I don't even know what a normal situation is, I said. But I do know when I feel safe.

Renata sighed a long sigh.

Okay, she said, I'm on board.

I turned and faced her, a lump the size of a melon in my throat. Thank you, I said in a whisper.

This now is no longer a patient-counselor relationship, Renata said, and pulled me into a hug.

I blinked rapidly, but a few tears dropped onto Renata's arm. I didn't know if they were tears of joy or tears of sadness. By joining a new family, I was leaving my mother for good. For possibly the first time in my life I had gotten what I wanted, what I had craved: I was united with that dot on my map, the dot that had been my lodestar right up there with the Pleiades for weeks. But I wasn't at peace.

My dream suddenly flashed back: I was in my old house and my mother was going from room to room frantically calling my name, my old name, and weeping; but I didn't respond, and she couldn't see me, it was like I was a ghost.

● ● ● ● ○ ● ● ● ●

That afternoon, I walked to Skip's. I told him that I had been questioned by a policeman who fortunately didn't search me, but I'd stayed away from the house to make sure he wasn't tailing me.

Good thinking, Man in the Moon, Skip said. I knew you wouldn't fuck up. Drop me a line when you get to Mexico. You never know, I may need a pad south of the border where I can lay low.

I retrieved my money from the shed and left Skip's for my new refuge.

That night I sat at the table with my new family to eat dinner, which was vegetables over rice with little cubes of what I thought was cheese, but Ben said was tofu. It's made from soybeans, he said.

It tasted like nothing. No wonder everyone around here is so skinny, I thought. It was the first time I had eaten with a family since the last time my old family had eaten together, which we did only when we all were hungry and at home at the same time and there was food available—a rare congruence of events.

I remembered that last time: my mother sitting in front of her empty plate cradling a glass of vodka, which she swirled between sips, staring hypnotically at the ice cubes as if she were seeking insight from pieces of frozen water, and my father slurping up canned beef stew so fast it was like he was vomiting in reverse, while simultaneously chewing out Jake for not changing the oil in the pickup. I wanted to die, right there at the kitchen table, just plop down dead.

I imagined that if I had, my mother would have kept swirling her glass and my father would have kept vomiting down his dinner and their lives would go on.

Shirley was cool toward me and we didn't make eye contact; she was not happy about the arrangement. Shirley was a small woman, but she filled the room as if she weighed three hundred pounds.

She talked about how if Richard Nixon won the election in November it would mean the end of America, if not of all life on the planet, and she made Ben promise to hand out flyers for some guy named Henning Blomen, who was running for president and would start the long-awaited revolution if elected.

Later that night I heard Shirley and Renata speaking in hushed but animated voices in their room, I assumed about me.

Shirley doesn't want me here, I told Ben.

Yeah, I know, he said. But it's not you personally. She's been looking forward to it being the two of them, without kids around. She's not into kids and it wasn't always fun growing up around her. But my mom loves her and they're a good couple. They complement each other. Shirley's all passion and fight and Mom's, well, you know, thoughtful and hard to upset. Combined they make a pretty sane two-headed person.

Maybe it wasn't about me personally, but I feared that Shirley would try and change Renata's mind.

Ben and Renata contrived a story to explain my sudden appearance in their lives: Renata's sister had been in an automobile accident that left her in a coma and her husband could barely cope, what with their four other children, so I had been dispatched from Iowa to live with my Aunt Renata in California. I had to call her Aunt Renata at all times, even when we were alone. Otherwise, you will slip up and forget, Renata said. Ben now was my cousin.

We'll have to get you registered at school, Renata said. It's one normal thing you're going to have to do, as much as you may not want to.

Schools concentrate, in one claustrophobic building, hundreds of kids who came in three types: Predators, Prey, and Onlookers. From day one, from kindergarten, the word Prey seemed tattooed all over me. It wasn't just a function of my size: Clarence Hall, who went by the nickname Bobo, was even shorter than me, but he liked sports and roughing it up with other kids and cursing and talking back to teachers, so he was promoted to Predator—a small and mean Predator, like a nasty little wolverine running with the wolves.

Once you are designated as Prey you're pretty much on your own, except for other Prey.

Most teachers were irritable women, who didn't care what happened to you in the hallways or on the playground or on the sidewalk after school or on the school buses. Gym teachers, always men, were the worst. They favored the Predators because they once had been Predators themselves. They despised the nonathletic, the bookish, the odd, the misfits. In gym class the Predators could hit you and taunt you and stomp on your foot and elbow you in the face and it was just all part of the game, whatever the game happened to be.

I liked learning—about space, the oceans, and lots of other things. I liked reading Asimov and Bradbury and Vonnegut. But once I had learned how to read and do basic arithmetic, school didn't contribute much to my learning. I never made good grades because I didn't do homework or pay attention in class. There were so many more interesting things to think about during a fifty-minute block of time than whatever the teacher was talking about.

Teachers would send notes home saying, He reads so far above his age level, I don't understand his poor grades. We need to schedule a parents' meeting. I would forge my mom's signature and the meetings never happened. Eventually the teachers gave up, and I did just well enough to keep getting promoted to the next grade, and I didn't misbehave, which is all they really cared about.

School seemed less about learning than it was about keeping children in line until they are adults, and then the police take over.

But I knew I had no choice; it was inconceivable to think that Renata would allow me to sit around the apartment all day reading and listening to music, as much as I would have liked that.

Registering for school is not easy if you don't have a birth certificate or school records. Renata told our story convincingly, and we agreed beforehand that my last name—the last name of Renata's imaginary brother-in-law—was Morrison. After Jim, of course, my idea.

The school registrar asked when the records from my old school district would arrive. My brother-in-law is taking care of that, Renata said, but he has a lot on his mind, as you can imagine.

The registrar excused herself and went to the assistant principal's office and closed the door. I was hoping she would come out and say, Sorry, he can't go to school here, he'll have to stay at home and do whatever he wants all day. But she emerged and said, Alright, we can proceed, but we'll need the records as soon as your brother-in-law can get to it.

I would be entering eighth grade, already several weeks into the school year. I could walk to school from Renata's apartment. I was down to a few ragged pieces of clothing, so Shirley gave me some tie-dyed shirts and several pairs of jeans from Zodiac, which was awfully gracious, seeing as she didn't want me to exist.

101

Renata bought my school supplies. I would have used my own money, but I didn't know how to explain why I had so much cash.

Schools and I had a traumatic history, and I was as nervous walking into that school building as I had been walking into that ramshackle building with Max. I imagined a powerful spotlight on me, following my every move, announcing to the world my status as Prey.

I found my locker, then proceeded to my homeroom one flight up. The stairs were crowded but everyone was talking and laughing and jostling and the spotlight seemed to dim a bit.

I handed my registration papers to the teacher, Mrs. Friedlander, who led me to my desk. A girl at the desk next to mine looked at me quizzically. She had big, almond-shaped brown eyes and a mop of thick brown hair that seemed never to have met a brush. Her mouth was too large for her face which made her look kind of like a stuffed animal, but a cute stuffed animal. She was wearing a lumberjack shirt and jeans and what looked like hiking boots. She kept looking at me so I, naturally, looked away.

Hey, are you new? I haven't seen you in class, she said in a tone more inquisitive than friendly.

Yeah, I said.

She smiled slightly and waited to see if I was going to produce any other words, but then the bell rang and we both faced forward. I got ready for fifty minutes of daydreaming. I planned to make a drawing of Saturn and its rings from the perspective of someone flying through the rings.

Class, may I have your attention, Mrs. Friedlander said. She came over to my desk. We have a new student joining our homeroom, she said.

Oh shit, I thought as an anxious wave swept up from my stomach into my chest.

Mrs. Friedlander rested a hand on my shoulder. I would like to introduce you to . . . She put on the glasses that were hanging from a chain around her neck and looked at the registration papers. Um, is this correct, dear? she said to me, pointing to the line that said First Name: Moon.

Yeah, that's right, I mumbled.

Oh . . . okay . . . Class, I would like to introduce you all to Moon Morrison.

A wave of snickers and whispers swept across the room. I wished an earthquake could strike at that moment—not a major one, just a disruptive one, about a 5.5 on the Richter scale.

Welcome to Mark Twain Middle School, Moon, Mrs. Friedlander said. Stand up and tell us about yourself.

I had boarded a bus into an unknown future, survived alone on the streets of Los Angeles, barely escaped a pimp's clutches, stonewalled a police officer, fled from a youth shelter, and worked as a drug runner, but at that moment in Mrs. Friedlander's room I was more terrified than I had been at any time since running away from home.

Mrs. Friedlander looked like a sweet little grandmother with her short gray hair and frumpy dress and kindly voice, but she was, in fact, a sadist.

In a classroom full of kids my age, a one-time drug-runner got transformed into a helpless and pathetic child. I felt like I was back home again. I felt like the old me, the me I had hated being, the labeled me I had run away from and, so I thought, had erased from history. But here he was, the old me, back.

I stood up; my hands were shaking; I put them in my pockets; I took them back out; I cleared my throat. Well, yeah, hi everybody . . . I, um, I like astronomy, and oceanography, um, and Vonnegut . . . and I like The Doors . . . and . . . yeah.

The room erupted into giggles and whispers. Did he say astrology? Freak alert! Look at his hair.

Mrs. Friedlander seemed to have been expecting a lengthy autobiography. Shh . . . no talking, class, she said. What school did you transfer from, Moon?

I glanced at the girl sitting next to me; I assumed she would be laughing too. But she was looking at me as you might look at a lost puppy caught in a rainstorm on a cold day, which is how I felt.

I needed to say something dramatic, something that would explain my appearance and my oddness, something that would stop the laughing and the humiliation. I had run away from home to start a new life, not to relive the horrible old one. I had to invent a new past, one that would make me special, an object of respect and not of derision.

Otherwise, I would relapse into the old me; school apparently had the power to do that. I squeezed my eyes shut and ceded to my mind, the mind I didn't fully trust, the control of my mouth, not certain of what would tumble out.

I moved to Venice a few days ago to live with my aunt because . . . because my whole family was murdered last summer while I was away at camp. These guys broke into the house at night, and when I got home the next day, I found . . . well, I still can't really talk about it. Things have been kind of hard.

I had never sounded so sincere in my life nor ever lied so grandly. I was squeezing my eyes so tight that a tear rolled down my face—a nice touch, I think, given the tragic situation.

The laughter and giggles stopped abruptly. I opened my eyes: Mrs. Friedlander's face was frozen in horror. The girl next to me looked as if she had just seen that little puppy in the cold rain get run over by a truck.

A massive boy with a crew cut—a Predator for sure—looked at me with mouth agape.

I'm . . . oh my, I'm . . . so sorry, Mrs. Friedlander said. She stepped closer as if she wanted to embrace me, but she settled for a shoulder squeeze. Her breath smelled like Listerine.

The class continued uneventfully, but everyone was stealing glances at me. I was a celebrity, of sorts. And from that point, the kids at school seemed fascinated by me, but also avoided me. Maybe they thought mass murder was contagious and if they got too close to me, they might contract it, only to return home from school to find their families' bloodied corpses.

They even left me alone in gym class—no one smacked me or stepped on my feet or elbowed me in the face. Not even the worst Predator would pick on someone who had been through what I had been through.

This was beyond my wildest dreams. I no longer would be Prey. I would be left alone.

I was sitting alone in the cafeteria a few days later, scribbling in a notebook, trying to compute how long it would take to reach the Andromeda Galaxy, which is 2.5 million light years from Earth, if I had a spaceship that could fly 10,000 miles per hour. I was getting lost in a sea of zeros and running out of room on the page.

Moon? May I join you?

It was the girl from math class. The only person who ever had wanted to sit with me was Jimmy Hollingsworth, so I immediately wondered if there was something wrong with her.

Sure, I said. She sat down opposite me.

Bummer about your family. I mean, that's so horrible. I mean, what you've been through. It must be terrible.

Yeah, thanks, I said, and took a big spoonful of chocolate pudding so that my mouth would have something to do other than speak.

I'm Jennifer, by the way, she said. I took another huge spoonful of pudding, without having swallowed the first. Are you from LA? Jennifer asked. I quickly and audibly swallowed the huge glob of pudding.

Yeah . . . I mean, now I am . . . but not, you know, before.

Where'd you live before?

Ohio.

Jennifer had managed to extract from me a fact that no one, not even Renata, not even the police officer, had been able to learn, and I didn't know how she'd done it. I was shocked and my face must have shown it.

Oh, shit, I'm sorry, Jennifer said. She reached across the table and took my hand. Oh God, I'm so insensitive. You don't want to talk about that, do you? Man, I'm such an idiot sometimes.

That's okay. I'm okay with it, I said. The bell rang at that moment, ending the longest and deepest conversation I had ever had with a girl my age.

I had been pot-free for over a week and missed it more than I imagined I would. I had grown accustomed to being numbed nightly, to having untethered thoughts emerge from my mind only to dissolve before I could capture them, and to feeling that full-bodied tiredness that made drifting off to sleep so effortless.

I had noticed that Ben quietly left the apartment most nights after Renata and Shirley had gone to bed, returning about fifteen minutes later with what I recognized as stoned eyes.

Renata and Shirley had retired early, Ben was sprawled on the couch reading *A Tale of Two Cities* for school, and I was sitting at the dining table reading a book of poetry by Allen Ginsberg that I had found on Renata's bookshelf. I never had read much poetry and struggled to understand him, but I liked the words, the rhythms, the way it sounded when I read it under my breath.

I put the book down, wadded up a piece of scrap paper, and threw it at Ben. We had spent most nights talking into the darkness of his room, like two disembodied voices testing the bounds of what we could share with each other. The wadded paper hit Ben's book. He grumpily peered over it. What? he said.

Can we get stoned? I know you have pot because I delivered it. And I know you go outside and smoke.

Ben put the book down. Look, he said, it's not even legal for you to be here. And now you want to smoke pot? Are you challenging fate on purpose? You shouldn't be smoking, you're too young.

You do it.

I'm seventeen.

When did you start?

When I was, I don't know, I think fifteen or something. Look, man, I've got to finish this book. Don't you have any homework?

I did it all, I said, but of course I hadn't. Let's share one joint, I said. It'll be quick. It helps me relax.

How long were you living with Skip? I can't believe he turned you into an addict so quickly.

I'm not an addict. It just helps me relax, that's all. I won't make it a habit. Really, I won't. Can't we just step outside and have a quick smoke? You were going to do it anyway, right?

I won. Ben put his book down and sighed, more like a groan. He got up slowly and looked down the hall. They're asleep, he said. You stay here, there's no way I'm going to let you see where my stash is.

He went to his room and came out a few minutes later. Come on, he said.

I followed him out the door and up the stairwell to the fifth floor, the top floor. There were two apartment doors and a gray metal door with the words Authorized Personnel Only stenciled on it. Ben pulled a key out of his pocket and unlocked the door; I felt outside air.

We climbed in darkness up a flight of metal stairs and emerged on the roof. The evening was cool and breezy. There was a new moon, and I could see stars far out over the Pacific where the glow of the city's lights didn't encroach.

Take off your shirt and leave it here, Ben said as he peeled off his T-shirt. Otherwise, it'll smell like pot. And don't go near the edge, there's no railing up here.

We sat with our backs against the flimsy wooden fencing that surrounded the rooftop air conditioning machinery. Ben took a joint out of his pocket and lit up. We passed it back and forth in silence. I could tell from how tightly the joint was rolled that Ben was a pro.

After a few deep tokes I started to relax. I looked up at the sky and found the Pleiades hanging over the Pacific. There's my mother, I said.

What? Your mother?

Yeah. She's hard to make out. She used to be easier to see. She loved me then, when she was easier to see. Now she's all blurry, you can hardly see her.

Shit, this stuff must be spiked, Ben said. Are you having visions?

Yeah, maybe I am. I held my arms toward the sky as if I were summoning visions: Right now I see my mom plastered, unconscious, on the floor, I said. And I see my dad at the tavern, drunk and pissed at everybody, about to have a fistfight with some other asshole and I hope he gets his butt kicked. And my brother is out cruising around in the pickup with his friends and a six-pack. And here I am in California getting stoned on a rooftop with you. But maybe you're not real, either. Maybe you're just part of my vision.

I started laughing at the thought that it was all a vision. Ben started laughing too, although I'm not sure he was laughing at the same thing.

Well, maybe I'm having visions, too, he said. I see my dad in Iowa with a new wife and my half-brothers and half-sisters, and I see my mom in bed with Shirley and maybe they're fucking the way lesbians do it, but I don't really want to see my mom fucking so I'll block out that part of the vision, and I see myself on the roof with some nut who probably should be in an asylum. Shit, we both should be in an asylum. We could share a padded cell.

Yeah, and your mom could be our therapist, I said.

We succumbed to spasms of laughter. It would subside, then one of us would crack up and it would start over again.

Ben lit another joint. Without thinking, I stretched out and lay my head on his lap and he rested his hand on my chest. I closed my eyes. He blew smoke in my face.

Hey, save some for me, I said, and reached up for the joint, but my hand, which was not under my full control at that point, went smack into Ben's nose.

Shit, man what's your obsession with punching me in the nose? he said, and we started laughing again.

The second joint had a calming effect and our laughter subsided. My head was still on Ben's lap, his hand still on my chest.

Guess what? Ben said. Melissa, that girl I told you about last summer? She said she'd go out with me. Isn't that cool? She said, I thought you'd never ask.

Yeah, that's great.

Eventually we fell into pot-induced sleep, sprawled next to each other on the hard concrete. We awoke around 3:00 am, hungry, thirsty, and headachy. We crept back downstairs and ate peanut butter sandwiches before going to bed just a few hours before we would have to get up for school.

Remind me not to do this again, Ben said.

But he didn't mean that, because we did it about twice a week at first and then three or four times a week. Not counting weekends.

Jennifer and I ate lunch together every day, the way Jimmy Hollingsworth and I would, only I liked it when Jennifer sat down across from me, and no bullies bothered us because of the mass-murder contagion thing. She was the only person I talked to at school and I had no desire to expand my circle. One friend was enough.

It was nice having a girl as my one friend. I didn't feel any of those bubbles down below when I was with her, although sometimes she would reach across the table and grab my hand and squeeze it for emphasis, and her small little hand holding mine felt nice.

Jennifer appeared to be friendless, but she must have chosen to be because usually only the ugly and awkward girls got left out of cliques and had no friends, and she was neither. But she was without doubt a misfit—the way she dressed, the way she took no interest in her hair, the fact that she seemed to like eating lunch with me.

She had felt bad that first time when she asked me what she thought was an upsetting question, but she exuded curiosity and I could tell that she really wanted to know more. She would be complaining about a teacher or something and then say, But I know you've been through hell and back.

So I began to give her details, gruesome details, and I enjoyed it: I was rewriting my life, which was far easier than erasing it. In my new life story, my parents had been bound and shot in the head, my brother had his throat slit and was submerged in the bathtub. I told her that when the bus from summer camp dropped me off at the designated location, there was no one there to pick me up, which was unlike my parents, and no one answered when I called home from a pay phone.

I eventually walked the five miles home and entered through the unlocked front door to find the grisly scene.

Did they catch them? Jennifer was leaning halfway across the table.

Yeah, they caught them. I had to appear at their trial. It was tough, but I got through it. They're going to fry. And then Aunt Renata adopted me and I moved out here.

The part of my story that I enjoyed the most was the fact that I had survived the trauma. In my story I was strong, brave, confident, and resilient. All the things that I wasn't.

I told Jennifer that my family had been close and had done all kinds of fun things together, things that were unimaginable in my real family—picnics, amusement parks, roller rinks, family birthday parties. I created a perfect family, a made-for-television family. It felt good pretending that it had all been true, that I had been part of a mythical family.

We talked about other things, too, like music and books and TV shows and teachers. Jennifer would say funny things about other kids and teachers, usually mocking and sarcastic things, and not realize they were funny until I started to laugh and then she would laugh too.

When I showed her my cartoon drawing of Miss Hartley, our strikingly unattractive math teacher, she laughed so hard she almost choked on an oatmeal cookie. Jennifer had a loud, explosive laugh, and sometimes would pound the table as well. I loved it.

After she saw my drawing of Miss Hartley, she started making requests. At her behest, I drew the scrawny old cafeteria worker with huge dangling ear lobes and gray stubble on his face and tufts of black hair like bird nests protruding from his nostrils. He served up food with a metal ladle and never said a word or looked up at you, not even when you said thank you. I drew him sitting inside a vat of stew, with just his head protruding out. Jennifer made me sign it and give it to her.

Jennifer lived with her mother and stepfather; her father lived in San Francisco with her stepmother; her much older sister was married and lived in San Diego. I was either a big mistake or a failed effort to save my parents' marriage, because they divorced before I was two, she said. Either way, I'm not really supposed to be here. I'm a fluke. A big, cosmic whoops.

My mother is a complete idiot—really, the only thing she's good at is being an idiot, and she's got that down well. I visit my dad for a month every summer and at Christmas, but he doesn't know what to do with me when I'm there, because he doesn't know anything about me and he doesn't care to, so I spend a lot of time watching TV and reading. His new wife is a fat sweat hog, but he treats her like she's Elizabeth Taylor. She wears all these big bangles and when she walks into the room you can hear her jingling, like a dog with ID tags on her collar.

As usual, Jennifer didn't laugh at her own words until I did.

The only person Jennifer talked about who did not evoke laughter was her mother's husband, Roy. He is vile and repulsive, she said. Every time my mother goes to San Diego to visit my sister and her kids, I have to stay at home with Roy. I can't stand it.

Why? What does he do? I asked.

He's so gross. I wish he would die.

I get it, but what does he do? I asked again. There were only a few things that could make Jennifer hate Roy so much, and I could think of only one thing that also would make her reticent to say why she hated him.

Compared to what you've suffered, it's nothing, she said. No one's dead or anything. She blew her nose in her napkin.

I think I know what Roy does to you, I said.

I wanted to tell her about Uncle Arnie, to let her know that I knew what she was going through, but I had portrayed my pre-massacre family life as a happy one. She cut me off and changed the subject when I tried to say more. Then the bell rang. See you later, Jennifer said.

111

Ben and Melissa started going out on weekend nights. Ben was smitten but tried to hide it behind his cool outward demeanor. Melissa was beautiful: slender and permanently tanned with wavy dark hair that she sometimes would stick a flower in, hippie-style. She always wore cutoff jeans, even on chilly nights.

I sometimes would go with them to the boardwalk after school or on weekend afternoons. Melissa once asked me how my mom was doing and I said, Who knows? Then I remembered my mom was supposedly in a coma, so I quickly added, It's touch-and-go, the doctors don't really know.

I had one mother, the one Jennifer knew of who had been bound and shot in the head, another mother Melissa knew of who was in a coma, and a third mother, the actual one from whom I had sprung, who was in a similar condition I had left her in. There was the old mother, too, the one who once had seen me, the one I never would have run away from. It was hard keeping all these mothers separate in my mind.

One Saturday when Renata and Shirley were at a political meeting, Melissa came over and we all went up on the roof to smoke.

You're really into pot for a thirteen-year-old, Melissa said to me. My little sister is the same age as you, and I don't think she'd even know how to light a cigarette.

Yeah, Ben said, Moon's been around the block more times than me.

In fact, I was fourteen by then. I didn't tell anyone about my birthday because I didn't want to celebrate it. I hadn't celebrated my birthday since Grandma died. She would take my mother and me to dinner and give me two presents—one was always a religious book about Jesus or a saint or a famous pope, but the other usually was a book I actually wanted. My mother would give me art supplies.

My father didn't seem to be aware that I had, indeed, been born. But after Grandma died and my mother changed, my birthday was barely acknowledged at all. My mother would wish me happy birthday and give me ten dollars, but she always acted sadder than usual. On my twelfth birthday, she was on one of her periodic and mysterious absences from home.

The anniversary of my birth seemed nothing to celebrate. All it meant was that I had ridden our planet around its sun-star one more time, like a carnival ride only not as much fun.

●　❨　❩　◯　❨　❨　❨　●

On election night, Ben, Renata, and Shirley watched poll returns on television while I lay on Ben's bed, reading a book on mushrooms that I'd bought for fifty cents at a used book store. Mushrooms, I learned, can get you stoned, but not the ones they put on pizzas.

I went into the living room just as Richard Nixon was declared the winner. Shirley burst into tears. Renata said to Ben, I am never letting them send you off to war, baby. Never.

I didn't follow politics or the news, so as we lay in the dark in his room, I asked Ben what it all meant.

It sucks, man, he said. This goddam war is going to go on and on even though no one wants it, just the crooks who're making money off it. And I'll have to register for the draft in a few months. Can you fucking believe that? Just as things are going so great with Melissa.

Can't you do something to get out of it?

Well, if I go to college, but they're being much harder about that now. Other than that, I don't know. If I had some kind of disease, like asthma or diabetes or a heart problem I could get out of it. But I'm healthy. That leaves Canada. If I move up there it'll be over with Melissa. Par for the course of my fucking life.

He turned off the light and rolled over, facing the wall.

I dreaded the thought of Ben fleeing to Canada. Our nights on the roof had become an important part of my life. I could be talkative or quiet up there with Ben, or giddy, or sad, or whatever. But always comfortable. He was my first real friend. The thought of him going off to war and getting killed was even worse, much worse.

Shirley's theory was that old men send young men off to war to reduce the competition for young women. They're not even aware that's why they're doing it, she said. It's primal.

It sounded like a crazy idea to me at first, but it was true that all the people making decisions about Vietnam were old men, and all the ones dying were young men. So maybe it wasn't so crazy. I imagined all those old men being like my dad, like the planet Jupiter, with nothing but a small cold rock at their core.

The next weekend Ben and Melissa asked me to go with them to the first postelection anti-war rally, and when I mentioned this to Jennifer she asked if she could come, too. It would be the first time we were together outside of school, so I wondered if this qualified as a date. The rally was large, with many speakers and a few folk singers and an army of policemen around the perimeter. I spotted Skip from a distance, working the crowd and moving in our direction. I tried to hide from view, but he saw me and walked over.

Man in the Moon! What a surprise. I thought you'd be taking a nice long *siesta* right about now down in Baja.

Yeah, well, I'm not.

Samantha misses you, Skip said with a wink. Then he nodded at Ben and sauntered away.

Who was that? Jennifer said. And what does he mean about Baja? And who's Samantha?

Yeah, who's Samantha? Ben echoed unhelpfully. I felt like I was at the police station again.

It's nobody, I said. Just some guy I met on the boardwalk. He's crazy, he doesn't know what he's talking about.

But who's Samantha? Jennifer said.

Nobody. She's nobody. Let's get some tacos, I said. Jennifer scowled at me but stopped interrogating.

I walked Jennifer home. It took much longer than it should have because Jennifer stutter-stepped to avoid sidewalk cracks, and insisted on crossing from one side of the street to the other several times for no apparent reason. She felt a need to touch every street sign we passed.

Since I was trying to walk in a straight line, she kept bumping into me. But she talked the whole time.

Melissa is very Hollywood, if you know what I mean, Jennifer said.

I didn't know what she meant but it didn't sound like a compliment.

I like Ben, though, he seems real, she said. I agreed with her on that. Jennifer said she couldn't wait for Christmas break, even though it meant she had to go visit her father and Sweat Hog in San Francisco. At least it gets me away from Roy, she said.

We reached her street and stopped in front of a tidy bungalow with a low chain-link fence around the small front yard. Jennifer sat down on the curb and put her face in her hands. I sat next to her.

I want to run away, Jennifer said. But I don't know where I'd go. My mom is blind. Or she doesn't want to see, I don't know which.

Inside, I was struggling. I had wanted to tell her about Uncle Arnie before, and now I wanted to tell her about running away. But I was stifled by my lie, by the story of my resilience and toughness in the face of the worst possible tragedy imaginable, the story that protected me against being Prey, that made Jennifer admire me. What Jennifer needed to hear but I couldn't bring myself to tell her was that I was a runaway misfit abandoned by his mother, hated by his father, molested by his uncle.

Can I tell you something really awful? Jennifer asked, interrupting my internal dialogue. It may upset you. You'll probably hate me for saying it.

You can tell me anything, I won't hate you, I said.

She was quiet for a few minutes, then looked me in the eyes with her big brown almonds and said: When you said in class what happened to your family and later told me about finding the bodies and all, I thought how great it would be if I got home and my mother and Roy were dead. I'd love it. Isn't that sick? What's wrong with me? Am I some kind of sociopath or something?

She rested her chin on her knees and tears dribbled down her cheeks. I considered putting my arm around her, but had never put

115

my hand on a girl before and didn't know how she would respond. But then she listed to the side and rested her head on my shoulder.

Now I had to put my arm around her, or I would fall over into the gutter. That doesn't make me hate you, I said. And it's not sick. I understand.

This may have sounded unbelievable to her, given that she thought my loving family had been brutally ripped from my life. But in reality, I too had fantasized about finding my family dead, even my mother, whose death I feared.

Jennifer wiped her nose on my shirt. Maybe I could look at the night sky with you sometime, she said. You can point out all those things you've talked about, like the Plebes.

It's the Pleiades. But sure, we can go to the beach. When the moon's not too bright you can see a lot out over the ocean.

It was getting dark. Jennifer kissed me on the cheek, held my hand for a few seconds, then went into her house. Her hell.

In Ohio we would have been preparing for winter snows. On Venice Beach, people were still wearing shorts. I often would go alone to the boardwalk to take in the street performers, hippies, body builders, and other oddities—my people—and join in any anti-war gatherings. If it were warm enough, I would stand barefoot in the sand at the point where the foam from the breaking waves would rush over my feet and then a few seconds later flow back in the opposite direction.

Standing perfectly still with my eyes closed and feeling the water rush toward shore and then back again made me feel like the only permanent thing in an otherwise churning world. It was a nice break from feeling like the only churning thing in an otherwise permanent world. I could stand like that for a long, long time.

Sometimes I felt a presence, as if someone were standing next to me, someone very familiar, someone comforting and loving. It was an odd feeling, kind of dreamlike but very real; I felt as if I could reach out and touch someone, hold someone's hand. But when I opened my eyes, no one was there.

The two-week holiday reprieve from school meant I could spend all day at the beach or in the public library, which had lots of astronomy and oceanography books. Without the imposition of teachers, I now could learn things that I wanted to learn.

I had not spent time alone with Renata since I'd moved in with her and her family. Four people in a small apartment made that difficult. Shirley still was cool toward me, and I still feared she would change Renata's mind or make an anonymous tip to the police, so I tried to stay out of sight when she was around.

I was well-trained at staying out of sight. I knew Renata was uneasy about our arrangement and feared we would get caught. She periodically would say, I can't believe they haven't asked about your old school records. In fact, I had received a note about this but didn't tell Renata.

On Christmas day we all went out for Chinese food. Ben left afterwards to meet up with Melissa, and Shirley left to spend a few hours at her married sister's house, where Renata felt unwelcome. It was just me and Renata and four fortune cookies. Let's go walk on the beach, Renata said.

So, what are you feeling today? she said as we walked in the sand under low gray clouds. Christmas can make people sad.

I'm fine, I said.

I asked what you're feeling, not if you're fine.

Oh, I'm sorry, I said. Is this a session? Do you work on holidays? Do we have group later?

You are such a little smart-ass, Renata laughed. Probably from hanging around with Ben, the Prince of Smart-ass.

She put her arm around me and pulled me tightly to her, the most affection she ever had shown to me. She was so thin I could feel her ribs. I put my arm around her, and we walked like that, our feet working in synchronicity. It felt good, an old familiar feeling, like being with my old mother but with a bubbly component which made it different. But good.

Well, I said, my home never was exactly filled with holiday joy. Not for the last five years, anyway. After my grandmother died, I didn't have to go to Christmas Mass anymore. I never liked going because it was long and boring, but it was the only Christmassy thing I ever did, and I liked some of the carols they sang.

Do you ever think about your family? Ever wonder what they're doing, what they're thinking about you?

Sometimes I wish they could see me, I said. I wish they could see I've survived without them, that I don't need them, that they can't hurt me anymore. That I'm better off. I really mean that—I'm happier living with you than I can remember being in a long time.

What I said was true, but I said it in order to bolster Renata, in case Shirley was lobbying her to oust me. And to make sure she would feel terribly guilty if she did.

That's nice to hear, Moon, but it's a very risky thing we're doing. I still wonder if it's the best thing for you. It's hardly an ideal family situation.

It's worked for Ben.

Oh, I don't know about that, Renata said. He can't be happy with how his family turned out. And why would he be? There's only one socially acceptable way to have a family and it sure as hell isn't this. It's been hard for him, all the lies and deceptions and not having a father. I wish it could've been different for him. But he somehow came out of it with good values, and I guess that's what really matters.

We stood at the water's edge and watched the sun set, our arms around each other. But I still wondered what Renata really felt for me, because deep down I knew she had been right when she said I was holding her hostage. Can you love your hostage-taker?

Truth be told, I'd thought about my family that very morning. My mother, especially. I wondered if she was trying to find me or if she had written me off for dead. Renata had been distraught when I ran away from the shelter. I couldn't imagine my mother, not the one of the past five years, showing any emotion at all, other than periodic rage toward my father. Perhaps she'd started drinking even more, I thought, if that were humanly possible.

Perhaps my running away had led to one drink too many and killed her. Maybe she blamed it all on my father and had left him for good. But she couldn't survive on her own. She'd held jobs from time to time but never for long.

I tried again to draw my mom's face from memory but couldn't. I remembered her hair and her eyes, but I couldn't visualize her face. I had no photos of her. The only photo I had taken with me was of Sirius, kept with my money in an inside pocket of my rucksack. All I had left was the melting face of my dreams. I drew a skull and then tore up the paper.

On New Year's Eve, I went to the boardwalk with Ben and Melissa. Hundreds of people had gathered for a drum circle on the beach, and built a huge roaring bonfire on the sand. Dozens of drummers were beating rhythms. A wild-eyed guy with waist-length hair, wearing only jockey shorts, was running around the bonfire banging on a hubcap, somehow keeping beat with the others. Pot smoke wafted everywhere, but the police didn't have enough officers to bust such a large crowd. They stood around the periphery.

Ben and Melissa merged with the masses, but I stood back to take it all in. The crowd quickly filled in around me. Someone handed me a joint and I took a few deep tokes before passing it on to a stranger's outstretched hand.

I closed my eyes and listened to the drums, which seemed to be coming from all directions at once. I was being jostled by the crowd like a buoy in choppy seas. I wasn't sure if I was still standing or was hovering above the sand.

I wondered what my mother was doing at that moment. I wished she could see me, and I could say to her: Look, Mom, I'm in California and I'm alive and I'm stoned, and no one can hurt me now. I'm free.

I'm free of you.

A sudden panic overtook me, and I opened my eyes. My face was about six inches from a man's hairy bare back. People were squeezed in on all sides of me. The drummers beat in full frenzy and the crowd had become like one large organism.

I caught a glimpse of Melissa clapping her hands over her head and swaying to the beat. I was breathing rapidly. I couldn't get enough air in my lungs. The drumming now seemed to be coming from inside my head. I turned around and barreled blindly through the crowd. I ran toward the ocean. I splashed straight into the water up to my knees. Then to my waist. Then to my armpits.

The ocean was calm but swells came up to my chin. It was the deepest water I ever had been in. It was cold and I started to shiver.

I looked up at the moon; it was a sliver, a waxing crescent, weak and frail, barely visible, the way I felt at that moment. My teeth began chattering. I fought a powerful urge to keep walking out into the deep. I imagined my head submerging, holding my breath in the pitch blackness for as long as I could until air exploded out of my lungs and then, like an uncontrollable spasm, I inhaled, and my lungs filled with cold salty water until I blacked out. And then it would be over. My lifeless body would drift out to sea and become shark food, then shark shit. And whatever tiny parts of me the sharks didn't eat would drift to the bottom of the ocean—marine snow, it's called—and become food for my fellow ugly misfits who live in total darkness.

I saw Jimmy Hollingsworth standing in front me, standing on the water like Jesus. I didn't imagine seeing him: I actually saw him, he was there, blood pouring out in a steady stream from where the shotgun blast had blown away a large chunk of his head. He motioned for me to walk farther into the ocean and join him; part of me wanted to.

Jimmy reached out his hand to pull me forward; I extended my arm but couldn't quite reach him without diving my head forward. I heard fireworks exploding on the beach behind me.

Jimmy started to fade, but his hand still reached toward me. When he disappeared, I retreated to dry land, numb with cold. I walked down the beach and then along the boardwalk, dodging drunks and revelers, a few of whom pointed and laughed at the boy in soaked clothes.

I headed back toward Renata's apartment, but turned down a side street along the way. A small house looked dark and uninhabited, so I walked up the short path, took a piss behind the hedge, then sat down on the front porch, hidden from view by the hedge, and took off my wet clothes—it was less cold wearing nothing.

I sat in a tight ball, my arms hugging my knees, my knees up to my chest, and listened to the distant din from the boardwalk. I heard people walking by, fragments of their conversations like random phrases from a book I'd never read. It helped me focus, while my body dried in the chill air. My nose had become stuffy and runny; it was only then that I realized I'd been crying.

Hey, man, where the hell did you go? We couldn't find you. I'm supposed to keep watch over you, Ben said when I finally entered Renata's apartment.

Renata and Shirley were staying overnight at a friend's New Year's party in Ventura and wouldn't be back until the next day. Ben and Melissa were on the couch, closer than Siamese twins, drinking beer and watching television replay that big stupid ball dropping down at Times Square.

All those people huddled in the street went wild in celebration of the calendar changing from December to January, celebrating midnight, something that happens 365 times a year. Well, fuck New Year's, I thought, and while you're at it, fuck all the Old Years, too.

I don't need anyone keeping watch over me, I answered Ben. I felt inexplicably angry.

Your clothes are wet, Moon. What happened? Melissa asked.

Nothing happened. Leave me alone, I'm going to bed.

I walked to Ben's room leaving a trail of damp footprints.

What's up his butt? I heard Melissa ask Ben.

He's moody, Ben said. You know, his mom's in a coma and all.

My feet were so numb from the cold, I couldn't feel them. I undressed, put on a Doors album, turned out the lights and curled up under the blanket on my homemade mattress on the floor, right next to the speakers so I could hear Jim Morrison's voice.

Moody, my ass.

I dreamed the ocean dream and drowned at the end as always, but it was different this time. I wasn't afraid. In fact, I wanted to drown. It was a relief.

I awoke early on January 1, the sky just beginning to lighten. Ben stirred and coughed but still was asleep. Melissa was in bed next to him. They both were fully clothed. I didn't want to be in the way if Ben wanted to lose his virginity, so I quietly got dressed and went to the roof to watch the new day begin.

Ben and Melissa indeed went all the way that morning and I scored points with Ben when I told him that I'd left the room for exactly that purpose. Thanks, cousin, he said. I owe you one.

I wanted to ask him what it was like, how it felt, but he didn't seem to want to talk about it and frankly was not as ecstatic about the milestone as I thought he would be. I couldn't help but picture it in my mind.

I felt light years away from going all the way with any girl. I couldn't imagine it happening. But pubes were sprouting like crabgrass down below, and every morning in the shower, with that morning hard-on begging for attention, a boy has to do what a boy has to do.

My first decision of every day was deciding who to think about while I did it. When I first started, back before I left home, the act itself was sufficient. The discovery that this handy organ, previously used only for peeing, had other talents was life changing. But the first image of another person that popped into my head: Jimmy Hollingsworth. This had horrified me, him being a boy, and creeped me out, him being a dead boy.

So, I declared a strict and permanent moratorium on the act, which I proceeded to break about twelve hours later. I tried to think about some of the girls at school, but this image always turned into them laughing at me, so that didn't work. But I soon had assembled a nice and safe cast of characters from television shows.

The girl who played Penny on *Lost in Space*, the one TV show I never missed, she was both cute and an astronaut. And she didn't seem like the kind of girl who would hang out with bullies. Elly May Clampett from the *Beverly Hillbillies*—she was crazy and dumb as dirt but she was funny and I thought I would have liked her, so she worked. And The Flying Nun was cute, although Grandma would have murdered me if she had known I was thinking about a nun while jacking off.

I continued to use these old standbys, and had added Samantha to the team. The image of her tits in my face at Skip's kitchen table was still vivid, and she was the only one of these characters I actually had met.

But the images often changed in the middle of the action and sometimes Renata would pop up, and if I really let my guard down—like if I was still half asleep after a late stony night up on the roof—I thought of Ben—not in any explicit detail but just his thin physique and his soft hair and his smell and the fact that he listened to me and talked to me about heartfelt stuff despite his I-can-take-it-or-leave-it attitude.

It was pretty hard to sleep in the same room every night with someone you've grown very fond of, both of you in nothing but boxer shorts, and then not think about him in the shower the next morning. Still, all those years of being called a faggot and a homo made it unsettling.

I didn't dare think about Jennifer. If I did, I would become nervous and awkward around her. I liked her, but if she started appearing in the shower every morning, things could get complicated. It was hard enough with Renata and Ben sometimes popping up. Jennifer was banned.

Something as manually simple as jacking off should not have been this complicated. I often doubted I ever would actually have sex with a real person because I didn't believe in my own desirability. But there was this: Once in sixth grade I had relented when Jimmy Hollingsworth invited me over to his house after school.

My mom and dad had been at it that morning. My mother had thrown an empty vodka bottle at my dad, which just missed his head and crashed into the refrigerator. My father kicked over the kitchen table and said, I'm going to piss on your boyfriend's grave (I had no idea then what that meant).

I only knew that if I went to Jimmy's house, I wouldn't have to go straight home. I hoped no one would see me leaving school with Jimmy. I was pretty certain I ranked below Jimmy on the Prey list, and I didn't want to get moved up by associating with him more than I already did.

We watched after-school television shows for a while, then Jimmy suggested we go to his room and read comic books. He had hundreds, and we spread them on the floor and dove in, reading especially good passages aloud to each other. I was in the middle of reading about the Green Lantern's epic battle with Goldface, the 24 Karat Villain, when Jimmy suddenly stood up and undid his pants.

You want to see mine? But you have to show me yours.

I was open to new experiences and thought it would be interesting to compare—I regarded it as a scientific observation of phenomena. So, I dropped my pants, too, and we stood there for a minute. Jimmy giggled.

Neither of us had entered puberty, so there wasn't a whole lot of scientific phenomena to see, but Jimmy rubbed himself and got hard. As I started to pull my pants up, Jimmy pushed me backwards onto his bed and jumped on top of me.

What are you doing? I said.

He didn't answer, but he didn't move either, he just lay there, pressing his body against mine, our organs mashed together. I didn't try to push him off, even though I could have; I wanted to see what was going to happen. I could feel his rapid, warm breaths on my ear. I think he would have stayed there a long time, but I eventually rolled him off and we pulled our pants up and went back to reading comic books as if nothing had happened.

I walked home before it got dark. I avoided Jimmy after that, even at lunch. He would stick notes in my locker, asking me to come over to his house, asking why I didn't want to be his friend anymore.

I wasn't angry at him, but when you're already Prey you have to be very, very careful about your associations. Three months later, Jimmy stuck that shotgun barrel in his mouth.

I wondered whether he felt bubbles back then. Maybe some kids feel bubbles sooner than others. Maybe Jimmy felt bubbles when he was laying on top of me. I hoped he enjoyed at least a few tingly bubbles during his short life.

I always had hated returning to school after Christmas break. It's not that the holidays at my home ever were fun, but I could spend the day at Grandma's house, reading or watching television while she knitted or baked pies for the church supper or played bridge with her friends. Returning to school after the holidays meant returning to boredom and to being Prey.

But now for the first time ever, I was eager to return to school because I had missed Jennifer. I enjoyed saying her name: It was like a piece of sweet candy rolling around in my mouth. She had sent me a postcard from San Francisco, on which she crammed more words in her tiny little handwriting than any postcard is meant to bear. I had to hold it close to my face to read it.

She wrote about her dad and Sweat Hog and how her father adored Sweat Hog's children and tried to make her hang out with them, but she refused to, so he got angry and called her a brat and she left the house and walked around San Francisco for hours until it got dark, hoping to frighten him, but when she got back, he hadn't even noticed she was gone.

All of this on one little postcard. She said she missed me and signed the card, Your friend and lunch-mate.

It was nice being missed. It was nice rolling Jennifer's name around my mouth.

I waited for Jennifer at the main entrance to school. She came up behind me, put her hands over my eyes and said, Guess who, cowboy? which was easy to answer because she was the only kid at school who spoke to me.

She launched into tales of Christmas break as we walked to our lockers. Jennifer talked a lot about painful things, like the way her father ignored her while gloating over his stepkids. But, like Ben, she bandaged her wounds with sarcasm, as if she really didn't care.

She said: We went to this restaurant in Chinatown that had ducks and geese and pig carcasses hanging in the windows. It was disgusting. I ordered just plain rice because it was the only thing on the menu that was normal food. My dad acted all pissy because his mother, my Grandma Ling, is Chinese, so I guess he thought I would naturally want to eat greasy bird carcasses.

He said, Well, it was a waste bringing you here, young lady, we should have left you at home. And I said, yeah, I wish you had. So, I was eating my rice, even though it was all lumpy like they had added paste to it or something, and everyone else was passing stinky food around the table, and I suddenly had this image of Sweat Hog hanging in the window, hanging naked from a hook by her feet, glistening with grease, and I started laughing. And I couldn't stop.

Rice was flying out of my mouth all over the table. I almost peed my pants. My dad got so hacked off and kept saying, Get a grip, young lady, but that only made it funnier. He didn't speak to me for the rest of the night.

Jennifer was good at bandaging her wounds, except when she talked about coming back home to her mom and Roy.

As soon as I saw my house, I almost puked, she said. I just wanted to turn around and run. You know, if it weren't for you, I wouldn't have had any reason to come home. I think I would've taken a bus to

Las Vegas or New York or Alaska or somewhere. I can't stand my life.

Then the bell rang, and class started.

I had started to feel about Jennifer the way I had felt about Sirius, which I would have recognized as love had I not been so frightened of feeling it. Or of acknowledging that I felt it. I had failed to protect Sirius from my father and had never forgiven myself.

At lunch, after Jennifer finished recounting how one of her stepsisters had spent an hour in the bathroom putting on makeup—so much makeup, I wanted to hang a sign around her neck saying Wet Paint, Jennifer said, and she's ugly as a bulldog so makeup won't help her—I said, Jennifer, we need to do something. You've got to tell someone what's happening to you. I can talk to my Aunt Renata, she'll know what to do.

No, no, absolutely not, Jennifer said and grabbed my hand. You can't tell anyone. If my mom doesn't believe me, why would anyone else? It'll just make things worse. I can handle it.

It only happens when my mom has a late shift at work or goes to San Diego. When my mom is home, I just slide my dresser in front of the door so he can't get in without making noise. Anyway, I shouldn't even complain to you about it. It's nothing compared to the horrible thing you went through.

I cringed whenever Jennifer referred to what I had gone through, since I didn't go through what she thought I had gone through, what I had made her believe I had gone through. I was sure it wasn't so much me she liked, as it was my story. She saw me as a strong person who had persevered in the face of unbearable tragedy.

If only she knew the truth; but I was in too deep to confess it now. It felt so good to be liked by her, even if it was based on a fiction.

Ben and I huddled together on the roof, passing a joint back and forth. Ben had a beer but he wouldn't share it, so I kept trying to grab it from him while he fought me off, and we both were laughing. He finally offered me the can, but all that was left was the backwash, so I punched him in the gut and we wrestled for a few minutes, physical contact I enjoyed, until Ben said, Enough already.

He lit another joint, the glow from the match briefly illuminating his face against the dark sky.

Did Renata ever hit you when you were little? I asked. It was one of those pot-induced questions, profound but apropos to nothing we had been talking about.

Nope, never, he said. You know her, she's all about peace and nonviolence and talking things out. Why'd you ask? Did your folks hit you?

My father did. All the time. He once knocked out one of my teeth, but it was coming out anyway. I got pretty good at avoiding him, but it was harder to avoid my brother because he was unpredictable. If I said or did something he didn't like, he would wait until later and punch me when I wasn't expecting it. Sometimes days later. My mother, she only hit me once. I ran away soon after.

Why'd she hit you?

I called her a fucking drunk and told her she'd be better off dead.

Well, that'll do it, Ben said.

It's more complicated, I answered. One night I was reading on the couch and my father came home and ordered me to get him a beer and I said, In a minute, and he said, No, now! He pulled me up from the couch and shoved me hard toward the kitchen. Sirius was at my feet and he jumped up and bit my father on the leg. It wasn't a playful bite or a warning bite, it was an I-want-to-kill-you-bite, and it started bleeding real bad.

My father kicked Sirius, so I grabbed him by his collar and ran to the backyard with him. A few minutes later my dad came outside with his hunting gun and says, Get out of the way, I'm going to kill that fucking dog. I got on top of Sirius and tried to cover him, but it was hard because he was growling and snarling and trying to get at my father, who kept yelling, Get off the damn dog or I'll shoot you too!

I didn't care if he did, I wasn't going to let him hurt Sirius.

Then my mother runs out of the house, and instead of going after my father, she starts pulling me off Sirius. I don't know, maybe she was scared my father really would shoot me, but when she pulled me off, he fired right into Sirius's neck, from about three feet away. Sirius was bleeding so bad, not moving.

I fell on top of him, screaming, and my mother tried to pull me off and she was crying. She tried to hug me, but I went ballistic. I mean, shit, she'd made it easy for my father. That's when I called her a fucking drunk and told her she should die. Actually, I screamed it at the top of my voice. Several times.

She finally slapped me across the face, and I fell over, back on top of Sirius.

Whoa. That's heavy, man, Ben said. I'm really sorry.

I leaned against Ben and he put his arm around me.

Why do people have kids, Ben? I said. Why do they go to the trouble to create a life just so they can destroy it?

I suddenly felt like I did on New Year's Eve on the beach, when I had to fight the urge to plunge deeper into the ocean, only it was worse, like I was in an elevator and the cables had snapped, plunging me faster and faster, out of control.

There was no railing on the roof. Ben, I'm scared, I said. Something's happening to me. My words were amplified in an echo chamber in my head, like someone else was speaking in my voice.

Hey man, it's all right, Ben said and held me tighter, now with both arms.

I squeezed my eyes shut but I couldn't stop the mental slide show: My mom slapping me across the face. Roy, as I imagined he looked, pushing against Jennifer's door. Sirius, blood-soaked and dying in the backyard. Jimmy Hollingsworth sprawled on his bed with brains oozing out of the remains of his head. Ben, dead in some rice paddy in Vietnam. Images kept coming, over and over and over, the elevator kept plunging.

Make it stop, Ben, please, make it stop, I whimpered. I was panting, trembling. Ben kept saying, It's okay, man, it's okay.

129

But it wasn't. I was hurtling alone through space. Nothing was okay. Nothing ever had been okay. Nothing ever would be okay.

Ben held me like a human straitjacket, my head against his chest, as if there were no boundary between our individual constellations of atoms. If he hadn't been holding me so tightly, I would have jumped off the roof. Not because I wanted to die but to stop those images in my head.

The elevator's plunge began to decelerate, the slide show slowly faded out, and the next thing I knew Ben was gently shaking me. C'mon, buddy, let's go to bed, he said. You had a bad high. It happens. It'll be okay in the morning.

He helped me up, and I walked woozily to the stairwell, pausing briefly to gaze at the moon in its half-quarter phase, hanging over the ocean in the western sky, reflecting the light of its sun.

I awoke the next morning feeling I had crossed the boundary line between madness and sanity, as I had on New Year's Eve. I was mostly back on the sanity side, but with an emotional hangover lasting several days. I wondered where that boundary line was—was it in my head all the time, just waiting for me to cross it? Or was that boundary line outside of my head, a place my mind went to before returning to the safer confines of my head? What would happen if my mind decided not to return, or got stuck and couldn't return?

Ben was very attentive for the next few nights and wouldn't even consider a visit to the roof. You're laying off the weed for a while, he said.

Jennifer told me her mother was going to San Diego to visit her sister, and she would be alone with Roy. She already had thrown up twice in the girl's bathroom. Neither of us felt like eating lunch, so we went outside and sat on the bleachers at the baseball field.

What time does Roy get home from work? I asked.

When my mom's not in town, usually around eight or nine o'clock.

He goes out drinking after work. Why?

I'll meet you at the corner down from your house at a quarter to eight.

And then what?

I don't know yet. I will by tonight. But you're not going to sleep at home tonight.

I can't go to your place, Moon. Your aunt will ask questions. I don't want anyone to know. It'll make things worse.

I know, I know. I'll come up with something.

It was Shirley's birthday, and Renata had planned for us to go out for pizza that night. I feigned illness. I went into the bathroom and made puking noises so hard that I almost puked for real—so Renata made me stay home, covered in blankets on the couch.

As soon as they departed, I packed some sandwiches and sodas in my rucksack, along with a blanket and Ben's transistor radio. I left a note on Ben's bed telling him not to worry, I would be back home the next day. I had to do something to keep Jennifer from getting hurt.

I ran most of the way to Jennifer's neighborhood and waited at the corner, out of breath and pacing, waiting. A few minutes before eight, I saw her coming down the sidewalk. C'mon, let's go, I said.

She looked at my stuffed rucksack. Where are we going?

To the beach.

The beach? Tonight?

Trust me, I said.

Jennifer did her quirky walking routine, with the stutter-steps and street-crossings, as we headed to the beach. Why do we have to keep crossing the street? I asked.

We just do, it makes me feel better, she said—in a tone that suggested I shouldn't ask that question again.

When we got to the southern end of the boardwalk, near the canal, I led Jennifer onto the beach and helped her crawl into the space between those two large rocks where I had spent the night once before. We nestled together in the sand hidden from view, the blanket draped over us.

Are we going to stay here all night? Jennifer asked.

That's the plan. By midnight it's pretty quiet. We can crawl out then and I'll show you the Pleiades and the Big Dipper and Sirius.

I opened a couple of sodas and ate a sandwich, but Jennifer ate nothing. We listened to the radio but didn't say much. It was a comfortable silence and Jennifer was safe so words weren't necessary. After a while Jennifer rested her head on my shoulder and fell asleep. I eventually drifted off as well.

I dreamed the ocean dream more vividly than ever before, perhaps because the sound of the actual ocean was in the background. I had stopped waking up from it in terror even though the ending always was the same. For some reason the drowning part was less frightening now, and the dream had become almost comforting, a continuity surviving the break with my old life.

Moon! Wake up! Jennifer was tugging on my arm. Let's go look at the stars.

We walked to the water's edge. There were no clouds. The sky was perfect for stargazing. I pointed out the constellations, but the Little Dipper, the most prominent part of Ursa Minor, was the only one whose shape made any sense to Jennifer.

I showed her Venus, which was so bright that even the lights of Los Angeles couldn't compete with it, and Saturn, the only other planet visible. I tried to show her the Pleiades but it's hard to see them unless you know how to look. We saw a few shooting stars and I told her they were meteorites, but she preferred the term shooting stars.

It was chilly and the ocean breeze was strong. Jennifer held onto my arm the whole time, as if she were afraid of being blown over.

I was looking at Saturn and wishing I had a telescope so we could see its rings, when Jennifer tugged on my arm.

What? I said, still squinting at Saturn.

Look at me, Moon.

I looked at her. She kissed me on the lips and held it for at least three or four seconds. I didn't exactly kiss back, but I didn't pull my head back either. She disconnected and rubbed her forehead on my shoulder.

A gaggle of boardwalk drunks were having an argument that escalated into a fistfight. When I heard police sirens, we retreated back to our nest between the rocks, huddled together under the blanket, and quickly fell back to sleep.

I awoke at the first hint of light. Jennifer was curled in a fetal position and I was snuggled behind her, my arm draped over her, my hand cupping her breast, my face in her hair. I contemplated the fact that I had slept with a girl and was at that moment in almost complete bodily contact with her.

I had my usual morning hard-on and felt those tingly bubbles rising from my crotch, tickling my stomach and chest. Jennifer made a few snorting sounds, smacked her lips, inhaled deeply, and resumed her slumber. I gently touched her cheek; it was soft and warm. I ran my hand through her hair. Despite its wild unruliness it was soft.

I remembered the kiss she had given me a few hours earlier, the feel of her lips on mine. The bubbles multiplied. It would be impossible now to keep Jennifer out of the shower.

I rolled over on my back and watched the sky grow brighter. Seagulls screamed at each other in the distance. Jennifer sat up abruptly, as if something had startled her. She scratched her head and rubbed her eyes. What time is it? she asked.

I don't know, I said, probably around 6:30. Are you hungry? She shook her head.

Don't you ever eat?

She just sniffed and stretched. I need some coffee, she said.

We went to a donut shop a few blocks away and then trekked all the way to school in our rumpled, sandy clothes. I spent the day trying to come up with a convincing story to tell Renata when I got home, but when the final bell rang, I still hadn't concocted one. I couldn't tell the truth because Jennifer had made me swear not to. As I emerged from school, I saw Ben at the bottom of the stairs; he already had spotted me, so it was useless to flee.

I can explain everything, I said, even though I had no idea what I was going to say next.

Good, because you owe me big time, Ben said. And the payback starts with telling me exactly what the hell you were doing last night. This better not involve Skip. And don't bullshit me, Moon. I covered for your ass. When we got home, I went in my room and saw your note and told Mom that you were sound asleep. You can't believe how hard it was to keep her from going in there and checking on you.

Then this morning I told her you were still asleep, and I even took you a cup of tea. So you're covered with her. But with me, you're in shit up to your eyeballs.

I thanked him profusely for keeping Renata in the dark.

Save your thanks for later, he said. He grabbed my arm and twisted me around so I was facing him. Look, he said, we're all skating on thin ice because of you. You better not fuck up this situation.

I told him everything. I had promised Jennifer that I wouldn't tell Renata, but I never said I wouldn't tell Ben. He had gone to so much trouble to cover for me.

Shit, man, this is bad, Ben said after he heard me out.

I know, but please, you can't tell your mom or Shirley. Jennifer begged me not to.

Yeah, Shirley would go over there with a kitchen knife and castrate that guy herself. But we've got to do something. She can't sleep on the beach with you every time she's in trouble.

Ben and I devised a plan as we walked home: Whenever Jennifer faced a night alone with Roy, she and I would sleep on the roof. Ben would create whatever diversions were needed to keep Renata and Shirley in the dark. But this won't work forever, Ben said.

At some point Jennifer's got to go to the police or the shelter. You need to convince her of that.

Melissa and Ben broke up—actually, she dumped him. She decided that being a committed couple was not cool. It's what our parents did, she told Ben, even though it was not at all what Ben's parents had done. Melissa wanted to pursue free love, where people don't tie each other down or have expectations or possess each other. I never want to commit to one man, she told him. I want to breathe love the way I breathe air.

Breathing love meant being with different guys and maybe even exploring girls and deciding on a day-to-day basis who she wanted to spend her Love Energy on. Ben might be one of those people on any given day, if she felt a need for his particular Love Energy, but he wouldn't be the only recipient of her love and they wouldn't be a couple anymore.

Ben was shattered. He became a different person. He still looked like Ben, but he was lifeless, just going through the motions of existence, breathing in and breathing out but not much else. He started smoking cigarettes. He would lie on his bed and stare at the ceiling, motionless except for the robotic movement of the hand that held the cigarette—to his lips, inhale, back to his side, exhale, repeat.

He stopped doing homework. He stopped eating. He stopped laughing. He only played music with the darkest and saddest lyrics. I didn't see him cry, but he sometimes would moan and then roll over onto his face.

The change in Ben was like my mother's—abrupt and total. Only with Ben, I knew the reason. But what reminded me so much of my mother is that Ben seemed empty and yet struggling with something. How can a person be both empty and tormented at the same time?

I wanted to tell Ben how much he had come to mean to me, more even than if we had been real cousins, but that seemed so inadequate compared to Melissa, like being told you had won ten dollars after you thought you had won a million.

Renata talked to him, but it didn't seem to do much good. There's nothing I can say to make things better, she told me. I feel terrible that he had to experience heartbreak so early in life. After the family life he's had, or hasn't had, I think Ben really wanted things to work out perfectly.

A few weeks after the breakup, Ben woke me in the middle of the night. Let's go get high, he said.

I was relieved, and not just because I had missed our sessions on the rooftop, which I had started to think of as our shared sacred space. I hoped it meant Ben was starting his emotional recovery, that he was ready to enjoy a good buzz and talk about things.

We snuck out, climbed the stairs and settled in our usual spot. We smoked in silence. I tried unsuccessfully to come up with a conversation starter. Ben was getting seriously stoned, inhaling deeply and holding it as long as possible, until the smoke burst out of his lungs. We knocked off a fat joint, and I lay on my back and looked at the sky. Ben stood up and stretched.

I closed my eyes and imagined what it would be like if gravity suddenly stopped working and everything on Earth flew off into space. People would flail about and collide into each other, but without gravity it wouldn't hurt, we'd just ricochet off things and fly in different directions. It might actually be fun, and it certainly would have brought a quick end to the Vietnam war if soldiers on both sides went flying off into space.

I rolled on my side, and saw Ben standing near the edge of the roof looking out over the city. I rose with great stoned effort and walked toward him. As I approached, I saw how close to the edge he really was.

What are you doing, Ben?

Contemplating.

Contemplating what?

I'm fucked up, man. Melissa made the right choice. I didn't know what I was doing. I didn't know shit. I thought I did. But I don't. I'm a fucking fool, Moon. My life's pathetic. It always has been and it's only going to get worse from here on.

What are you talking about? Melissa's the fool. She's just one girl.

It's not her. I couldn't make it work out. The problem was me. It'll be the same with any girl. He put his hands on his head and squeezed hard, like he wanted to crush his thoughts.

Don't stand so close to the edge, I said. Step back. Please.

I'm just too tired of it all. Nothing in my life has been real. I can't keep pretending like things are normal.

Ben, you're freaking me out. Move back.

I had frozen in my tracks about five feet from Ben. I could see now that his bare toes were literally over the edge. One slight sway forward and he would plunge onto the asphalt parking lot below. Pure, raw terror rose up from my gut, through my chest, into my throat; I began to tremble.

Ben, please. Step back, I begged him. I craned my neck and peered over the edge; it made me dizzy, but I took three small steps forward into the terror, grabbed Ben's arm and leaned backwards. Come away from the edge, I said.

Why should I? Ben said. Tell me why my fucked-up life is worth living. My father must be pretty smart. He must have known how I was going to turn out. Tell me why I shouldn't jump.

Because I love you, that's why, I said.

The words ejected out of my mouth, bypassing the editor. They were not the result of thought. It was the first time I had told someone I loved them since the last time I had said, I love you, Mommy.

I gripped Ben's arm tighter. I was sobbing and sputtering. If you jump, I'm not letting go, I said. I'm going over with you. You're going to kill me, too. I mean it.

I kept pulling on Ben's arm with all my strength until he suddenly fell over backward, away from the edge and on top of me. I started pounding him with my fists in rage—rage at him, rage at Melissa, rage at life. He shielded his head from my pummeling but otherwise took it like a punching bag.

Okay, okay, he finally said. I'm okay.

His voice was weak, little more than a whisper. He sounded frightened. I think he had terrified himself. He put his face in his hands and started to sob, his body doubled over in pain, his anguish total.

I got up off of Sirius's dead body and ran into the woods behind our house and kept running, along the rusty fence bordering the railroad tracks. I ran without seeing, stumbling over fallen branches. It was a primal urge to flee pain. I tripped over a stump and landed facedown with a thud. I pounded the ground with my fists and screamed into a pile of wet leaves. I screamed so hard, I made no sound, a suspended cry. Until well after dark, I lay shivering on those cold wet leaves, made wetter by my tears, until Jake showed up with a flashlight. Jake—my brother, my scourge, the cause of daily misery—gently and wordlessly picked me up and carried me back to the house. He helped me out of my wet clothes, put me in my bed, covered me with a warm blanket, and sat at the foot of the bed until I had sobbed myself to sleep.

Ben finally was depleted. He sat with his head on his knees, breathing in shallow and irregular breaths. I offered my hand, pulled him upright and guided him back downstairs. He fell into bed without even taking off his clothes, facing the wall. I got into his bed and lay against his back. I still was trembling.

I wondered whether Ben had heard what I blurted out on the roof; the words still echoed in my head. If he had, I feared it would be the end of our friendship and thus the end of my safe refuge. Guys didn't tell other guys they love them.

I was about to climb off the bed when Ben reached over, grabbed my hand, and pulled my arm over his chest so we were embracing from the back, nestled like two spoons. He squeezed my hand so hard it hurt, and pressed it tight against his chest, as if my hand were his life preserver, the only thing keeping him above water.

I would have chopped it off and given it to him if that's what he needed to keep from drowning. My face was against his neck; his soft hair tickled my nose with each breath I took, his smell encircled me.

He rolled over and faced me, then put his arm around me. His breath smelled of pot smoke and salty tears. Perhaps my long hair, which was almost shoulder-length by that point, and smooth beardless face reminded him of a girl. Perhaps he had heard what I'd blurted out on the roof and was giving me his response. But everything happened wordlessly as if it were meant to be. And nothing hurt.

I awoke the next morning, my arm draped over Ben's chest, feeling confused and a little scared about what had happened, what we had done. But I also felt happy. I felt beloved.

For the rest of the day Ben and I mostly avoided eye contact.

Renata didn't know how to celebrate Ben's eighteenth birthday. His mood had improved, but he now would be eligible for the draft, so it was hard to make it a happy occasion. I want to sleep all day, that's how I want to celebrate it, Ben said.

Shirley bought a cake, but we refrained from singing Happy Birthday because it was not a happy birthday. Later that night Ben said, C'mon, let's go to the roof. That'll be my party.

Can we go someplace you can't jump off of, I said. Like the sidewalk? I don't think you could hurt yourself jumping off the curb.

Ben laughed, the first time I'd heard his laugh in a long time. I'm okay, he said. I'm serious. My life sucks but I'm not going to off myself. I promise.

I've faced it, man, Ben said as we settled in our usual spot and lit up. My life has been fucked up pretty much from day one. Why did I expect that I could turn out normal? I've got to stop expecting anything good to happen. Maybe I'll live alone my whole life. That would be better than being, you know, not normal. Better than trying to make things work and then getting fucked over in the end, don't you think?

He was posing this question to someone who had assumed that life would be a continuation of middle school: The cool guys and Predators get the best girls, the onlookers get whatever is left, and the Prey, like me, get nothing, or at best they get each other. But here was Ben, by all measures a cool guy, good looking, with friends and at least for a while a girlfriend, asking me to agree with him that he should live a solitary life, that he should accept unhappiness as his destiny.

That's the stupidest thing I ever heard, I said. Trust me, I know more about this than you do.

Well excuse me, Professor Moon, Ben laughed. Tell me what you know.

I'm serious, I said. Some people have no choice. They have to be alone in life, that's just the way it is. But you have a choice. Melissa fucked you over, and that sucks. I get it. But people like you. You'll always have people in your life who love you. It may not always work out perfectly, but at least you don't have to be alone if you don't want to be.

Ben lit a cigarette. What I'm saying is that I don't think I can make it work with any girl, he said. I mean . . . look, the other night when you and I . . . don't you know what I mean?

I knew what he was referring to, of course, but I wasn't sure I knew what he meant. He was missing Melissa, and I had reminded him of Melissa and I was there. I assumed he regretted it.

But you and Melissa, I said, you went all the way, right? I saw you two together, kissing and hugging and all that. Just because it didn't work with her doesn't mean it can't work with any girl.

Ben looked at me and smiled weakly. There's a lot of fucked-up shit going on in my head, Moon. There has been for years. Thanks for being supportive. But let's talk about you now: what about this Jennifer chick. She seems to like you. And you took a big risk for her, so it's pretty obvious you like her. Right?

She doesn't really like me, I said. She likes the person she thinks I am. She thinks I'm someone else.

But you are someone else. Even Mom and I don't know where you came from and what your name used to be. If you want her to love you then you have to let her inside. You don't like letting people inside, do you?

That's not fair, I said. I've told you and Renata lots of things about my past. You know a lot about me.

But you've never told us anything that would make you vulnerable. It's like you don't trust us, like we would screw you over if we had the chance. Are you afraid we'll send you home if we find out where you came from? That I'll go call the police?

I didn't say so, but yes, deep down I was still afraid that I would wake up one day and Child Services or the police would be in the apartment waiting to cart me off.

Alright, alright, I'll tell you, I said. I'm from Ohio. Akron, Ohio. Are you happy now? Does that change anything?

Akron was not a large city. One call to the police there and they would certainly have known about the kid who disappeared in May, 1968. I had just made myself completely vulnerable to Ben.

So, have you told Jennifer about why you ran away from home? Ben said.

No. I kind of screwed up, I said, and then told Ben about my grand lie on the first day of school and how it had saved me from becoming Prey, but how Jennifer believed it, and how I was pretty sure that was the only reason she liked me.

Oh man, Ben said. That's some story. Did you have to make it so damn dramatic? When are you going to tell her the truth?

Are you kidding? I said, I can't tell her the truth now. She's the first girl that ever talked to me because she thinks I'm this strong kid who saw his whole family butchered and somehow survived. If she knows the truth, I'll be a nothing to her.

Truths have a way of coming out, Ben said. At least you know what your truth is and what your story is. I'm still confused about mine.

Ben had changed the subject to me and Jennifer, but I thought about what he was trying to tell me before he did. I thought about Jimmy Hollingsworth and about how Ben sometimes popped into my mind when I was jerking off, and about the words that had flown out of my mouth when he was contemplating suicide, and about Samantha's tits,

141

and Renata's sweet smell, and about being labeled faggot and homo before I had even known what the words meant. And about feeling beloved.

Eventually we stumbled back downstairs, undressed, and without really thinking, I crawled into bed with Ben. He didn't seem to mind. Happy birthday, I said. He propped up on one arm and looked at me lying next to him. We both smelled smoky. Thanks, man, he said. I wouldn't have lived to see this birthday if it hadn't been for you.

The next morning was another no-eye-contact morning.

Ben got his induction notice just a few days after his birthday. The only thing standing between him and Vietnam was an interview and a physical. Shirley wanted Ben and his friends to do active resistance—burn their draft cards, protest in front of the induction office, get arrested, that sort of thing. Shirley liked to fight, and she didn't even mind losing as long as she believed she was right.

Ben and his friends just wanted to stay out of Vietnam. Renata and Shirley got into a big argument about this. Renata wanted Ben to go to Canada if he passed his induction interview. I don't want him hauled off to jail, she said. If that's what this country wants to do to him, then fuck it, he should go to Canada.

But if he stays and resists, he can be part of changing the system, Shirley said. So what if he goes to jail? Martin Luther King went to jail. And anyway, it will be easier to visit him in jail here than in Canada.

Ben was silent during this argument even though it was his life they were talking about. We eventually retreated to his room, put on a Bob Dylan album, and slouched on his bed, side by side, backs against the wall.

So, what do *you* want to do? I asked him.

I don't know, man. I don't want to go to Nam. I don't want to kill people who haven't done anything to me, and I don't want to die for a bunch of old men. I don't want to go to jail either. And you know what else? I don't want to be in Los Angeles anymore. I really don't.

Don't leave because of Melissa, I said. She's not worth it.

It's not that, Moon. I told you, I don't even blame her. Let's face it, I have no home. Me and Mom are here, my father's in Iowa. I wonder if that asshole even realizes I may be headed to Nam. I've got to figure out who I am, what I am. And I won't be able to do that getting shot at in some jungle and I won't be able to do that in jail and I won't be able to do that working at a menial job and going to Santa Monica College. I've got to get away and figure things out.

So you're going to Canada? I said. My heart was sinking.

I need to be on my own, Ben said. I need to see what happens. I need to see something different every morning when I open my eyes.

But what if you can get out of going to Nam by flunking the induction interview? I've read how people act insane or mentally handicapped or fake an asthma attack. You could try something like that.

You're not hearing me, Ben said. I need to get out of here. And anyway, I don't want to act insane or pretend to be sick or whatever. That's cowardly. This war is wrong. The people making us fight it are wrong. And Shirley thinks we're going to change it by burning induction notices? Shit, people have been doing that for years and it hasn't made a damn bit of difference.

Ben turned and looked at me and shook my arm until I was forced to look at him.

When I first met you at the shelter I thought, shit, this little fucker has bigger balls than me. You left home and went across the country all on your own and you never broke. You never called your mommy and asked her to come get you. Can't you see why I need to do that, too? Or at least see *if* I can do it, because maybe I can't.

So that was that. Ben was going to Canada.

I knew I couldn't change his mind. I hugged my pillow as I tried to fall asleep that night, the way I did when I was sad or confused or missing Sirius. After a while, I crawled into bed with Ben; his steady breathing lulled me to sleep.

● ➍ ➊ ➋ ◯ ◖ ◖ ◖ ●

It was one year since I had arrived in California, one year since I had tried to start a new life. Ben graduated from high school and prepared for Canada. He played it straight at his induction interview and got rewarded with an A-1 status, which essentially meant, pack your bags, you're headed to Nam.

Shirley connected him with some people in Canada who helped American draft dodgers; she knew all about that kind of stuff. Renata was grief stricken that her only child was leaving. She was exhausted all the time and lost weight, of which she had little to spare.

I hoped things might change at the last minute, like maybe Nixon would stop the war or Ben would break his leg or contract some disease—nothing fatal, just something serious enough to keep him from going to Vietnam without otherwise affecting his quality of life or preventing him from smoking pot.

Ben spent a lot of time with friends he knew he wouldn't see again for a long time, if ever, but he saved the late night for me and the roof, our sacred space. We got high but we didn't talk much. We didn't need to.

As if losing Ben to Canada wasn't hard enough, Jennifer had decided to spend the summer in San Francisco with her father and Sweat Hog. She wasn't happy about it, but her mother had quit her job and was planning to spend more time in San Diego with Jennifer's sister, leaving Jennifer with two choices: Roy or her dad.

Jennifer and I had started hanging out on weekends, going to movies, eating French fries and kettle corn on the boardwalk with all the crazy people, spending lots of time in record stores but purchasing nothing, going to the public library to do homework (or rather, Jennifer did homework while I read books on whatever interested me).

We spent one Saturday night on the roof together when Jennifer's mom went to San Diego overnight for Easter Sunday. Ben facilitated things, as he'd promised, so Renata never knew that the child she was illegally sheltering spent the night with a girl on the rooftop above her head. It was a cloudy night so we couldn't look at stars, but we had a transistor radio and some sodas and a package of Oreos.

I used blankets to prepare a bed. Once we were sitting comfortably, I sprung the question: Do you want to get high?

Yeah, sure, she said. I've never tried pot. I steal beers from the fridge at home, but they just make me dizzy and need to pee.

I handed her the joint. She rolled it in her fingers and sniffed it. Smells weird, she said. Let's do it.

I lit up and demonstrated how to inhale and hold.

How did you become such a pro? she said. She took a toke but only held it in for a few seconds. We took turns but by the end I had consumed about eighty percent of that joint, and I felt it; with Ben I was lucky to get forty percent.

Jennifer turned up the radio volume. C'mon, let's sing, she said, and started singing along with the radio. I normally sang only when I was certain I was alone. But I was stoned, so I was convinced I actually sounded good. Jennifer and I looked into each other's eyes, singing with great passion. She took my hand and swung her arm with the beat.

I wanted to put my mouth on hers, I wanted to pull her in to me, to squeeze her body against mine, to merge together. We kept singing louder and louder as the song reached its crescendo.

A window opened on the floor below. Shut the fuck up, a man yelled.

Bite me, Jennifer yelled back.

Shhh, I said, we don't want to get caught. I turned down the volume and we lay on our backs, laughing.

Jennifer's head was six inches from mine. A movie star would have rolled over, straddled her delicate body and given her a long and passionate kiss. She'd rub her hands through his hair and moan with pleasure. Then the scene would cut to thirty minutes later, lying together in bed, smoking cigarettes, satin sheets shielding her boobs from the moviegoers.

But I wasn't a movie star. I was a kid who never had made out with a girl. I may have been stoned, but was cognizant enough to know that.

I'm hungry, Jennifer said. Still on my back, I handed her the bag of Oreos. Thanks, she said, still on her back, and then spent about five minutes trying to open the bag. It finally ripped open. Oreos rolled out all over the place, but we ate them anyway, the entire bag.

While we were eating cookies, I thought about coming clean and telling Jennifer the truth about my life. Maybe I was wrong: maybe she liked me for reasons other than my having survived my family's massacre. But she thought I was someone I wasn't, so even if she liked me, it was not the me I really was, it was a fictional me, though of course it contained lots of the real me in it, or at least the real new me I'd become since moving to California. The old me, the me I was trying to forget, she didn't know anything of him.

I wasn't really sure who she liked. Or who I was.

Jennifer put her hands behind her head and stretched out, which pulled her shirt up well above her belly button. I could see the top inch of her panties. She closed her eyes and took a deep breath, black Oreo crumbs on her lips.

Her breasts had become more pronounced since I'd known her. Her thin little waist. Her legs clad in tight bell-bottom jeans, crossed at the ankles. Her bare feet. She had a slight smile on her face as she fell asleep; her nose twitched now and then, like a bunny's. I imagined running my hands over her naked body, over her breasts, feeling her soft pubic hair between my fingers.

I was getting all bubbly and stiff and it was a good eight hours before my morning shower and the possibility of relief. I feared I was setting myself up for frustration and disappointment. I had never believed girls would be part of my life, and I had good reasons to believe this: The pretty ones hung out with the Predators. The not-so-pretty ones were mean, because they didn't want to worsen their lot by hanging out with Prey. Just about all the girls were taller than me, so I literally was under their radar.

I assumed girls found me ugly: My nose was big, and my ears

protruded, although now they were covered by hair. Grandma's friends used to say things like, you are such a cutie. I assumed they meant cute in an elfin sort of way, a not-quite-human-but-not-scary way.

Girls also must have found me boring. They weren't interested in outer space and the oceans or Asimov and Vonnegut. They preferred the Monkees over The Doors. So what would I talk about with a girl? They must have thought I was stupid: I barely got promoted from grade to grade, I stuttered and stumbled when teachers called on me in class. No girl would dream of asking me for help with homework.

Ugly, boring, and stupid do not make a girl-magnet.

Maybe I had become unappealing to my mother, the way I was unappealing to other girls. Or maybe whatever it was she needed from me, I couldn't provide. I used to think about this a lot, sitting in the backyard with Sirius, and I never came up with answers.

But there was this: A couple years ago I woke up in the middle of the night to find my mother sitting on the floor beside my bed, reading a postcard by flashlight while caressing my cheek. The pile of postcards in her lap looked to have foreign stamps.

Neither of us said a word. I reached out from under the covers and took her hand; she gently rubbed my back and wept quietly. We looked into each other's eyes until my eyelids got heavy and I fell back asleep, still holding her hand. My old mother who loved me had come back, I thought. But the next day she was gone again.

Ben came up to the roof at daybreak. He brought me coffee and sat next to me while Jennifer slept. I was in my sacred spot with the only two friends I'd ever had.

Renata was in mourning over Ben's imminent departure. She took time off from work to be with him, but mostly spent those days in bed or lying on the couch smoking cigarettes. Shirley diagnosed it as emotional trauma and blamed it all on Nixon and the military-industrial complex. She made Renata drink all sorts of foul-smelling herbal teas she got from a Chinese doctor who claimed they would revive her, but they didn't.

Shirley said that as soon as Ben left town, she was going to take Renata to a shrink that she was seeing, some guy in Santa Monica who performed a new kind of therapy where you get all worked up over your problems until eventually you scream—a blood-curdling Primal Scream, according to Shirley—but you felt a lot better when it was over. It sounded awful to me but Shirley swore it had helped her.

The problem, Shirley told Renata, is that you don't express the depth of the anger you feel toward your family, who disowned you and Ben because of who you are. You need to let yourself feel it and be angry. And now Ben's leaving, so it's bringing up lots of old shit about leaving and being left. Holding in all that anger is hurting your body. It's not healthy.

Renata didn't think primal screaming would help. Once Ben's settled in Canada, once I know that he's safe, I'll feel better, she said.

I agreed with Shirley. Renata rarely showed anger, even when I knew she must be feeling it. She always tried to understand what the other person was feeling. That's a good trait if you work in a refuse bin for runaway kids, but in the real world it's good to get pissed every now and then.

I had the advantage of a short fuse, which made it much easier to get pissed. And Shirley was always angry about something or other, so I frankly didn't see why she needed to pay a shrink to help her scream about things.

Our seeing Ben off was torture. Maybe it was standing next to that bus, just like the one I had fled on. Maybe it was watching Renata say farewell to her only child, a silent farewell, a wordless but tender embrace. Or maybe it was when Ben asked me to look after his record collection, made a joke about my having the room to myself, whispered in my ear where he kept his stash, and then wrapped his long skinny arms around me and squeezed tight.

I pressed my face into his chest. There was a volcano in my throat, a burning pressure welling up and ready to blow, so I didn't dare try and speak. We watched the bus lumber out of the station.

When we got home, Renata went to bed, Shirley went to a political meeting, and I went up to the roof and let the volcano blow.

All three of us got letters from Ben several weeks after he got to Canada. He sent them via a friend of Shirley's because we feared the authorities might be snooping around the apartment and going through our mail, since Ben had failed to show up for induction. He already had gotten a threatening letter from the Army.

Shirley got a two-page letter telling her about all the radicals and other draft dodgers he was meeting in Vancouver. They were sleeping in the basement of a church whose members were providing meals and helping them find jobs.

Renata got a three-page letter that made her cry, but I didn't ask her for details. I got the longest letter, five pages, with an account of his journey and his reflections along the way and some older-cousin advice about not getting too stoned too often and not doing anything to screw up my living arrangement with Renata. Reading it made me feel like I was sitting with him on the roof.

I also got two postcards in one week from Jennifer, each one recounting an egregious act by her father or Sweat Hog or her stepsiblings—the Hogettes, she called them. Each one was laugh-out-loud funny, each one signed, sarcastically I assumed, Your Lover and Mistress.

In the second postcard she told me that her father threw a fit when she told him about me. He told her that she was too young to be carousing with boys and that he wasn't sending her mom a check every month to raise a slut. At the bottom she wrote, I miss you sooooo much, and underlined it three times

I missed her too. I was surprised at how much I did, never having had a girlfriend before or even a girl who would speak to me. Jennifer was now a regular in the shower every morning.

Renata started running fevers at night. After trying every herbal concoction that Shirley prepared, to no apparent benefit, she finally went to a real doctor, who ordered a bunch of tests. She also started to worry about money. The tests were expensive, and she had been working only part-time for several weeks. She had given most of her savings to Ben, but if he couldn't get a job in Canada, she soon would have to send him more money.

I was concerned that the extra expense of hosting me would become a burden, not that I cost much to feed, but with Ben gone, I feared Shirley might look for ways to convince Renata it was time to evict me. I trusted Renata, but in her weakened state I wasn't sure what she would do.

Ben's stash was almost depleted, so I soon would need money for pot, which was going up in price along with other staples. I needed a summer job. And possibly a new refuge, if Renata started talking about foster families again.

Man in the Moon, what a pleasant surprise, Skip said as he opened his front door, cautious, with a gun in his hand, the way he always opened his front door, peeking through a crack until he could identify the knocker.

We sat at the kitchen table which as always was covered with loose pot and baggies. The house still had its familiar smells—stale pot and cigarette smoke, spilt beer, dirty clothes, mold. It was nostalgic. Joe Cocker's deep sandpaper voice drifted from the stereo speakers.

I need to make some money, I said. Can I work for you until school starts again?

What's wrong with a paper route? Or making milkshakes at the drug store? I thought you'd gone straight on me, man. I mean, shit, going to school and everything?

Yeah, well, staying in Venice seemed better than Mexico. And I've got a good arrangement. But now I need to make some money.

Well let's see now, where in my enterprise can I use someone with your extraordinary skills? Skip said. He handed me a beer, stared out the window, and rubbed his chin for a while as if he were thinking, but I'm pretty sure he already knew what he was going to propose.

Tell you what, Man in the Moon. I could use someone with your outward appearance of—let's call it youthful innocence—to pick up deliveries for me. You won't be handling money. Just inventory. Same rules as always: if you're nabbed, you're on your own. I'll pay you $15 per delivery and a nickel bag as soon as it's safe and sound in my possession.

So, I became a working stiff again, only this time I had to go to a boarded-up house in an East Los Angeles neighborhood, far from Venice, where some Mexican guys would give me a vinyl sports bag with a Los Angeles Rams logo on it, stuffed with twenty pounds of pot, which I would then lug back to the bus stop, looking as innocent as a fourteen-year-old schoolboy on summer break, and head back downtown to make the transfer to Venice.

It took about two hours in all, and $15 for two hours work was a lot more than I could have made in any other summer job. I did this two or three times a week. I knew I was taking a bigger risk than before, one that could get Renata in trouble, too. Ben would have been irate. But I swore to myself if I got caught, I wouldn't talk.

I regularly stuck $10 bills in Renata's wallet. She never caught on.

Renata was diagnosed with Hodgkin's disease. Shirley said it was very serious, kind of like cancer, and that Renata would be injected with powerful drugs and then blasted with radiation. It was the first time I ever saw Shirley in distress. She always had the answers to problems, even if they proved to be the wrong answers, but now she was lost. She hugged me tearfully and said, Oh my God, we can't let her die, Moon, we can't let her die.

Die? I thought. Is that how this could end?

I went to Renata's bedroom later that night. Her eyes were closed but she was awake. I climbed onto the bed and lay down next to her. She looked older than when I had first met her at the shelter; her cheeks were hollow, her skin wan. During the past year she had been the one constant, the stable planet I orbited around. A crazy, mixed-up orbit, but an orbit nonetheless. Her gravity kept me from flying off into space.

Even when I'd lived with Skip, I knew where she was, where she lived and worked. Knowing that she was there helped me get to sleep all those nights in Skip's backyard. Maybe that whole time I had wanted her to find me, to bump into me on the street as I delivered pot.

We didn't talk regularly now, the way we had when she was my counselor; but her presence alone, her acceptance of me, was all that I needed. If she were to die . . . well, what would happen to a moon if its planet died? It would spin out of control.

She opened her eyes. Hi, kiddo, she said. What did you do today?

Nothing important. How do you feel?

I'm scared, she said, but at least I know what I've got, and they have a treatment plan. She closed her eyes again.

I slid closer and kissed her on the cheek three times, and she smiled and gently rubbed my back like my mom used to do. I felt like kissing her on the lips, but I wasn't sure if she would like it. I watched her chest as she inhaled and exhaled. She looked so vulnerable.

She opened her eyes abruptly, as if she had a sudden thought. Moon, she said, you can't tell Ben that I'm sick. I know he would try to come back home and if he does, he will get arrested. I don't want him to know about this. He's got too much to deal with now. He doesn't need to worry about me. I'll get through this.

I promised but I didn't feel good about it. I already had written Ben the week before and told him that Renata was better, which was a lie even then, but it was in part wishful thinking. Now that I knew the truth, I would have to write a conscious lie. That would be hard to do to Ben.

Renata came home from the hospital after her first treatment and was violently sick from the drugs they pumped into her. She threw up all night long, well after there was nothing left to throw up. Shirley and I tried to get her to take sips of water, but it kept coming right back up. She finally fell asleep, Shirley sitting on the bed by her side stroking her hair, me sitting next to Shirley holding Renata's hand.

Shirley and I finally bonded over something: We loved the same woman. Usually when two people love the same woman it creates animosity; in our case it did the opposite.

I went to the roof but was afraid to get high. I was tottering on an emotional edge and Ben wasn't there to take care of me if I had a bad trip. I didn't want to end up splattered on the asphalt in the parking lot. I looked at the stars and thought about my mother and Renata, Ben and Jennifer. I spotted the constellation Canis Major and that made me think of Sirius.

And then I remembered: This was the night Apollo 11 would be landing on the moon. I thought about how the moon had lived in peace for eons, circling the Earth and reflecting the light of the sun, and now, greedy, mean, destructive human beings like Roy and Max and Uncle Arnie and Hunter Posey and my father were going to walk around on it as if they owned it, as if they'd conquered it.

Didn't they know that the moon controls the tides and the waves, that it can look straight at the sun and reflect its light, that it's far more powerful than our tin can spaceships ever will be?

I felt a surge of anger, of rage: Rage at NASA, rage at Richard Nixon, rage at the military-industrial complex, rage at Hodgkin's disease, rage at Roy, rage at my father. And rage at the Pleiades for leaving me all alone in the world.

I pounded my fists on the ground and screamed—a primal scream that sucked all the oxygen out of my lungs and all the thoughts out of my mind. Afterwards, I lay exhausted on the roof, depleted and empty. It was a relief to be empty.

I read about Hodgkin's disease in the library. It was named after Thomas Hodgkin, the Englishman who discovered it. Hodgkin himself died of dysentery, which is diarrhea that kills you. And I learned this: Hodgkin's isn't like cancer, as Shirley had said. It is cancer. It was a hot summer day, but I felt a chill as I sat in the library.

My grandfather had died of cancer when my mother was ten. She kept a framed photograph of him in her bedroom. He was in a suit, sitting on the front steps of a small brick house, and my mother, who was about three or four years old, was sitting on his lap. He wasn't smiling but his face looked kind. He had a thin little mustache and slicked back hair.

My mother told me he'd immigrated from Lebanon when he was a child and met my grandmother, who had immigrated from Ireland when she was a child, at a Catholic church social. Grandma said that my grandfather's death was a blessing because he had suffered so much. She said he died of the Terrible Disease, and then she would make the sign of the cross to ward off the Terrible Disease.

My mother told me that the disease was called cancer. My grandfather got it in his lungs.

Mary Russell's mom died of cancer when we were in fourth grade. Miss Bailey made an announcement before class, without uttering the word cancer, and told us to write a condolence note to Mary. She explained what condolence meant and wrote the word on the blackboard and made us all repeat it. I hoped that Mary's mom appreciated the fact that her death provided a useful vocabulary lesson.

I didn't know Mary because she sat on the other side of the room, so I wrote: I am sorry your mommy is dead. Miss Bailey told me that my card was not very sensitive. Tell her what you really feel and say something that will make her feel better, she instructed me. And don't use the word dead.

That was what I really felt: I was sorry her mommy was dead. And how could I write a condolence note without mentioning that someone was dead? So I wrote, I am very sorry about what happened, and signed it, Your friend (which I wasn't). Miss Bailey frowned and shook her head but placed my card with all the others in the shoebox we'd decorated with cheerful stickers.

It's hard to think of cancer without thinking of death. I used to worry about my mother dying, especially when I would see her unconscious on the floor or hear her vomiting and groaning in the bathroom at night. I would put the pillow over my head to block the sound.

Sometimes it seemed like death would be a better option for her than living. It certainly couldn't be any more miserable. I feared her death because I would then be left alone with my father and Jake. The mother I loved and who had loved me was gone, but at least her shell was there, and she still would defend me against my father or Jake when she was sober enough.

I think one of the reasons I ran away is that I didn't want to be there when she died. I didn't want to see it happen. I chose to be all alone because I didn't want to be left all alone. And now Renata had a disease that could take her from me too.

I didn't believe Renata's strategy of keeping Ben in the dark could be sustained for long, but I had promised to go along with it. I wrote him and said: The doctors are still doing some tests (true), but her spirits are good (kind of true), I think she's looking a lot better (huge lie), I hope they have some answers soon (even bigger lie, they already knew what she had), and I will tell you as soon as I know (I already knew).

Three lies and two truths.

Ben wrote me back—a short, one-page letter. Is Mom really doing okay? he wrote. And don't bullshit me. Be straight: Do they know what she has? What's causing this? I called for her at the shelter this afternoon, and they said she hadn't been in all week. You don't stay home all week to wait for test results. Tell me what's going on. Send it by the fastest mail possible. I'm counting on you, man. The truth.

I was straddling one of those fault lines: On one side, I could do as Renata wished and keep Ben in the dark. But Ben already suspected something, so I couldn't keep him in the dark for long. On the other side, I could tell Ben the truth and break my promise to Renata. If Ben then tried to come home and got arrested and thrown in jail, it would be my fault.

I stared at the blank piece of paper, stuck with one foot on each side of the fault line. I didn't know what to do, so I put my head on the desk and fell asleep. I awoke about an hour later, sweating from the heat of the desk lamp. I took off my shirt, opened the window, and let the breeze waft over me, then wrote this:

> *Your mom has a kind of cancer called Hodgkin's. They are giving her drugs for it. I am sorry I didn't tell you, but she made me promise not to. She is scared that you will try to come home, and you will get arrested so please stay there, you can't help her if you are in jail.*
>
> *I read all about Hodgkin's and it's not the very worst kind of cancer. They can treat it. Your mom is strong. She didn't even get upset when her hair fell out from the drugs. It makes her feel better to believe you aren't worrying about her. Please don't tell her I told you this, and I promise I will not keep anything from you again. I wish you were home. I don't like having the room to myself.*

I mailed it special delivery. Ben wrote back right away and told me to tell him everything that was going on and gave me the home telephone number of the minister at the church in case I needed to reach him in an emergency. He said that if Renata got worse, he would sneak back into the country by crossing the border on foot in the wilderness and then hitchhike to Los Angeles.

People from the induction office were calling the apartment every few days asking for him and I was sure they would nab him if he came back, but I knew I couldn't change his mind.

Jennifer returned in August after her mother got back from San Diego. We spent every afternoon together, walking on Venice Beach, wading in the ocean, going to anti-war protests, and eating pizza on the boardwalk.

We wandered to the topless area of the beach one day and I dared Jennifer, only partly in jest, to take off her shirt. She said that she would go topless if I went bottomless. We both laughed, then blushed and went silent for a few minutes.

I was shocked by my own brazenness and relieved when Jennifer took my hand as we walked on. One afternoon we snuck in by the fire escape door to see *Easy Rider*, an adults-only film. We sat low in our seats in the back row so no one would see us. Jennifer held my hand the entire time and when Wyatt and Billy got shot at the end, she buried her head in my shoulder and cried. I wanted to kill the guys who shot them.

I fulfilled my business obligations for Skip first thing in the morning, before Jennifer and I met up in the afternoon. I spent the evenings with Renata, reading and watching television and getting her whatever she needed. She had started the radiation treatments, which left her exhausted, but didn't make her throw up, so she could eat again and gained a few pounds.

I still was terrified she would die, but as long as she wasn't getting worse I was able to suppress the thought. There was a new dynamic in the apartment, with me and Shirley taking care of Renata; it created a closer bond between me and Shirley, which was further bolstered by my now-fierce opposition to the war.

I wrote Ben regularly to keep him updated, and he called every few weeks.

Jennifer and I both dreaded the thought of starting Venice High and once we did, we both were determined to hate it. It was big and confusing, and we didn't have the same lunch period. The senior boys were adult-sized, and some had facial hair. I was nervous my family massacre story might no longer protect me from becoming Prey.

The teachers were strict and said things like, you're in high school now, so we're not going to baby you—which would have been wonderful if it meant they'd leave me the hell alone. But that's not what it meant. They assigned homework on the first day of school, which I had no intention of doing, but it offended me on principle.

After the first week, Jennifer and I decided on our way home to treat ourselves to hamburgers and a bitch session. After we got our burgers and sat down, I told Jennifer how Renata, Shirley, and Ben all were vegetarians. Maybe that's why they're all so skinny, I said. They literally have no meat on their bones.

Why don't they eat meat? Jennifer asked, as she carefully removed the pickles, lettuce, and tomato from her burger, then tore the patty into little pieces. Jennifer and food had a peculiar relationship with one another.

They think it's cruel to kill animals, I said. And it is, but I can't help it. It tastes good. And anyway, these cows already are dead, so we might as well eat them.

Oh gross, Jennifer said. Why'd you have to say that? Now I can't eat it. She shoved her tray to the side with a look of disgust.

I licked ketchup off my finger. I know it's hypocritical of me, I said. I'd never personally kill or hurt an animal. I really shouldn't eat meat.

Me neither, Jennifer said. It's cruel. And what about people who hunt? They're the worst because they do it for fun. Someone should hunt them for a change.

Yeah, tell me about it, I said. It's already hunting season in Ohio. I bet next weekend my dad and my brother will be out there shooting deer, like it's some great feat to hide in the bushes and blow an animal's brains out. Maybe this year a big stag with antlers will charge them. I'd love to see those two assholes throw their guns down and run like cowards. I started laughing at the thought.

Jennifer wasn't laughing. She wasn't even smiling. She was staring at me, unblinking, motionless.

Then it hit me. I stopped laughing and froze with my mouth open, most likely with an indictable look on my face. Every gray cell in my brain tried to come up with a way out of this one.

What did you just say? Jennifer said with an eerie calmness, but her chest was heaving and her face reddening.

I swallowed hard. Well, what I mean is . . . well . . . if they were still alive . . .

My gray cells were failing me.

Moon, I want you to tell me something and it had better be the truth. Jennifer pronounced each word very distinctly as if she were talking to a naughty child, which is what I felt like. What happened to your family? she said. Were they all murdered, like you told me?

It's kind of complicated, really, I said, trying to sound self-assured as my mind frantically sought a pathway to safety.

That was all the answer Jennifer needed. You've been lying to me this whole time, haven't you? she said. You bastard! You're just like every other man I know. You're a liar. Was that bullshit story your way to make me like you, so I'd feel sorry for you, so you could get down my pants? Is that what it was all about, getting down my pants? Her voice quaked and grew louder all at once.

Other diners began staring at us.

No, no, that's not it, Jennifer, please, let me explain.

Explain what? she said. Explain why you made up that horrible story about your family being murdered? What kind of person are you?

Jennifer stood up and leaned over the table. Her petite body suddenly seemed large and menacing, as if her anger had inflated her. I thought you were . . . I thought . . . She started to sob. You are such a fucking bastard, she yelled, then grabbed her book bag and ran out the door.

Jennifer, wait, I called after her. I sounded pathetic.

My fears were confirmed: Jennifer didn't like me. She had liked someone else and I wasn't him, and now she knew I wasn't. Who had I been fooling?

I actually had started to believe I'd somehow survived a terrible ordeal and come out of it strong and confident. That I really did have a wonderful family that was murdered, instead of a horrible family that rejected my very being.

I hadn't survived the brutal murder of a loving family. I had bought a bus ticket to a city two thousand miles away to escape a horrible, sunless life. I was a loser, a runaway kid who should've been dead or dying slowly in a juvenile home or an insane asylum.

I became aware all eyes in the room were on me. A man sitting in the booth across from me chuckled and said, Puppy love, kid. You'll get over it.

Fuck you! I yelled at him. The restaurant hushed. The proprietor craned his neck over the cash register and glared at me.

Fuck all of you! I said as I headed for the door.

I half-walked, half-ran down the sidewalk as if I were fleeing, which I was: fleeing hurt and humiliation and rejection and shame and the cold truth that I was unlovable. No matter how fast I stumbled along, those feelings kept pace, like a jeering crowd running alongside me. The tears in my eyes made everything look blurry. I must have walked for half an hour, crossing against traffic lights, bumping into people, kicking a few newspaper boxes along the way, muttering to myself, wiping my eyes with my shirtsleeve. I had no destination.

Or so I thought: I found myself in front of Skip's house. I heard music coming from inside. I wiped my face and knocked. No response. I knocked louder. I pounded. The music got quieter and I heard footsteps coming to the door.

Well, well, what a lovely surprise, said Tony. I brushed past him without saying a word and collapsed on a couch. The cushion was damp and smelled of spilt beer. Tony sat down next to me. What's going down, Moon? he asked.

Nothing, I said. Do you have a joint?

I may have, but what's going on with you? Your vibes are pretty stressed out right now.

I don't want to talk about it. I didn't think I could make my life any more fucked up than it already was, but I just did. Now I want a joint.

Oh, Moon. Tony put his arm around me. Sometimes it seems like we've fucked everything up, he said. Believe me, Tony-boy here has an Olympic gold medal in fucking up. But the great thing about fucking everything up is that things can only get better from there. Am I right? Most of your life is ahead of you, darling. Whatever has happened can be repaired—I mean, you're still alive.

I wasn't sure still being alive was such a great thing and said so.

Tony went into the kitchen and came back with two beers and a bottle of little red pills. You are clearly way too stressed out. Here, take one of these little red devils and we'll calm down together. Then maybe you'll feel like talking. Not that I'll be of any help, but I do have a good pair of ears. And I've been through some messy shit, that's for sure.

I took the pill with a swig of beer; then I took another one. I didn't care what they were as long as they made me feel better.

I think you'd better stop at two, Tony said.

By the time I finished the beer I was breathing deeply, and my body felt like a soggy cornflake at the bottom of a bowl of milk. I could still see the horrible things I was feeling, but it was like being in a cozy, warm room looking out the window at a fierce storm; I felt safe from those horrible feelings. My nose itched but I didn't have the energy to reach up and scratch it.

Feeling better, darling?

I nodded yes.

Tony reached around and squeezed my shoulder. I listed to the side and lay my head against his chest; it was rising and falling with each breath he took, and I could hear his heart beating deep underneath; its steady, rhythmic thumping was reassuring. It felt good to be close to another person, a caring person. I reached around and hugged him tightly.

I sank into a fluffy cloud, my body completely inert. I don't know how much time passed, but when my eyes flittered open, it was dark outside so it must have been a few hours. I was sprawled across the couch; my shoes and pants were off.

Strange dream fragments popped in and out of my mind: My mom cradling Sirius's dead body, weeping; Renata lying in a casket, but still alive and smiling at me; Ben hugging me tight; Jimmy Hollingsworth lying on top of me, his face in mine, yelling, help me! over and over; my brother Jake, lying crumpled in the woods, blood pouring from his mangled body, a large stag standing over him, triumphant.

And then Jennifer, storming out of a restaurant, out of my life. But that wasn't a dream fragment. That was real.

Tony came from the kitchen. I tried to make you more comfortable, he said, and handed me my pants, which he had folded neatly on the coffee table. He sat on the couch next to me. You said some interesting things, Moon, Tony said, do you remember?

I shook my head.

From the sound of it, you love very easily, Tony said. And you hurt very easily, too. You're like me, that way. That can lead to a lot of pain.

I started putting my pants back on from a sitting position just as the front door opened and Skip and Clyde walked in.

Well, what have we here? A little afternoon gaiety? Skip laughed.

Clyde's face was turning red. You fuckin' faggot, he said, and charged toward Tony.

No, I yelled, get away from him.

I tried to get between Clyde and Tony but my pants were only halfway up, so I couldn't move quickly. Clyde grabbed Tony by the collar, pulled him up off the couch and punched him so hard in the face I could hear Tony's nose break. He fell backwards onto the pile of empty beer cans and full ashtrays on the coffee table. Blood began seeping from his nose. He was out cold.

I rammed into Clyde with all my weight—which wasn't much compared to his muscular bulk—while Skip pulled him from behind.

Hey, Skip said to Clyde, Tony's my best sales agent, let him be.

Clyde kissed his fist and stepped back, then looked at me: I always thought you were a little faggot, he said.

Fuck yourself, I said, which was not a smart thing to say to someone more than double my weight, who also carried a gun. Clyde took two steps toward me and slapped me so hard, it made my father's slaps seem like caresses. I fell over onto Tony, and the coffee table collapsed; my pants were still only half up.

Skip jumped in and pulled Clyde back. I think you should go now,

Moon. Whatever you and Tony were doing, I don't need the grief. You need to stay away from here.

We weren't doing anything, I said. He didn't touch me.

But Skip just pointed to the door.

I had just lost my girl and my job on the same day.

Still woozy, I walked down the front steps. The side of my face pulsed with pain and my ear was ringing. Tony's blood was on my shirt.

I stood on the sidewalk trying to figure out which way to go, where to go, whether to go. I considered parking myself on the curb and passively watching the world go by as my body slowly decomposed. But that could take weeks.

I don't remember how I made my way back to Renata's.

By the next morning my brain had unscrambled and reassembled itself and Jennifer was the first thing I thought of. She joined me in the shower, which only made things worse. I could fantasize all I wanted, but that wouldn't change the fact that she now hated me.

Fantasies bring pleasure when there is a chance, however remote, that they might come true. Otherwise, they're torture.

I made fried eggs for Renata and we ate breakfast together. I picked at my food. The side of my face hurt so bad it was uncomfortable opening my mouth.

What's wrong? Renata said. Your face is swollen. You look upset.

I walked into an open locker door at school, I said. And I have a big test today.

She looked at me skeptically; she knew I couldn't care less about tests. But it was the only excuse I could come up with on the spot.

Moon, everything's going to be alright, Renata said. I'm not going anywhere, and neither are you. As soon as I'm stronger, you and I are going up to Canada to see Ben.

Renata now was working half-days at the shelter. She wrapped a scarf around her bald head, and we left the apartment together. She dropped me off at school but as soon as she drove away, I headed to the beach. I couldn't deal with seeing Jennifer.

What if she spread the word that I had lied about my past? My defense against being Prey would be gone. I would be the target of bullies again, even more so than ever, and Jennifer would be on their side.

I went to Santa Monica and walked to the end of the long pier. I leaned over the rail and watched the swells as they rose and fell against the pier's wooden posts. I was a fifteen-foot plunge away from ending it. I always had blamed other people for my misery, but this time I had no one else to blame. Jennifer was right and I was wrong. I couldn't hate her even though she hated me. It's so much easier when you can blame your misery on others.

I went to see *Easy Rider* again. Only one other person was in the theater. I remembered how Jennifer had held my hand for two straight hours. I left about halfway through, went to a pizza parlor and ordered a Coke, and thought about how disappointed Ben would be that I had fucked things up, especially since he had told me to tell Jennifer the truth.

Maybe I should hop a bus to Vancouver and join Ben, I thought. Maybe Skip had connections there I could work for. Maybe it would be me and Ben against the world. Maybe we could live together in a little house by the ocean.

Maybe, maybe, maybe.

I thought about my story, the one I had made up, the one Jennifer had believed and liked me for, and I thought about how all we are is our stories and I bet everyone's story contains lies, maybe more lies than truths, and maybe we all come to believe some of our lies because we need to believe them.

When we dream at night our minds make up stories that aren't true, yet we believe them while they're happening. Maybe our waking lives are the same, just a bunch of stories we believe really happened even if they didn't. Maybe we make them up because we wish they were true, because they make us feel better.

I wished I'd grown up in a wonderful loving family, a family I never would have wanted to leave, a family that was brutally taken away from me instead of a family I couldn't bear being part of anymore. Maybe there is no truth, just a bunch of stories that make us feel good and fulfill our needs, a stew of lies and exaggerations and fantasies with a tiny bit of truth mixed in.

No, I knew the story I'd told Jennifer was a lie, even if it was a lie I wished had been true, and that it had made me feel like a stronger person. The unforgiveable thing was that I had knowingly deceived Jennifer.

Ben knew my real story, or most of it, and he liked me anyway. So maybe my real story would have been good enough for Jennifer to like me. But not now that she knew my old story was a lie, and a conscious lie to deceive her.

One year before, I'd not even known Jennifer. But now I felt a gnawing pain in my gut because she had stormed out of that restaurant in a rage, because she hated me and no longer would be in my life. She hadn't been in my life for my first fourteen years. I didn't miss her then, so why was it so unbearable now?

I had left my family without regret, but I couldn't bear being left by someone I had known for only one year? It made no sense. Did this mean I had fallen in love with Jennifer? If being in love is a temporarily blissful illness for which the cure is fatal, then yes—I had fallen in love. Jennifer's rejection, even though I deserved it, was one rejection too many, one rejection over the line, the final blow.

I returned home at the usual time, as if I had come from school. Renata was on the couch reading. How was that big test? she asked.

Test? Oh, yeah, it was fine, I said. I dropped my rucksack on the floor and sat next to her. She ran her hand through my long hair, last cut in Ohio, in my earlier life. Can you spare some of this? she said. I could use a little.

Yours is going to grow back, I said. When you're well, and the Hodgkin's is cured.

I know you pretty well, Renata said. Better than you probably think, and certainly well enough to know when something's wrong. Do you want to tell me what's going on?

It's true, Renata did know me well. Or at least the parts of my story that she knew, she knew well. She didn't know I had worked for a drug dealer. She didn't know about me and Ben's sacred place on the roof and how close he and I had become, or not the full extent of it. She didn't know where I was from or what my name used to be. So there was a lot of my story she didn't know.

But I think she knew the me that was not part of any stories, true or not. She knew the me who told the stories. She may have known that me better than I did.

At that moment part of me wanted to explode like a burst emotional pipe, to let it all flow out of me until there was nothing left but a few drips. But another part wanted to withdraw into my turtle shell and hide from my truths. Turtles must suffer from lots of unpleasant truths.

I've kind of had this girlfriend, I said. But I lied to her about something important, and now she hates me. She dumped me, and it's my fault.

I couldn't tell Renata why exactly Jennifer was angry. The story I had told Jennifer was not the official story that I'd sworn to Renata I would stick to—about my mom being in a coma. Thankfully, Renata didn't push for details.

Relationships are difficult, Renata said, especially romantic relationships. There's nothing I can say that will make you feel better. But you will, over time. I can assure you of that. I don't know what the details are, but I know enough about you to ask you this: Did you let her in? Did you let her see who you really are? You've had to hide so much in your life. I think hiding is second nature to you. But it's fatal to relationships.

Renata didn't know the details, but she sure as hell had figured out the problem. I felt like crying but I was almost fifteen years old, so I swallowed hard and took a deep shaky breath instead. Can I ask you something personal? Did you love Ben's father? You married him; you had a baby with him. Were you in love?

It's funny you ask that, she said, because Ben never has. I suppose he doesn't want to know. The truth is, no, I didn't love him. I was nineteen when we married. I was doing what I thought I should do, what my friends were doing, what my parents wanted me to do. I was living everyone's life except my own.

I was up there at the altar and I had a terrible crush on my maid of honor—my best friend—and I looked at Donald and felt nothing. But I still said those two words—I do. I'm happy I said them because otherwise I wouldn't have Ben. But it sure ended up causing a lot of unhappiness.

She leaned closer: I was never attracted to boys. I loved my best friend and thought it was sinful and wrong and perverted. So, I know about hiding. I thought if I did the right thing everything would work out. I prayed to God every night to fix me, cure me, make me normal. What did I know about anything? I was just a child.

I took Renata's hand. But you left, I said, and you found your sun.

Look, Renata said, whatever happens with this girl, you've got to start loving that boy who erased his family. He will never be able to become a strong person unless you do. Believe me, I know, because I hated that girl who loved other girls. I despised her. It took me a long time to learn how to love her. I didn't find my sun just by leaving; it took a lot of work.

Renata cradled me in her arms, the bald cancer patient filled with radiation comforting the long-haired runaway filled with lies.

For what it's worth, she said, I love you, kiddo. It was the first time she had used the L-word with me. I melted into her arms. It felt warm and safe.

I went to school the next day because if I skipped again, they might call Renata and maybe start trying to figure out again why the hell I had no school records. But I felt like I was attending my own funeral as I walked into the building. English class was torture: We were reading *The Tempest* out loud and the teacher pointed at me and said, You read Ariel's part.

I had no idea what the play was about, or who Ariel was, but after I read a few of his lines—Louder, please, louder! the teacher kept admonishing me—it seemed that Ariel was some kind of ghostly thing, or not completely human, maybe a boy, and maybe a girl. The role matched how I felt—perfect casting.

My next class was on the second floor. I was climbing the stairs with the chattering masses, when I saw Jennifer coming down the stairs as she always did at that time. Our eyes met briefly but she brushed right past. A dagger went through me. She was so close I could have touched her, but she was gone, like a ghost.

I stalled for a second, and the big kid behind me, a hulk wearing a varsity football jacket, crashed into me and said, Hey, you little twerp, what the fuck? and I wanted to say, Oh, sorry, sir, I'm picking up the shards of my broken heart. But instead, I sped up and got out of his way.

Halfway through the next class, I asked the teacher if I could go to the nurse's office. I told the nurse I felt dizzy and nauseated. She told me to lie down on a cot, and I spent the rest of the morning counting the ceiling tiles over and over, first in one direction, then another, then diagonally.

There was a big hole in me where Jennifer had been, right next to those big holes where my mother and Sirius had been. I was Swiss cheese and I wondered how many holes a piece of Swiss cheese can have before it disappears? I snuck out of school at lunchtime and spent the rest of the day at the beach, standing in the surf, feeling the waves break over my feet.

Let her in, Renata had said. But I wondered why Jennifer would want to come in where I was. I'm in here permanently, I thought. I'm stuck in here for life and it's not very pleasant most of the time. My mother had been in with me for eight years—little kids naturally let their mommies in—but then she left. If I let Jennifer in, it might only confirm why she wanted out, why she wanted nothing to do with me.

Still, I had nothing more to lose at that point. The worst outcome of letting her in would be no worse than what I already was feeling.

I wrote Jennifer a letter that night. At four o'clock in the morning, my waste basket filled with crumpled attempts, I finally completed my confessional: In twelve pages I wrote about my father and Jake and both versions of my mother, about Sirius and how he had died, about being Prey and about Jimmy Hollingsworth, about my days on the streets of Los Angeles, and about the shelter and how I had really met Renata.

I told her about Uncle Arnie and how that was why I had known what Roy was doing to her and how awful it was. I told her about living with and working for Skip, and the fact that I was living with Renata under an arrangement that endangered both of us. The only things I left out were my old name—which I no longer wanted to utter, much less put down in ink—and what Ben and I had not even spoken about ourselves, which I still was both happy and confused about.

I also reminded her how we had slept on the beach together and looked at the stars. And this: I told her that I loved her.

When I had thought Ben was about to leap to his death, those words had come out of my mouth without thinking—unadulterated, unfiltered truth, driven by the terror that I was about to lose him.

But it was hard to write those words, that truth, to someone who I was pretty sure hated me, someone I already had lost. It wasn't until the final draft that I wrote them.

The next morning, after the first bell rang and the halls had emptied, I slid the letter through the vents of Jennifer's locker. I held on to it briefly before letting go; I was about to reveal my true self to someone who, at that moment, hated me. I must be in love, I thought, to do something so crazy.

I released my grip. The letter disappeared and I heard it flop down inside. It was only then I realized the full implication of what I had done. Jennifer not only could reveal me to other students, she could inform the school administrators that my official story was a lie and Renata was harboring me without authority. I could end up in a juvenile home, and Renata could be without a job.

The remainder of the day was agonizing. I couldn't concentrate or eat lunch and I had diarrhea so bad that I used the bathroom at school, something I never in my life had done; school bathrooms are not safe territory for Prey.

By the end of the day, I was exhausted and feeling faint from lack of nourishment and the fact that the night before, I'd had only a few hours of sleep.

I got home and checked on Renata, who also was exhausted. In her case it was from being radiated that afternoon. I fell asleep snuggled next to her on her bed until Shirley got home and Renata arose.

I kept sleeping until Renata came in with a thermometer to see if I was sick. I assured her I was fine, went into Ben's room and collapsed on the bed. I wanted to fall right back into unconsciousness but couldn't: I tossed and turned, stared at the streetlight out the window, tried counting from a hundred to zero, but never got past eighty-seven, turned on the radio but soon turned it off because every song they played reminded me of Jennifer or Ben. I tried to imagine in explicit detail what it would be like to jump off the roof and land on the asphalt and feel my legs shatter underneath me like matchsticks.

When I finally fell asleep, things only got worse: I dreamed that Jennifer was making out with Hunter Posey, and I watched them until I couldn't take it anymore and ran into the next room, into Renata's comforting arms, only when I looked up it wasn't Renata but my mother, and her face started to melt, dripping down on me like candle wax until I was covered in melted flesh. I ran outside and found Ben crumpled dead on the pavement and I started screaming until I woke up.

I was on the floor, having fallen out of bed. And I thought about that image of Jennifer and Hunter Posey making out and how passionately she was kissing him, and even though I wasn't in the shower I went at it right there, and it felt wonderful and miserable at the same time.

● ❭ ❭ ❭ ◯ ❪ ❪ ❪ ●

I had planned to give Jennifer a week to ponder my confessional, but after three days without a word from her, despite several ships-passing-in-the-stairwell incidents, I was going certifiably insane.

I spent most nights tossing and turning until dawn, playing out various scenarios and dialogues in my head. I gained a new appreciation for the fetal position. I stayed away from pot, but still had several plunging-elevator episodes come on without warning.

After four days, not knowing had become worse than the worst scenario. At the end of the day, as the school emptied, I hid behind the shrubs at the bottom of the steps outside the main entrance.

Jennifer came down the stairs slowly, fiddling with her book bag. I stayed hidden until she'd descended and started walking down the sidewalk. When she was about twenty paces ahead, I began following her.

I was feeling bubbles just watching her walk: her unruly hair bouncing against her back with every step, her round little butt squeezed inside her jeans, her erratic gait as she tried to avoid stepping on sidewalk cracks. After two blocks I sped up until I was just behind her and then, after taking a deep breath, was by her side, but with a good three feet between us, well out of punching range.

Hi, Jen, I said. It came out weakly and tentatively, more like a question than a greeting.

She maintained her pace, looking at the ground just ahead of her as if she had known the whole time that I was behind her. Hello, she said without looking at me.

That was a bad sign: No one says Hello unless they're angry. Otherwise, they say Hi or Hey or something like that. Hello was not good. Can we talk? I asked.

So talk, she said.

This was almost as bad as Hello. But it wasn't as bad as Fuck Off.

Did you get my letter?

Yep.

171

Well, that letter's the truth. Some of the stuff in there I haven't told anybody ever, not even Renata. I didn't mean to keep lying to you, but I didn't know what to do. I was nervous that day in class, I had to say something and then it just got out of hand and I couldn't fix it, even though I knew I should. I really did, you can ask Ben, because we talked about it. He told me I should tell you the truth, but I was an idiot. Can we sit down somewhere? I'll buy you a soda.

I could've been talking to a stranger. She kept walking for half a block, then side-glanced at me and said, We can sit over there—she nodded toward a bus stop shelter.

Once there, she sat down, crossed her legs away from me and stared straight ahead. I sat next to her but at a respectable distance.

I was afraid if I told you the truth you wouldn't like me anymore, I said. I thought you liked my story, but never would like me. Now you know everything about me. I'm not who you thought I was, but I did leave my family and I haven't been in touch with them, and they don't know where I am and probably don't care, so it's like they're dead, at least to me they're dead. And who knows, maybe they really are dead by now. So, I'm just a loser, a runaway kid, nothing special. I'm no big hero. I'm sorry. I really am. I'll never lie to you again, I promise.

Halfway through my monologue Jennifer looked directly at me for the first time and her eyes still were fixed on me when I fizzled out at the end. She pulled her legs up and hugged her knees.

I wanted to get down on my knees and kiss her feet and beg her to forgive me. Her hair fell over the side of her face, covering her left eye, but she still was looking at me, expressionless—not angry, not friendly—as if her eyes were performing an X-ray analysis of the freakish boy next to her.

I knew exactly what was happening: Jennifer was straddling a fault line. On one side there was me, a strange boy of questionable character and bizarre behavior, who had lied to her for the past year and now had come clean—but only after getting caught—and who professed to love her and wanted desperately to make up.

On the other side was the possibility of a normal boyfriend, who had a normal family and normal friends and did normal things and thought normal thoughts.

But would that normal boyfriend have spent the night with her on the beach or on the roof of an apartment building to keep her safe from Roy? Would he laugh at her tragic-comic stories of her dad and Sweat Hog? Would a normal boy share her disdain for just about everyone at school, students and teachers alike? Would he have written her a long letter revealing deep and embarrassing truths?

Jennifer was weird: normal boys probably wouldn't go for her. An elfin-looking runaway ex-drug-runner may be the best she could land. That was my hope, my one ace card. But it didn't seem wise to point that out.

I sat quietly while her jury of one deliberated.

A bus drove up, stopped, and then roared away after we waved it off, leaving us coughing in a cloud of blue smoke.

What if she rejects me, I thought? What if the three feet that separate us is as close as I will ever be to her? What if I never feel her hand in mine again?

The longer I waited, the worst scenario was becoming likelier. I could sense the elevator cables were about to snap; I gripped the rim of the aluminum bench.

Jennifer suddenly reached over and fingered the end of my hair. Your hair's getting awfully long, she said matter-of-factly. You have terrible split ends. Do you want me to trim it for you?

I didn't want her to touch my hair. I'd planned to grow it to the middle of my back. Judging from her own mismanaged hair, I doubted the outcome would be good, but if she trimmed my hair, she would have to get close to me, even touch me.

Sure, that'd be great, I said.

Okay, come on, she said in a commanding voice, as if I were a dawdling dog on a leash. We walked in silence to her house. I didn't dare reach over to take her hand. She unlocked the front door and directed me to the kitchen.

Take off your shirt and sit there, she said, pointing to a chair at the breakfast table. She draped a towel over my shoulders, laid some newspapers on the floor, and got a pair of scissors from a kitchen drawer. It occurred to me that she might be planning to stab me repeatedly with them. But I didn't move.

Don't worry, she said, I've watched my mom trim Roy's greasy hair. If she can do it, a baboon can do it. She started snipping, periodically turning my head one way or the other.

I gazed out the window, relishing my being the object of her attention. The tick-tick-tick of the kitchen clock registered the moments. She muttered Oops and Uh-oh a few times, which was not reassuring, but I didn't budge. It could have gone on all night, as far as I was concerned.

Jennifer stood in front of me and looked closely, her eyes asquint. I think we're done, she said. I think that's better. She handed me a mirror.

She had taken about two inches off the left side and maybe three inches off the right, although numerous individual strands jutted down below the lines. I felt the back: It was equally uneven. I don't think a baboon would have done any worse.

It looks good, I said, violating my promise never to lie to her again.

Maybe I need to touch it up a little. Jennifer was still squinting and assessing her work.

No, no, it's good. I like it, I said. I wanted to keep the damage to a limit.

Jennifer removed the towel and I brushed the hair off my stomach and pants. I started to stand up, but she pushed me back down in the chair forcefully, then punched me in the gut. She punched harder than I would have thought she could; it was a rage-fueled punch.

I doubled over to catch my breath, which gave her the opportunity to start pounding my back with both of her fists.

Okay, okay, stop, I gasped as I almost slid off the chair.

She pulled me back up into a sitting position and sat down hard, angrily, on my lap facing me, her feet dangling over the floor, her hands around my neck like she wanted to strangle me. Our faces were inches apart. I still was trying to catch my breath. She stared into my eyes.

So you deal drugs? she said.

Deliver, not deal, I said, as if that was an exonerating distinction. But I'm not doing that anymore. Honest.

And Renata is your shrink, not your aunt?

When I was at the shelter she was, but now she's . . . I don't know, she's like my unofficial foster mother. I know she cares for me, and Ben does, too. They are my family now.

So what's your real name? She squeezed my neck tighter.

This question posed a dilemma. Of all the memories I had tried to erase, the memory of the boy I used to be was the one I most wanted to be free of. I didn't want to speak his name.

Please, I don't want to say, I said. That person doesn't exist anymore, it's not who I am. I told you in my letter what it was like being in that life—what I was called then doesn't matter.

Well, whatever the fuck your real name is . . . you are such a . . . oh, I don't know what you are. You're an asshole, that's what you are. And you're nuts, that's also what you are. Totally fucked up.

I know, I said. It's a problem. I'm working on it.

Jennifer's anger was arousing—it meant that she felt something toward me. As were her hands around my throat, which meant she felt enough to possibly kill me. She was sitting right on my crotch and millions of bubbles were rising from below; I was getting hard and I was sure she felt it. I could see my reflection in her eyes, we were that close.

And getting closer. Her face suddenly melded with mine, her lips pressed hard against mine, now her open mouth covered my mouth, and my lips and mouth and tongue, without ever having read an instruction manual, seemed to know exactly what to do. But it was a first for both of us, so it was sloppy and a bit off target.

Up until now, we had just kissed on the lips, with mouths closed, like extended pecks. Now she drove into me until I feared the chair might fall over. We came up for air and then started all over. After several rounds we were breathing like a couple of racehorses.

Jennifer rested her head on my shoulder. My arms wrapped around her. I wanted the world to end. I wished an errant asteroid would strike the Earth, ending all life in a split second, so that our last split second would be this one, and Jennifer and I would be frozen in our embrace and never again would feel sorrow or pain, just the bliss of this moment.

My mom will be home soon, Jennifer whispered into my ear. You've got to go.

But I held on to her and didn't let her get up. She giggled her high-pitched giggle and said, I'm serious, she'll be home any minute.

She got off my lap and I put on my shirt, which I left untucked to conceal the bulge in my pants. Jennifer held my hand as we walked to the front door. She looked over my shoulder to make sure her mom was not in sight, then kissed me and held it for a few seconds. Go home, she ordered after we disconnected, and closed the door.

As I turned onto the sidewalk, I heard the door open again. Hey Moon, you know I'm in love with you, don't you? Even though you're an asshole. The door slammed shut before I could respond.

I walked back to Renata's slowly, Jennifer's taste in my mouth, my shirt untucked, my hair mangled, my entire body enveloped in a warm, sweet, beautiful cloud. I went to the roof that night, smoked a joint, looked at the Pleiades out of the corner of my eye and said, Someone's in love with me, Mom.

It was my fifteenth birthday.

Jennifer and I spent another night on the roof a few weeks later; she had come over pretending that we were going to do homework together, then I pretended to walk her home, and after Renata and Shirley had gone to bed I joined her on the roof. We smoked a joint and made out under the blanket.

Let's run away together, Jennifer said, as we lay together curled up like two puppies, me in a sea of bubbles. Every time I walk into my house I want to throw up, she said. And you hate school, so what are we doing here? We could go to Las Vegas. Anywhere. Just away from here. We could make it together; I know we could.

If we ran away together, every night could be like this—minus the schoolwork, which made it an appealing thought. I was fifteen, so I could get a part-time job flipping burgers and we could sleep in cheap motels and when Jennifer turned fifteen in a few months, she could work, too.

Eventually we would go all the way, although I was in no rush, at least not in my mind; other body parts were far more eager. I don't think Jennifer was in a rush either, but one day it would happen. For the first time in my life, I felt confident about that. But I couldn't walk out on Renata, not while she was sick. Ben had written to me that he would sneak back into the country if she got sicker, and I had promised to help him arrange a safe place to stay. I couldn't just disappear from their lives, not even for Jennifer.

But Jennifer got increasingly desperate. She showed up unannounced one night at around midnight. Renata and Shirley had retired, and I was sitting at the dining table drawing landscapes of imaginary planets and listening to the radio. The pounding on the apartment door was so abrupt that my pencil skipped and ruined what was supposed to be a delicate extraterrestrial plant in full bloom.

Jennifer's face was tear-stained, she was barefoot, and her left foot was bleeding. She fell into my arms and buried her head in my neck. She didn't say a word. She didn't need to.

Renata and Shirley came out of their bedroom, and we helped Jennifer to the couch; she rested her bloody foot in my lap. What happened to you? Renata asked.

We have to tell them, I said to Jennifer.

She nodded consent, and then haltingly recounted how her mom had gone out with a friend, so she'd barricaded herself in her room knowing her mother would be out for only a few hours. But she had to use the bathroom and when she got back to her room Roy was waiting for her.

She ran toward the front door, but he caught her before she got there. He held his hand over her mouth and when he stuck his other hand down her pants, she bit the hand that was on her mouth and was able to run out of the house. She had run all the way to Renata's, barefoot.

Shirley was spitting fire and wanted to call the police, but Jennifer begged her not to. Renata tended to Jennifer's foot and said she could stay with us for that night. We made the couch into a bed. I slept on the floor next to her. She dangled her hand over the side so that I could hold it and remind her I was there.

In the morning Renata insisted that we go to school as usual, while she and Shirley figured out what to do. Jennifer made Renata swear not to call the police. We walked hand-in-hand. About three blocks from school, Jennifer abruptly stopped and pulled me back. She stared straight ahead, eyes wide and fearful.

A man I assumed was Roy stood leaning against a street sign, watching us, no more than thirty feet away. He actually looked like a nice guy, well-groomed with a trimmed mustache, kind of like a television sportscaster.

My instinct was to run, but Jennifer was rigid as a statue, and anyway I think Roy would have caught up to us, so I stood my ground too, facing him down like in a Wild West gunfight. The only thing missing was a large tumbleweed blowing across the street.

Roy started walking toward us. When he was about ten feet away, I pulled Jennifer forward and tried to walk around him, but he blocked our path.

Where did you run off to last night, young lady, Roy said. I was worried sick. I covered for you with your mom, said you went to a girlfriend's house to do homework. And now I find you with a boy. What's your mom going to say?

He took a long drag on his cigarette. So, what were you kids up to all night?

I tugged on Jennifer's arm and tried to squeeze past Roy. We have to go to school, I mumbled.

What's that? I didn't hear you.

Get away from us, Jennifer said. I'm not coming home. And you can tell Mom I'll call the police if she tries to make me come home.

Call the police? Roy said. About what?

We tried again to walk around him, but he grabbed Jennifer's arm and pulled her up so that she was standing on her toes. Don't you fuck with me, little lady, he said. I'll make your life hell.

Seeing Roy's hand gripping Jennifer's arm detonated fifteen years' worth of rage in me. I pulled my arm back and punched Roy in the jaw with as much force as I ever had exerted in any physical activity I had ever done. That single punch was like a five-fingered atom bomb.

Roy's head snapped to the side. He let go of Jennifer and staggered backward like a drunk and then fell to a sitting position.

I pulled Jennifer by the arm and said, Let's go.

Roy, blood dripping out of his mouth, stood up and took a step toward us; I raised my arms, bracing for a punch, but instead he kicked me in the gut, karate-style. It felt like his foot had made it all the way through to my spine.

I crumpled to the ground and landed hard on the side of my face. I heard scuffling sounds above me and Jennifer shouted, You bastard! I hate you! and a man's voice yelled, Hey, what's going on over there?

I looked up and saw Roy waving toward the house from where the voice had come. It's no problem, we're just horsing around, Roy said, and then turned and walked quickly down the sidewalk, holding his jaw.

I still had not taken a breath because my lungs refused to take in air, although miraculously I was still conscious. Jennifer sat next to me sobbing and stroking my head, and eventually my lungs started to work at half-speed. A few kids from school walked by and stared.

We made our way to a drug store and Jennifer bought alcohol and cotton balls and rubbed alcohol on my face, which was scraped and bleeding from landing on the sidewalk. I winced and squirmed like a four-year-old and tried to push her hand away.

We walked to Santa Monica, slowly, because I still was having trouble breathing, and arrived in time to see the first showing of *Easy Rider*. I was so angry when Wyatt and Billy were murdered that I pounded the seat in front of me and cried tears of rage.

Renata called Jennifer's mom that night, as Jennifer and I hovered over her to listen in. Renata made an offer: Jennifer would stay with us for the time being and Roy would stay away from her or we would call the police.

Jennifer's mom denied everything and called Jennifer a liar and a tramp.

Very well, then, Renata said, I'll hang up right now and call the police.

Calling the police would have been a huge risk for me and Renata, so I didn't know if it was just a bluff, but if it was, it worked: Jennifer's mom quickly backed down and accepted Renata's terms, but only after accusing Renata of destroying her family. I'll make you pay for this, she said to Renata as she hung up the phone.

I'm sure she's happy to be rid of me, Jennifer said.

Shirley talked of assembling a posse of women to deal with Roy, but I didn't think she really would have done it. She was just primal screaming.

We pushed the couch to the corner of the room and Shirley brought a folding screen from her store to put in front of it so Jennifer would have some privacy. Renata decreed that Jennifer could not be in Ben's room, now my room, after she and Shirley went to bed, but that didn't keep me from slithering into the living room when the lights were out. Jennifer and I would snuggle on the couch behind the screen, but she eventually would shove me off because two people couldn't really sleep on that couch and I would fall asleep on the floor next to her.

●❍❍❍○❍❍❍●

Renata's doctor told her the Hodgkin's was in remission. She could stop the drugs and the radiation for now, but if the Hodgkin's recurred, the doctor said, it would be more aggressive than before.

Now that her treatment was over, Renata finally told Ben about the cancer. He of course already knew, I had told him everything in weekly letters, but he pretended not to know.

We're going to Vancouver over Christmas, Renata told me after she hung up the phone with Ben. I can't stand being separated from him like this.

I hugged her and let her cry on my shoulder. I was now her comforter as much as she was mine, and there was no way I would leave her. And the fact that she was taking me with her to Vancouver told me that Renata and Ben now truly were my family.

Shirley would stay in Venice to keep Zodiac open for the busy Christmas season, and Jennifer would spend Christmas with her dad, as usual.

She had not told him about her new living arrangement. He doesn't need to know anything about my life, she said. If he found out, he might insist that I move to San Francisco and live with him and Sweat Hog. He wouldn't really want me to live with them, but he'd do it just to spite my mom.

Renata and I took the bus to Vancouver, and Jennifer went with us as far as San Francisco, where we had a connection. Her father was waiting at the curb outside the station to pick her up. I extended my hand, which he took reluctantly and said, Why don't you get a haircut, boy?

I had no answer.

Get in the car, Jenny, let's go, he said.

Jennifer and I embraced, and she affixed her lips to mine in a long and passionate Hollywood-style kiss, as much to piss off her dad as anything else, and when she started rubbing her hands in my hair he barked, Hey! Enough of that! and pulled her toward the car, causing our lips to audibly detach.

She looked at me and laughed a silent and victorious laugh, having accomplished the goal of pissing off her dad.

We arrived in Vancouver late at night. Ben met us at the bus station and couldn't hide his shock at how his mom looked after months of being attacked from the inside by cancer and from the outside by drugs and radiation.

Ben had moved out of the church basement and was living rent-free in a room in a neglected, sparsely furnished house he shared with two other American draft dodgers and a bearded, chain-smoking, middle-aged Canadian named Fletcher who owned the house, which he'd grown up in. Fletcher described himself as an anarchist and a poet.

Ben insisted that Renata sleep in his room. He and I bedded down in the small front room using sofa cushions as pillows. An old radiator hissed periodically but gave off little heat. We lay on our backs under several blankets and talked into the darkness, just like old times.

My life is so fucked up, Ben said. This is not where I want to be. But I'm stuck here, maybe forever. And Jesus, Mom looks like hell, man. Why didn't you warn me?

I did tell you about her hair falling out, I said. I didn't want you to get scared. But she's in remission. She's better now. As long as the cancer stays away.

Yeah, if it stays away, Ben said. This is my biggest fear, man. Without Mom I've got nobody. And it had to happen right as I left the country, maybe for good. Fuck, man, I may have gotten out of Vietnam but there's a war in my head that I can't run away from. At least they've got good pot in Vancouver.

Ben told me that he was seeing a Canadian girl he'd met at the restaurant where he worked as a busboy. She's not a girlfriend or anything, he said. We mostly get stoned and then try to screw. It usually doesn't even work. Maybe we get too stoned or maybe, I don't know, maybe I'm just not into it.

We talked about me and Jennifer and Venice and busing tables and the war until it started to get light outside. I rolled over, put my arm across Ben and snuggled next to him. I started to drift off, but he shook me awake.

Listen, man, I've got to come home, he said. I've been looking at maps and there's all kinds of little roads that cross into Idaho or Montana that probably don't have border stations. I wrote to our old friends from the commune days, and they said I could stay with them in Ojai, and only you and Mom and Shirley would know. I think it'll work.

But if you get caught, they'll send you to jail, I said. They're serious, Ben. I hear about it all the time. They're ruthless. They're throwing dodgers in jail.

I don't care, he said. I'd rather be in jail in California than this far away from Mom. If she . . . if she were to . . . if the cancer . . . if she doesn't make it through this, I've got to be there, even if I'm in shackles. They can fucking execute me later if they want, but I've got to be there.

I knew I couldn't talk him out of it and I didn't try to.

He said: When this is all over, when the war's over, when I don't have to hide anymore, I'm going to Iowa. I'm going to confront my old man. I've got to look him in the eyes. I'm going to knock on his door and when he answers, I'm going to say, I'm your son, you son of a bitch. But you've got to go with me, Moon. You promise?

I promised I would. My temper could come in handy in a situation like that.

Tears were sliding down Ben's face and we embraced. I had thought that maybe I was a stand-in for Melissa those other times, but this time I don't think I was. I think I was me. I was Ben's planet just as he and Renata were my planets. We all were orbiting around each other.

And the next morning, we did make eye contact.

Our time in Vancouver sped by, a blur made blurrier by the fact that the pot in Vancouver was indeed good. Ben and I would sit huddled close together on the creaky back porch, trying to stay warm against the cold dampness that is winter in Vancouver, listening to music on a little cassette player. And even through the clouds and fog, I sometimes could see the moon, the only guaranteed constant in my life, the only thing that, even if I live to be a hundred, will still be up there going through its cycles, looking the same in 2054 as it did when I was born, in 1954.

Ben and I stayed up late every night, and he then rose early to spend time with Renata. They would go out for coffee and walks. I'd awaken around noon to an empty house, except for Fletcher, who padded around in slippers all day, sipping whiskey out of a coffee cup while listening to opera records. One day he handed me a copy of Vonnegut's latest novel about World War II, and I read it that afternoon while Ben was at work and Renata napped.

Fletcher was a fellow Vonnegut fan so we talked about the book, about time travel, and about how illogical war is, and he served me whiskey as if I were just another unshaven forty-year-old poet and anarchist.

Most days it rained off and on, and the sun was pale and weak, the coldness and darkness reminding me unhappily of Ohio. Renata cooked Ben's favorite meals at night and insisted that the other two draft dodgers join us, for which they were immensely grateful. Fletcher preferred to eat canned sardines on toast and drink whiskey, but he joined us at the old wooden dinner table and shared with us the merits of anarchism.

Ben and his fellow draft dodgers mostly talked about home and the things they missed. If we had anarchism, Fletcher said one night, there would be no government to send you off to war, to make you choose between killing for your country or leaving your country.

We departed on New Year's Eve for the thirty-hour bus ride home, leaving Ben to face the new decade alone under Vancouver's heavy skies. The weather became sunnier and warmer as we rolled southward, but my mind and spirit remained stuck in Vancouver's grayness.

Renata and I didn't talk much on the bus, but we took turns using each other's shoulder as a pillow, and she often would reach over and take my hand. I went straight to bed when we got home, not having slept well on the buses, and felt sad when I lay down in Ben's bed and thought of that little house in Vancouver with chipped paint and rusted radiators that was now his refuge from the rice paddies of Vietnam. But it never could be a refuge from that huge black hole in his heart, which, like all black holes, sucked up any light and life that dared venture too close to it.

That black hole would be with him wherever he went, and I feared it might suck up Ben's light and life.

Jennifer returned from San Francisco a few days later, and her mom called, but Jennifer refused to speak to her. She locked herself in Ben's room and blasted the radio. Renata tried to push me away, but I kept my ear near the phone receiver and heard it all: Jennifer's mom was leaving Roy—For reasons that are none of your goddamned business, she told Renata—and was moving to San Diego to live with her older daughter and her grandchildren.

She insisted that Jennifer move with her. She's my damn daughter and you can't keep her against my will, she said. That's kidnapping, and I'll call the police.

Later that night Jennifer pleaded with me through tears of rage and powerlessness and fear, the kind of tears I knew very well: I've got to run away—let's do it, let's go together.

I didn't blame her for wanting to flee and I wasn't one to argue against running away from an unbearable life, but I had promised Ben I would help him get home and would go to Iowa with him, and Renata needed me now as much as I needed her.

Maybe we could go live with Ben and his friends in Ojai, I said. The three of us could live there together, and Ojai's not far away from Renata.

But we don't know when Ben will get it together, or if it will happen, Jennifer said. My mom wants me to move now. We don't have time to come up with other ideas. I've got to get away. With or without you.

I thought of Jennifer living on the streets, as I had. I thought of her meeting someone like Max.

Renata suggested a temporary solution: Jennifer would stay with us so she could finish the school year at Venice High, and then could move to San Diego to join her mother and sister. It's the best I can come up with, Renata said. We don't have any legal standing here. And none of us want the police involved, right? It's really up to Jennifer's mother, though. All I can do is make the case.

Jennifer's mother agreed to the arrangement without much argument, but with the added condition that Jennifer spend every other weekend in San Diego. Jennifer still wanted to run away but I convinced her this arrangement would give us time and maybe Ben could get home by then, and we could join him in Ojai.

I had not received a note about my missing school records since I'd started at Venice High, so I assumed the issue had disappeared into the bowels of the school system. I was wrong.

Renata got a call asking her to meet with the school counselors to discuss some issues related to her ward, which was my official status. I was to attend as well. Renata was pissed. This is all because of your crappy schoolwork, she said. Can't you at least give enough of a shit that you don't raise a red flag? We've got to keep this con going for three more years.

We waited in the small room outside the counselor's office until a plump woman with a nasally voice and a pageboy haircut came out and motioned us into her office. You appear to be struggling some in your schoolwork, the woman said to me. So, we reviewed your files and realized there are some records missing—in fact, lots of records are missing.

Renata explained that her sister, my poor mother, remained in a coma and that it was much better for me to stay in California with her. I think it would have been very difficult for him back home, she said.

I nodded agreement and tried to look both sad about my comatose mother and happy to be living with Aunt Renata. And then—this was the *coup de grace*—Renata insisted she had in fact received my school records from home and had personally delivered them to the office at Mark Twain Middle School the year before.

I didn't make copies of them, she said. I'm sure they have them at Mark Twain and I don't know why they didn't send them over to you.

The woman looked skeptical, but Renata was very convincing, at least to me.

I made a lame comment about trying harder in school and said how happy I was to be at Venice High.

Well, at a minimum we need proof of your ward's medical vaccinations, the woman said. Legally he cannot be in school without proof of vaccination.

I walked Renata to her car. She still was pissed at me, and for good reason. Her son had fled to Canada, she was exhausted from cancer treatments, and now I had brought attention to our extralegal arrangement. If you're going to live a lie you have to work at protecting that lie.

I promised her that I would try harder at school, and I really meant it. It wouldn't be fun, but I would do it.

The next day I was sitting in the waiting room of the free clinic on Sunset Boulevard, to get the vaccinations the school required. It was loud and disorderly. Sneezing, coughing children were spewing germs like sprinklers on a golf course. A magazine cover caught my eye. It was a *Life Magazine* from the past summer, sitting in a cluttered pile of other dated magazines and coloring books. The headline was, The Faces of the American Dead in Vietnam—One Week's Toll.

I picked it up and started thumbing through it. Inside were the photos of two hundred and forty-two Americans who had died in the war during one week in June, with their names and hometowns printed underneath. Some of them looked like Ben's friends; many of them were Black or brown. None of them were old men.

I had started watching the television news every night to try and understand what was happening, what the war was all about, and for the periodic stories on American draft dodgers in Canada. The newscasters would talk to old men in Washington, some in suits and some in generals' uniforms, who voiced their opinions with certainty—some in favor of the war, some against it, but none of them at risk of getting shot at or stepping on a booby trap in a faraway jungle.

Newscasters talked to protesters: college-aged kids who either had not yet been drafted or had figured out a way to avoid getting drafted, priests, college professors, and movie stars. And they showed films of bloodied soldiers being loaded onto stretchers and into helicopters, sweaty and unshaven soldiers who talked of firefights and night patrols and ambushes and booby traps, deer-eyed soldiers who said, Love you, Ma, as they looked into the camera.

On Fridays the newscasters gave a weekly tally of dead Americans and dead communists, as if the whole thing were some sort of sports competition. We always seemed to be killing a lot more of them, but for some reason the war kept on going.

As I was about to flip a page of the *Life Magazine*, my peripheral vision caught the word Akron, my hometown for my first thirteen years. I looked at the accompanying photo and time stopped: The young man looked just like my brother, Jake, but with close-cropped hair and wearing a military uniform.

I felt a tingling in my chest, a chill wave over my skin. I tried to keep my eyes from looking at the name under the photo, but you know what eyes do when you tell them not to look at something. They looked: Jake Bruno, 19, Private First Class, Akron, Ohio.

I never had seen my brother's name in print—and in a national magazine, no less. Strangely, that was the first thought that crossed my mind.

I looked back and forth from the photo to the name a few times then tossed the magazine back on the pile as if it were radioactive. My instinct, as it so often was in those days, was to flee.

But just at that moment the receptionist called out my name, so I could at least flee to the exam room. The nurse asked me a few questions which I must have answered correctly because she proceeded to jab me four times, twice in each arm. Don't be nervous, it'll only pinch a little, she said, mistaking my quivering arms for fear of needles and not for emotional crisis.

I left the exam room smelling of alcohol wipes and headed for the front door. Wait, the receptionist called out, we need to give you copies of your records.

Of course. That's why I was there. I sat down on the other side of the room, far away from the *Life Magazine*. But I could see a soldier's photo on the partially torn cover, a close-up of his face. His eyes were looking right at me, and even when I moved to another seat they followed me.

It seemed to take forever for them to prepare the vaccination record. When it was ready, I walked quickly to the desk, grabbed it from the startled receptionist's hand, and half-ran out the door with my head down so the soldier's eyes wouldn't meet mine again.

I went to the cemetery in Hollywood, the one I had used as a refuge during my early days in Los Angeles. It was crowded—famous movie stars were buried there and viewing the site where a beloved star's body has decomposed is a popular tourist attraction—but I knew the quiet areas near the graves of the less famous. I sat under a tree, buried my face in my hands and wept. They could have been tears of grief, or of confusion, or of frustration, or of anger—or some alchemical combination.

And I remembered things: Jake and his friends locking me in the basement closet when they knew I had to pee desperately, and finally in tears I peed in the corner of the closet, and when my father got home he smacked me repeatedly and then made me clean it up, as if I had willingly chosen to pee in the closet.

Jake pinning me against the wall of my bedroom and threatening to break my nose when he found evidence that I had been using his turntable (I had forgotten to turn off the power button).

Jake setting off a string of Black Cat firecrackers behind me as I sat in the backyard reading, causing a coronary event that most likely will shorten my life.

Jake laughing and doing nothing when his mean, pimply-faced friend Russ pinned my arms behind my back and suggested they use me to practice fucking. He's kinda like a girl, Russ said, and started pulling at my pants. I broke free and ran outside and down the street.

Most of all, I remembered Jake, like my father, refusing to see Mom as she got sadder and drunker, and he should have seen, because he was older than me, and yet I saw. I was the only one who saw, and it was lonely and scary being the only one who saw her sorrow.

But I also remembered this: Lying face-down in the cold wet leaves in the woods behind our house, depleted of tears, determined to lay there until I died and could join Sirius in eternal nothingness, preferable to remaining in unbearable somethingness, and Jake came with a flashlight and picked me up and carried me inside and put me to bed.

He said, Dad's a fucking asshole. He sat on the edge of my bed and periodically patted my back, while I cried. And for the first time in my life, on the worst day of my life, I had a brother, and though that moment passed and everything returned to its normal abnormality, that moment was real and is still there in that place where moments remain when time leaves them in its wake.

And I thought of my mother, who—if she were still alive—had now lost both of her children. At least she knew what had happened to Jake. Presumably his body, or whatever parts of it were left, had been sent back to Akron.

But my disappearance was a mystery: I had left no note. For all she knew, I'd fallen into the creek and drowned and my body had made its way to the Cuyahoga, floated lazily up to Cleveland, and then discharged into Lake Erie. The idea that I might be living two thousand miles away in a new family of my own construction couldn't have crossed her mind.

Until I learned of Jake's death, I had not really considered the possibility that my mother may have been grieving over my disappearance, or at least feeling any deeper grief over it than whatever it was she had been grieving for the previous several years.

I had imagined life in that miserable family had just continued as usual, minus me. But now both her children were gone forever, and she would be left all alone with my father, if they were still together. If they weren't, she would be completely alone.

It is hard for the powerless to feel guilt.

For most of my time on Earth, I had lived at the mercies and whims of others, most of whom had disliked me. The first act of personal power I ever had taken was to run away, to try and find my sun before it was too late, to die trying if necessary. But as I sat under that tree in the cemetery, I felt guilt because of what my act of power—my act of survival—possibly had done to my mother.

I had wondered at times whether my running away might push her over the edge, but it was an edge she already had been drunkenly stumbling toward. Guilt had not been part of those thoughts.

Until now. Until I knew that she had buried one of her sons. Until I considered that she might be alone. I had not run away from home so that she would be alone. I had not done it to punish her for leaving me.

Or had I?

I called Jennifer that night—it was one of her mandatory San Diego weekends—and told her everything. My new pledge of full honesty had been liberating. I no longer had to edit myself as I talked.

Jennifer and I shared nuclear family disasters. Jennifer, like me, thought kindly of her grandmother, but her grandmother spoke only Chinese, so their relationship was limited. We both sought to erase our families from our lives, if not literally—as in my fantasy story—then by fleeing them, forgetting them.

But none of those people we so hated, who had caused so much misery to us, whom we wished to forget, actually had died. Until now;

until Jake. And family deaths reverberate, even to those who thought they had erased their family and its influence from their lives.

Although this was happening to me and not to her, Jennifer's natural empathy got the better of her: Oh my God, your poor mother, were the first words out of her mouth. Unknowingly, she intensified my feelings of guilt.

Yeah, I said. I've been thinking about that. I think I had assumed that she knew I wasn't dead. But how would she know that? It's like every time I looked at the Pleiades, I assumed they were looking back at me. She probably thinks both of her sons are dead now. And she'll go to her grave thinking that, unless . . .

Unless what?

Unless she's already dead.

Or unless you get in touch with her. Isn't that what you were really thinking?

It now was clear to me that one of Jennifer's many talents was mind reading, but I wasn't going to admit that yet.

I don't know what I was thinking, I said. But I feel really sad at the thought that she might believe both her children are dead.

Have you ever thought about getting in touch with her when you turn eighteen? When you are a legal adult, and they wouldn't be able to force you to go back to Ohio?

I haven't thought that far ahead, I said. I don't even know what I'm doing next week.

And that was true. I hadn't considered whether the erasure of my family was to be permanent. Jake's death now made me realize that my family could be permanently erased by things other than me.

Here's an idea, Jennifer said, but promise you won't get mad at me.

I grunted my agreement not to get mad.

Why don't you write her a letter or a postcard? she said. Just to let her know you're all right. You don't have to give a return address or a phone number or anything.

What would I say? Hi Mom, sorry Jake is dead, but at least I'm not.

Don't be snarky, Moon. I'm serious. Maybe you don't give a shit about her at all, but I don't think that's the case or you wouldn't be so upset about this. You can't pretend it away.

I know. You're right. I've just got to think about it.

Why the hell did I pick up that magazine, I thought as I lay in bed trying to fall asleep that night. It was a random event. An infinite universe is filled with random events, and it's those random events that change the trajectories of our lives. I felt—I feared—my life trajectory was changing, but I didn't know in what way. And I wasn't at the steering wheel.

Jennifer returned from San Diego the next evening, and we spent the night watching television with Renata. I sat between Renata and Jennifer, holding each one's hand like they were two tethers keeping me attached to Earth.

Let's go to the roof, I said to Jennifer as soon as Renata and Shirley retired. I started to roll a joint, but Jennifer stopped me.

No. You hide behind pot all the time. I want to talk to you, not to a stoned-out version of you.

Okay, but let's still go to the roof. I want to see the Pleiades.

Jennifer waited patiently while I contemplated the sky's most beautiful object through my binoculars. With strong binoculars you can look right at the Pleiades without the blind spot problem, and I did, for a long time. Jennifer finally nudged me. Let's sit down and talk, she said.

The Pleiades were getting blurry now anyway, because of my tears; I put the binoculars away, wiped my eyes and sat down next to Jennifer.

I don't know what to do, I said. I've lived in fear that I would be forced to go back there. I never thought once about contacting them. I guess I saw it as a mutual breakup: they hated me, and I hated them. So why does it seem different now?

Jennifer pulled my head into her lap and stroked my hair. You've never talked about your mother hating you, or you hating her, she said.

I've noticed she's the only one you don't seem to despise. And that's who this is about, isn't it?

Jennifer was right: I never had thought my mom hated me. She had just stopped loving me, which in some ways is even worse than being hated. If someone hates you, you can hate them back. But if someone you love stops loving you, if you no longer are their beloved, there's nothing you can do. Except leave.

Why did she stop loving me? I said out loud. I wasn't asking Jennifer—I was posing the question to the universe. Or maybe to the Pleiades.

I suddenly felt like a small child, not just any small child but the small child that once was me, in my bed in Ohio, asking Sirius: Why doesn't Mommy love me anymore?

I don't believe my mother loved me from the get-go, Jennifer said. I was an accident. A fender-bender baby. She didn't want me. But your mom did love you. So, something happened, Moon. But it couldn't have been anything you did. You were eight years old for shit's sake. What could an eight-year-old do that was so bad?

I wish you could have seen them, I said. The before mom and the after mom. They were two completely different people.

That's what I'm saying, Jennifer said. She was the one who changed. Something happened with her, not you.

Jennifer's observation seemed so obvious, so clear, I wondered why I'd never thought of it that way before. I knew my story. But I had not considered there may have been another story, a story I didn't know. My mother's story.

I suggested you send her a letter or a postcard, Jennifer said. That way she would know you're alive. But that wouldn't give you any answers. I think you should call her.

I lay silently, eyes closed. Jennifer continued gently stroking my head.

A cavalcade of old memories and images passed through my mind. Maybe Maurice was right, and the past doesn't forget you. It's like a long tail that extends behind you, stretching back out of sight, and no matter how fast you run or how suddenly you turn, it's still connected to your ass. I clearly had not succeeded in severing my tail—Maurice had warned me it was hard to do—and Jennifer now suggested I stop trying, that I reconnect the jagged edges of the tail I had managed to tear but not sever.

I don't ever want to go back to Akron, I said. Nothing my mother says could change my mind about that.

I'm not saying go back. Shit. You know I don't want you to do that. I'm saying call her. You can do it from a pay phone. She could never track you down. This is a big city.

I sat up. Three crows were idling on the edge of the roof. Two were fighting over a mouse carcass, flipping it in the air between them. The third crow looked toward me, its head cocked. At that moment I knew I would call my mother.

It was as if the decision had been made by a secret mind, a mind I didn't know, a mind that made its own decisions and then told my other mind what to do.

I hadn't told Renata anything about my brother or my memories. I couldn't. I felt like I was cheating on her, planning a clandestine date with my ex-mother. She drove me and Jennifer to school.

Jennifer got out of the car, but I stayed in the front seat, staring straight ahead.

Are you okay? Renata said.

I looked into her green eyes, which still fascinated. Her face had aged from the Hodgkin's. Or maybe from taking care of two freeloader kids, while her only child was a thousand miles away at risk of going to jail. Or from all those years of living a lie, of being unable to love Shirley outside the confines of that small apartment, of having her family hang up the phone whenever she called.

I'll never go away, I said. Whatever happens, I'll never leave you.

I leaned over and kissed her on the lips, as I often had imagined doing, then got out of the car before she could respond, before I could see her response.

I walked with Jennifer to the front entrance of school and stopped. I'm skipping today, I said. I'm going up to Sunset; I'll find a phone there.

Do you want me to come with you?

No, I have to do this alone I said. Jennifer kissed me and hugged me tight.

I stopped at a bank on the way to Sunset Boulevard and got five dollars' worth of quarters. They jangled in my pocket as I continued my trek. I passed many pay phones along the way, but I wanted to be far from Venice in the event my mother was able to have the call traced. I thought about what I would say, what I would reveal, what I would ask.

I finally stopped at a row of four pay phones attached to the outside brick wall of a drugstore. I sat down on a conveniently placed empty wooden crate and put my head in my hands. Am I really going to do this, I said out loud, a statement, not a question, because I knew I was going to do it.

I chose the second phone from the left and picked up the receiver. I didn't know what long-distance calls cost, so I dropped two dollars' worth of quarters into the slot. I dialed my old telephone number by rote, without even thinking. I didn't so much remember the numbers as the movement of my fingers, the pattern that sequence of numbers made on the rotary dial.

After a few seconds of clicking noises the call went through. The phone was ringing in my old home—once, twice, three times. I was making noise in my old home. I was a presence there again.

Yes?

It was the way my mother always had answered the phone. She never said Hello. It was like she wanted the caller to state their business and forego the niceties.

I suddenly felt unsure of what my business was. Hearing her voice for the first time in two years caused me suddenly to picture her face again, a clear and exact picture, a picture I thought I'd forgotten. I tried to form words, even just one word, but all that came out was a breathy guttural sound.

Charlie?

I slammed the receiver down and took two steps back, staring at the phone as if it were pointing a gun at me. The sound of my old name, coming from my old mother's mouth, was like the invocation of a curse, as if by simply hearing my mother call me Charlie made me Charlie again, as if my mother had the power to erase Moon with one word. It unleashed a flood of memory, not specific memories, but rather amorphous memory, a blob of memory.

I retreated to the wooden crate. How had she known it was me at the other end of several thousand miles of copper wire? Or did she believe or wish or hope that every unidentified caller was me?

One thing was certain: I had not been forgotten.

I went into the drugstore and bought a small tin of aspirin. I didn't have a headache, I just felt that I needed to take something, anything. It gave me something to do.

I went back outside and watched people walk by as I chewed an aspirin. An old lady pulling a grocery cart looked at me and smiled kindly and toothlessly. I wanted to ask her what I should do, but it would have required too much explanation. And no matter what, she probably would have said, Of course you should call your mother; children always should call their mothers.

I put eight more quarters into the phone—this time, the one on the far-right end—and my fingers followed the pattern they knew so well. The phone rang only twice.

Yes? Who is this?

It's me, I said, my voice surprisingly weak and low.

This better not be another of those goddamned prank calls, she said. Her voice was quivering.

No, it's really me.

Then tell me this: What were the stories I told you at night when you were little?

You mean Simon? The adventure stories?

It went silent on the other end, but only because her sobs were soundless at first. Then not. My leaking tears were quiet as I listened to my mother's joyful anguish. She was struggling to speak.

Where are . . . how are you . . . are you safe . . . She struggled to reduce a thousand questions into one.

I'm fine. I'm good. My tone sounded angrier to me than I felt. Or maybe it was exactly how I felt.

I understand why you ran away from me, she said, as if she had been waiting all this time to say that. And it struck me how right she was: I had not run away from home. I had run away from her. She had known that even better than I had.

I'm just so thankful that you're alive, she said, and started to sob again.

The phone started to beep, so I inserted all my remaining change into the slots.

I'm sorry about Jake, I said when her sobbing subsided. I just learned. That's why I'm calling. For some reason, I needed to let her know that, had I not learned of Jake's death I would not have called. It sounded mean but it was the truth.

They wouldn't even let me see his body, Mom said. He had been so eager to sign up. I think it was his way of running away. Like you. But Charlie, there's a lot of things you didn't know. It's not your fault, it's my fault.

I knew what I needed to do to keep from dying, I said.

Oh, I'm not questioning that, Charlie. And you kept me from dying when you ran away, because there was no further down I could go. I had only two choices: to die or to live and maybe, just maybe, see you again. The detectives said that if thirty days went by with no sign of you then most likely you were dead. But I didn't believe them; I knew you were alive. I've always known it. Just like when Jake left for Vietnam, I knew that I never would see him alive again.

There's things you need to know, important things, things I should've told you, things I wanted to tell you, things I dreamed of telling you. But I want to tell you to your face. I want to see you so bad. She spoke as if she had been rehearsing for this conversation, had said it out loud to herself a hundred times.

I'm not coming back, I said.

I wondered if the call had been traced, if police cars were about to scream up to the pay phone. I looked over my shoulder both ways down Sunset to make sure.

That's okay, I'll come to you. I won't try to make you come back. I have to move out of the house soon. Larry moved in with Arnie a year ago, and I can't pay the rent here. So there's no place for you to come back to. I will come to you.

The phone started beeping.

I have to go, I said. I don't have any more money.

Call me again, she pleaded over the beeping. Please, Charlie. I have to tell you about your father.

The line went dead.

I walked slowly back home. Jennifer was waiting for me outside the apartment building so we could walk in together as if we both had come from school. But Renata had received a call from school about my unexcused absence and she was irate, angrier than I had imagined it possible for her to be.

Don't you have any common sense at all, she yelled at me. I'm doing everything I can to keep this charade working for the two of you, and you keep trying as hard as you can to fuck it up.

I stammered apologies. She retreated to her bedroom and slammed the door.

Why don't you tell her what's going on? Jennifer said.

I can't. Not yet.

She's a counselor. She may be able to help you figure things out.

I need to keep this family separate from that family. It's like I'm two people, and when I spoke to my mother, I was the old me again, and I didn't like it. I don't want to mix things up.

I told Jennifer about the call, and my mother's curious last words.

You've got to call her again, she said. It sounds like she has something she really wants to tell you.

Yeah, but I'm not sure I want to know what it is. What could she possibly say about my father that would be so important for me to hear? He hated me and I hated him.

I wrote a letter to Renata before I went to bed and left it on the kitchen table in a sealed envelope. I told her that she and Ben were my family, the only family I wanted to have. I told her that taking me in and then rescuing Jennifer proved she was a better person than I ever would be. I thanked her for putting up with my inconsiderate behavior. And I told her that I loved her.

I stood in front of another row of pay phones, this one in Santa Monica, closer to home. Now that I had done it once, I was less fearful of the call being traced.

Hi, I said when she answered the phone. It's me.

Oh, sweetheart, oh my God. I am so happy you called again. I wasn't sure it was real. I'm on all these medicines and sometimes I don't trust my memory of things.

What did you want to tell me? What do I need to know?

I heard her light a cigarette and then exhale the smoke.

I don't drink anymore, Charlie. I dried out in the hospital, in the psych ward, and they put me on all these drugs—Nardil, Librium—all this stuff I can't mix with booze. So my choice was to be sane or be drunk.

That's good, I said. I wish you had . . .

Yeah, I know. I wish I had, too. I so wish I'd been there for you. And for Jakey. But I was dealing with things, or not dealing with them. I was just drowning everything in booze. I've only realized in the past few years how ill I was. In the head, Charlie. That's what the drugs are for. She sniffed and took another deep drag on the cigarette.

I put more coins in the phone even though it wasn't beeping yet.

Charlie, this is what you need to know: Larry Bruno is not your father. He's Jake's father, but he's not your father.

What are you saying?

When I was in high school, I fell in love with this guy. Madly in love, crazy in love. And he loved me—believe it or not, I was wild and fun in those days. I drove Grandma nuts. Anyway, he loved me, but he wanted more than anything else to see the world. So after we graduated, he went up to Cleveland and finagled his way into a job on a freighter headed for Europe. And from there he sailed all around the world, doing all kinds of jobs. He sent me letters and postcards—oh, God, every week.

He always told me he loved me, but I knew he was happy and I didn't know when he was coming back, or if he ever was. Well, I met Larry in the meantime, and we started going out, mostly getting drunk and going bowling and stuff. I know it seems hard to believe but Larry could be fun, sometimes even fun enough to keep my mind off of Simon.

The phone beeped. I inserted more quarters.

Simon? I asked when the call resumed.

Yeah. That's where those stories came from. They were his stories, with maybe a few embellishments by me. Anyway, next thing you know, I was pregnant with Jake. Larry and I got married—really fast, too, because we knew people would do the math. People like Grandma.

So, who's my father?

Several years after Jake was born, Simon came back to Ohio for his grandfather's funeral. It was the first time he'd been back in the country and the first we'd seen of each other in years. We were gonna just meet for a beer and talk about old times, but it was love at first sight all over again. It hadn't faded at all. That was the happiest week of my life. And that's the week you were conceived, Charlie.

So, I'm a bastard? I'm a mistake, I said.

A bastard? she said. I wasn't married to your father, if that's what you mean. But you were conceived in love. A mistake is something you wish had not happened, something you wish you could undo, so no, you are definitely not a mistake.

Where is he now? Simon? My father?

Simon died when you were eight, Charlie. And I guess you know what that did to me. I mean, I've been emotionally unstable my whole life, up and down. But that was a down I couldn't come out of.

The phone beeped. My hands were shaking as I stuck the last of my quarters into the phone.

Tell me about him, I said. I want to know.

Charlie, I so badly want to see you. Tell me where to come. After that, if you want me to go away forever I will, I swear I will. But I just have to see you one more time. I have so much more to tell you.

So, you're not going to tell me more unless I agree to see you?

She didn't answer, but it didn't matter, because now I wanted to see her. I wanted to hear her story—which now was my story, too. I wanted to see pictures of Simon. I wanted to know everything that had happened. I wanted to know who I was.

I'm in Los Angeles, I said.

Call me tomorrow, Charlie. I'll find a motel there and let you know where I'll be.

The phone beeped.

Everything was moving so fast, as if I'd been floating down a choppy river, had rounded a bend, and suddenly was in the midst of ferocious rapids. I didn't know whether going through those rapids would lead me to calmer waters or to a fatal plunge over a waterfall.

I often had wished Jake were dead; I never could have envisioned the chain of events his actual death would cause. My mom moved quickly, perhaps to prevent me from changing my mind. When I called her again, she had plane tickets and gave me the address of a motel on Century Boulevard, near the airport. Los Angeles is so big, she said, and this was all I could afford. I hope it's not too far from where you are.

I had forty-eight hours before my old life, the life I had tried to erase, would collide with my new life. I knew seeing my mom again would create a San Andreas-sized fault line, and virtually every second of those forty-eight hours—including the sleeping ones, awash in feverish dreams—was an emotional amalgam of fear, anticipation, anger, and sadness. Only Jennifer knew what was going on.

I still couldn't bring myself to tell Renata, either from fear that if she knew she would think I was going to leave her, or from fear that if she knew she would encourage me to leave her. After all the love and devotion she had shown me, I still managed to have doubts about what I meant to her.

I had no doubts about what I meant to Ben, but I didn't tell him what was going on because he had enough worries of his own without hearing about mine.

Those longest hours of my life passed, and I was on an airport express bus, on a Sunday morning. Jennifer was in Venice that weekend but had not even suggested accompanying me, and I would not have wanted her to.

I didn't want my two lives to clash so directly. I didn't want Jennifer to hear my old name. I wasn't sure I wanted to hear my old name again. I got off at the airport and started walking the mile down Century toward the motel. I felt surprisingly calm for the first time in weeks, perhaps because I knew there was no turning back now. So far, at least, I had survived the rapids.

I stood on the sidewalk in front of the dumpy two-story motel. The sign said Motor Hotel, but they weren't fooling anyone. There were no more than a dozen rooms on each floor, and a separate office the size of a backyard shed. A small neon-tube sign flickered Vacancy. The marquee announced Color TV and Air Conditioning; it didn't say anything about Painful Family Reconciliations.

I didn't see any police cars or paddy wagons poised to nab me, so I climbed the concrete stairs and proceeded to Room 206.

I knocked.

I heard the latch being turned and the chain lock slide open. And then my mom was standing in front of me. Or a woman who looked a lot like my mom, for she was even thinner and smaller than I had remembered, and her hair was streaked now with gray. Her face looked familiar and yet different, not quite right, like an amateur's painting of someone you know.

Her eyes met mine and widened; she too was seeing a painting of a strange but familiar face. We looked at each other's portraits for what seemed like hours, though it was only seconds.

Oh my God, she whispered, Oh my God. She took one step toward me but then stepped back so I could enter the room.

She sat on the bed, her eyes never leaving mine. I stepped inside and closed the door; my mother reached out toward me, her hand shaking, but I was afraid to take it, afraid to make physical contact, afraid of raising things to a whole new level. But what had I expected? That we would sit and chat like old friends and then go about our day?

When I looked into her eyes, I realized what I had done, but it was too late: I was Charlie again.

My mother drove home that fact: Charlie? Charlie? Oh God . . . Charlie, she said over and over.

I took a tentative step toward her but my legs felt wobbly, so I sat down on the floor and leaned back against the door; maybe to maintain some physical contact with the exit.

My mother fell to her knees, crawled forward, and collapsed on top of me. It was not a hug; it was more like a fog bank rolled in over me, blurring my boundaries with the world. I smelled cigarette smoke and shampoo and her clothes closet and our house. I smelled the first thirteen years of my life.

I rested one hand on her back, but it was like putting a cork on a volcano. I put my other hand on her back and held on to her tighter and tighter until it became an embrace.

I felt constriction in my chest and throat, and blinked rapidly to fend off the pooling tears, but they started to flow. I had lost the battle of control and the volcano had erupted, but I felt safe, like a small boy again, in my mother's arms. The thing I had fought so hard against ever feeling again felt good.

We remained like that, two distinct and separate agglomerations of stardust entangled in memories and tears, for a long time, until we were drained of tears.

Afterward, Mom and I walked down the corridor, wiping our eyes, still sniffling. She held out her hand, but I didn't take it. She kept glancing up at me—I now was taller than her by at least three or four inches—and in silence we made our way to a table in the coffee shop next door to the motel.

We sat across from each other and I stared at the sugar packets, stacked nicely in the little metal holder that they shared with the salt and pepper shakers. I grabbed a packet and kneaded it between my fingers. My nose was stuffy from crying and my eyes felt hot.

We ordered coffees from the waitress, and Mom lit a cigarette.

You've grown so much, she said. You look healthy. Do you like it here?

Yeah, and I'm staying here, I said. I want you to know that.

I do know that. You're free, Charlie. I love you more than the air I breathe. That's why I want you to be wherever you are happy, and I know that can't be with me.

Good, I said. I mean, thank you.

I'd like to hear about your situation out here, and I'd like to be in your life—on your terms, of course. I hope you have a good situation here, and I trust you if you say you do.

I was kneading the sugar packet so hard, it ripped and sugar spilled out onto the table; I swept it into my hand and dumped it in my coffee. I looked up at Mom.

I won't disappear again, I said. I wasn't confident I could keep that promise but I didn't know how to make it conditional, or what the terms might be. She wasn't going to try and make me go back to

Ohio, so my first condition was met.

I had so many questions, so much I wanted to know. But the question that came out first surprised me: Did Dad, I mean Larry, did he know I was not his son? Is that why he hated me?

Mom snuffed out her cigarette, coughed, and lit another one. He knew, she said, because he and I weren't having relations at that time. We agreed to stay together after I got pregnant with you because we couldn't afford to split up. He agreed to be your dad. Or to play the role of your dad. I know he didn't do it well. I can't fully blame him. After all, I did cheat on him.

So is that why you let him hate me? Why you never did anything, why you looked the other way while he hurt me? Because you didn't blame him? You felt guilty?

She didn't answer right away. It was a powerful accusation. I was satisfied to let it hang in the air.

Maybe, Charlie. Maybe, she finally said. I don't know. I haven't figured everything out. Those years are such a cloud in my mind. Simon told me he was going to come back, that we would be together one day. I guess I thought when that happened everything would become clear to you, and you would have a father who loved you.

And what about Uncle Arnie, I asked? Was that part of your atonement, too?

What are you talking about? She furrowed her brows and leaned slightly forward. What about Arnie?

Oh, fuck it all, I said, and rested my face in my hands. I suddenly felt nauseated. I wondered if volcanoes felt nauseated just before they blew their lava vomit. I took a sip of water.

Charlie, what about Arnie?

It's too late to talk about it now. It's done. Forget it.

Charlie . . .

Forget it!

The cook standing at the grill turned around and looked at us. My mom settled back in her seat and stared away from me, out the window. I took another sip of water to calm the lava in my stomach.

Did Simon know about me? I said quietly.

My mom hesitated before answering. I wasn't sure if she was thinking about what to say or if she didn't want to change the topic.

I told him about you the year before he died, she finally said. I would've told him earlier, but Simon was living his dream. If you love someone, really love someone, you let them live their dreams. I shared Simon's adventures with you through those stories I'd tell you at bedtime.

Then things started to get really bad between me and Larry. He was having affairs and, well, you saw it all. So, I sent Simon a letter, with photos of you, and I told him you were his son. I was trying to lure him back.

Mom started to weep softly, and fiddled with her hair.

He wanted more pictures and a lock of your hair and he wanted to know everything about you—your favorite things, what you liked to do, your quirks, everything. I told him how you loved to look at the stars and read about outer space. How smart and curious you were, just like him. I sent him some of your drawings.

So, if you loved him and he loved you, why didn't you go join him? Why'd you stay with Larry when you could've married Simon?

Life's messy, Charlie. Jakey was my son, too. I couldn't just walk out on him while he was still young. And Simon was following his passions, he didn't want to be tied down. I didn't want to get in the way of that, it wouldn't have been fair. And marriage? Not as long as Grandma was alive. She never would've stood for that.

Why not?

She didn't believe in divorce. And anyway, Simon was Jewish. Grandma would have stepped in front of a freight train before she'd allow me to marry a Jew. Grandma never liked Larry, she thought he was beneath me, but at least he was raised Catholic, at least he had that going for him. My dad would've been fine with it, because he never took the religious stuff that seriously.

Did Grandma know I was Simon's child?

Oh, she never said anything, but I'm sure she knew. She knew

Simon had been in town nine months before you were born. She knew how much I liked him. And she could look at your face and see Simon. That's why she insisted on taking you to church every Sunday. I think she was trying to wash away my sins.

How did Simon die? I asked.

She met my eyes. She took a breath and looked down. He was murdered. That's about all I know. He'd been living in a small town in Mexico, teaching English and learning about some Indian tribe in the area. It was his latest passion. I'm telling you, Charlie, his mind was never still. He had learned their language and their music and their religion and everything. And he'd met this Indian man—some kind of spiritual guy—and they became close friends and Simon wrote that he finally was beginning to understand his life. He had changed, he had grown.

The really hard part, Charlie, is that several weeks before he died, he sent me a letter saying he was ready to settle down, that his adventures were over. And he wanted me and you to join him out here, in California, where he was going to buy a small farm with money his grandfather had left him. He wanted to be with us.

Anyway, this letter came in the mail—I got a post office box that Larry didn't know about just so I could get mail from Simon—and you know what? I finally was ready too. Jakey was old enough then, he didn't need a mommy anymore, and he was closer to Larry anyway. It would've split up our family, but it wasn't much of a family, right? And I didn't care anymore what Grandma thought. She could cut me off for all I cared, I just wanted to be with Simon and you. I was ready.

And then, a few weeks later, I got word from his brother that he'd been murdered. All I know is he was stabbed. Many times. They shipped his body home. I couldn't even go to the funeral. I couldn't get out of bed. I couldn't do anything. For a few short weeks, Charlie, my life's dream had come true. I was so happy, happier than I ever had been. And then it ended. Only a few weeks of true happiness, that's all I got in this life.

When Simon died, I died, too. But I guess you saw that. And you were way too young to have to see that. I am so sorry you had to see that. Mom sobbed into her folded arms. She was mourning her lost life, her lost love, her lost happiness, her decimated dream—a dream that included me and my father. My father, who never held me in his arms or bounced me on his knees, who never read me a story or tossed me a baseball, who never taught me all he knew about life.

I never would talk to him, or touch him, or hear his voice. But he had conceived me in love. And he had wanted to start a new life with my mom and me. When my mom's dream was shattered, so was mine; when her happiness came to an abrupt end, so had mine.

My mother reached into her purse and handed me a photograph. It was the first time I'd lain eyes on my father.

My life story was being rewritten. I had fled to California to become someone different, but I had been someone different my whole life and hadn't known it. My whole life had been a lie and I had fallen for it. At that moment, I couldn't have picked myself out of a police lineup. I was reeling.

No longer inside my body, my mind hovered next to me in space, as if it could fly away at any moment. I feared it would, leaving my body slumped there on the vinyl seat in that booth. I gripped the sides of the table.

My mother put her head down, again sobbing into her arms. The noise in the coffee shop was getting louder, like someone turned up the volume.

I was breathing fast and shallow. I maintained my grip on the table, trying desperately to stay connected to something physical. I wanted to stay with my mom, but my survival instinct had only one thing in mind: flight.

I stood and backed away from the table.

Mom raised her head. Charlie, where are you going? she asked.

Her face started to melt, just like in my dream. Everyone was looking at me.

What's wrong, Charlie? Mom kept saying, even as her melting

face dripped into her lap and onto the table. Her voice echoed, as if we were in a canyon. I turned and ran toward the door.

Charlie, don't leave me, Mom called, and then I heard everyone in the coffee shop chanting, Charlie, don't leave me—

I ran out the front door and down the sidewalk and saw a bus, loading passengers. I charged aboard just as the doors were closing, emptied my pockets into the pay machine, made my way to the empty back row, the long row, and lay facedown on the cracked vinyl seat with my arms over my head. I listened to my rapid breaths and the rumbling of the bus's engine just a few feet from my ears, but I could still hear the voices—Charlie, don't leave me!

The steady vibration of the engine as the bus lurched along its route was like a sedative, and the voices faded as we got farther away. Suddenly the bus driver was shaking my arm. Get up, kid, he said. This ain't your bedroom.

The bus was empty except for me and the driver. The scene outside the windows looked unfamiliar. Where are we? I said.

Cypress Park Bus Yard, end of the line. Where you headed?

Venice.

Well, you need a better compass, kid. You ain't nowhere near Venice.

Somehow, I navigated my way back to Venice. I still felt like my mind was outside my body, but at least my body was doing what my mind told it to do, because I had to make several bus transfers. As I waited at bus stops, I paced in circles and tried to steady my breathing. I wanted to get back to the safe confines of Renata's apartment, back to the familiar little world I'd carved out in Venice, the Slum by the Sea, and the family of misfits I'd joined there.

As precarious as that little world was, it seemed safer than what was outside it, where my entire life—my sense of who I was, my story about myself, my understanding of what was real and not real, of what had happened and not happened—had been overturned in one nondescript southern California afternoon while the rest of humanity was going about its business.

The puzzle pieces of my life now were scattered, again, all over the place. I feared I was slipping into insanity, that only the thinnest of threads were keeping my thoughts connected to one another, that at any moment those threads would start snapping, and I would become one of those rambling and incoherent people I'd encountered on Hollywood and Sunset during my first days in Los Angeles.

Jennifer looked relieved when I got home, meeting me at the door. She'd become fearful I might indeed have been nabbed and forced back to Ohio.

I can't talk about it, I said. Not yet. I don't know where to start. I think I'm going crazy. I'm not sure I can hold on. Just stay with me, please.

I lay on my bed later that night, in the safe cocoon of Ben's room. I wanted to turn the clock back to when Ben and I shared his room, listened to records, got stoned on the roof, talked in the dark, and fell asleep to the sound of each other's breathing.

I heard Renata and Shirley turn off their television; in a few minutes they would be asleep. I turned off the lights and waited for Jennifer.

Jennifer quietly turned the doorknob and slipped in, against house rules. She crawled into my bed and lay down next to me, her head resting on my bare chest, her arm draped across me, her feet entangled with mine. I buried my head in her hair and she caressed my face.

So? she said. Do you want to talk about it now?

In a whispered voice I told Jennifer the story of my life, the third version she'd heard in less than two years. And it turns out there was some truth to the first version she'd heard: One of my parents had, in fact, been murdered.

I revealed it all. I was a completely open book, in boxer shorts.

So do you still love me, now that you know I'm a bastard child? I said.

You idiot, of course I do, Jennifer said. More than ever. We'll get through this.

211

She'd said, We will get through this, not, You will get through this. Her choice of personal pronoun moved me to tears. I felt aroused and anxious at the same time. I didn't know what to do.

Technically, I knew how it was done, but there's a big difference between that and knowing what to do. We kissed softly four or five times. Jennifer slid her hand down my boxers and we kissed harder. Millions of years of mammalian reproductive instinct took over from there.

Afterwards, I rolled over and faced the wall. I didn't want Jennifer to see my tears. They were tears of sadness because I knew that happiness doesn't last, joy evaporates, and love abandons. Nothing so miraculous lasts forever. I thought about how happy my mom had been for a few short weeks, believing that she and my father and I were going to share our lives together, were going to flee our collective unhappinesses and move to California.

Jennifer squeezed up behind me and wrapped her arm around my chest. I took her delicate little hand in mine and squeezed it. She kissed my neck.

I awoke abruptly, with a gasp.

The clock on the bedside table said 3:07. Jennifer was asleep, breathing deeply. I crawled out of bed and went to the window. The world was quiet. I looked at Jennifer, her mouth partly open, her hair splayed across the pillow. I had lost my virginity on this strangest of all conceivable days.

I got dressed and slipped silently out of the apartment and up the stairs. I unlocked the metal door and as I started up the staircase to the roof, I saw a flickering light at the top, growing brighter as I climbed. There were more stairs than usual, or so it seemed. I climbed and climbed. When I emerged at the top, I saw a roaring fire, right in the middle of the roof. But nothing around it was burning.

It was like the Biblical burning bush. I looked around but I was all alone.

I approached the fire until I was about five feet away. I could feel its intense heat and started to sweat. I watched the flames as they danced upward into the night sky. Every few seconds there was a pop, causing sparks to fly. The flames danced to a rhythm, a pulse-beat, and before long it matched my heartbeat, which had become strong and loud, so loud, I feared it would awaken people downstairs.

The flames now were dancing and roaring upward, combining into fiery shapes and forms. The flames laughed—a mischievous laugh—until a sudden gust of wind silenced them and caused them to huddle together into one large flame that writhed and shifted and then grew again. The fire was confined to that one spot in front of me and I didn't understand why it was not spreading.

And then I saw Jimmy Hollingsworth. He was standing right in the middle of that large flame. But he wasn't burning. The fire lapped at him but seemed to do him no harm. He looked at me sadly, longingly, tenderly.

I felt profound despair; I wanted to cry; I wanted to hold Jimmy in my arms and comfort him. But he was standing in the middle of a fire.

I'm sorry, Jimmy, I said. A loud pop came from the fire, like a gunshot, and sparks flew all around Jimmy. Bright red blood poured from his head and flowed into the orange flames, and fueled them like gasoline to an even greater intensity. The fire now started to consume Jimmy, his hair and his clothes and his flesh. He looked horrified, the way being consumed by fire would look, and reached out toward me.

Charlie, Charlie, help me, he called out, as the flames engulfed him.

I wanted to jump into the fire and pull Jimmy out, and I would have, but it was as if a mighty weight were pressing down on me and I couldn't budge. I watched Jimmy writhe in agony and heard his high-pitched screams as burning flesh slid off his bones. With every scream I saw him inhaling flames. He burned until only his skeleton remained, then it too was consumed by the flames.

I felt seasick, as if the entire building were bobbing in turbulent waters, and I was losing my balance. I got on my hands and knees.

I heard a dog barking in the distance. Why would someone be walking a dog at this hour, I wondered. The barking became louder and closer. It sounded like the dog was on the roof. And the bark now sounded familiar.

Sirius? I said. Sirius? I said again, louder.

I strained to see, but the night was pitch black and the fire was rapidly dying out. I heard an animal scampering and panting on the roof.

Sirius? I called out.

The dog stopped abruptly at the sound of his name and barked: It was a bark I knew so well, a happy bark, a playful bark.

Sirius, I screamed, as I stood up and stumbled blindly into the darkness. I smashed right into the roof-top fencing that surrounded the machinery, and fell to the ground, but I heard Sirius panting nearby and started crawling toward him.

Sirius, come here, boy, I said.

He was to the left of me, then to the right. He thought we were playing. I couldn't see him and didn't know which way to go.

Sirius, where are you? I begged.

I felt his sloppy wet tongue on my cheek and smelled his familiar doggy breath, and I could just make out his face in the dark. I wanted to hug him and kiss his snout and roll on the ground with him, but I was paralyzed, unable to move while my dog licked my face and nuzzled my neck. I started to weep and Sirius lapped up the salty tears. Then he stopped abruptly as if he had heard something. He growled and started sniffing the air.

It's okay boy, stay here, it's okay, I said. But Sirius responded to his ancestral instincts, not to my words. He barked and scampered about, trying to find whatever it was he heard or smelled. Come back, Sirius, I yelled. But it was hopeless; his bark became fainter and fainter until he disappeared into the night.

I curled into a ball and cried myself to what I thought was sleep.

I dreamed I was floating in a peaceful ocean under beautiful blue skies . . . you know the rest of this dream. But this time, when the sea turned angry, it turned very angry: The sky was roiling, lightning flashed constantly, the waves surged higher than ever before, and I flailed about, helpless. I was exhausted, unable to tread water any longer, when a boat appeared.

A man was rowing toward me, and he, too, was struggling with the waves. He looked to be maybe thirty years old and from the way he was fighting the waves, he seemed strong, though his body was slight. His hair blew wildly in the strong wind and his ears, like mine, poked out. I recognized him from the photo my mother had shown me.

Just as I was about to surrender to the sea, the boat finally came within reach; my father leaned over and extended his hand. I extended my hand, expecting him to pull me on board, but he didn't: He just touched my fingertips, ever so lightly. And for that brief second that we touched, we were one person, one organism, one unit of energy in the universe.

For that brief second, I didn't feel alone, or scared, or sad, or in danger. But I still wanted him to pull me aboard. I wanted to be with him, to sail away with him. Help me, I said.

He smiled and said, I already am helping you.

But he wasn't pulling me out of the water. His boat began to drift away, and I struggled to maintain contact with his fingers, but a large wave lifted the boat up and we separated.

No! Don't go! Come back, Dad! Come back! I yelled.

But he was drifting away, not even trying to row back in my direction. He smiled at me lovingly. I saw a knife sticking out of his back; his shirt was stained red. I screamed. Not words, just a scream, a horror-film kind of scream, a primal scream.

It did no good. My father floated away. But the sea calmed. The sky cleared to blue again, and the water once again was holding me up. I felt brave and I cautiously stuck my head under water, and then pulled it right out. I tried again, and this time I dared to open my eyes under water.

I saw schools of silver fish swimming and a family of manta rays, gliding with the current. The water was blue and clear, and it took me a moment before I realized that I was swimming under water, effortlessly. I looked up toward the surface and saw the sun, jiggling and dancing as its light hit the water's surface.

I looked down and my body was gone. It had been absorbed into the ocean. I was just a thought. But this didn't scare me. It felt wonderful: for I now was the ocean, infinite and vast and deep and powerful. I was everywhere at once. I was the ocean's thought. I started to laugh with joy, but as I had no body, it really was more just the thought of a laugh.

I awoke slowly and reluctantly. I wanted to stay in that dream forever, to remain an infinite, joyful, laughing thought of something large as an ocean. But alas, I was back in my body. I leaned against the fencing and looked up at the night sky. I found the Pleiades and as usual I looked out of the corner of my eye, and as usual I thought of my mom.

The star cluster began to grow brighter, so that soon I could look straight at it. Then the seven stars began to throb and pulsate. They grew bigger and bigger until they took up my whole field of vision; it was as if I were in a spaceship rapidly approaching the Pleiades. I had never seen them before so closely or so clearly.

Oh my God, I thought, the Pleiades are going to supernova. All seven stars are going to explode into huge celestial fireballs. The Pleiades will cease to exist, and I am flying right through the middle of them and will be consumed.

I covered my eyes with my hands, but the Pleaides were still there. I lay on my stomach and buried my head in my arms, hoping to make the pulsating Pleiades go away. Slowly, they did. The screen in my head went blank, but I dared not move.

I heard the sound of a wailing woman, faintly at first, but then her cries grew louder and louder. I was horrified at the depth of her sadness.

I opened my eyes: It was my mother: I could see her now, on the roof in the ashes where the fire had burned out. She was kneeling over a man's lifeless body and his shirt was wet with her tears. Beneath the man was a pool of bright red blood.

Mommy? Mommy? I heard a child's voice calling. Mommy, where are you?

A little boy, perhaps seven or eight years old, edged toward my mother, hesitant. He was frightened by the sight and sound of her despair.

Mommy, I need you, he said, but she didn't respond. She had buried her head in the dead man's chest and was heaving convulsively. The boy reached out his hand as if he wanted to touch his mother, but then thought better of it. He looked down at the blood, leaned over and dipped his finger in the puddle. He raised his hand and studied the red stain on his fingertip. Mommy? he said one last time, but she didn't respond.

The little boy turned slowly and looked me in the eyes. It was Charlie Bruno, a boy I used to know. A boy I used to hate. A boy I used to be.

He started walking toward me, his eyes locked on mine, steady and determined. He was holding up his bloody finger. My mom sobbed in the background.

Stop! Go away! I said.

But he kept walking, coming closer and closer until our noses touched. He kept going until our faces merged together, our eyeballs squished together. I opened my mouth to yell but he opened his at the same instant, and our mouths fused together. And then he was gone, or inside of me, or maybe I was inside of him.

I jumped up to run away, to flee from that boy, from Charlie Bruno.

But I was on the roof and there was nowhere to run. But, no, I thought, there is somewhere to run: I can run straight ahead and leap off, soar into the sky for a few blissful weightless seconds, then let gravity do its thing and bring an end to this unhappy biological organism. But what if my disembodied mind lived on, I worried, unable to shut itself off? Floating for an eternity above that apartment building in Venice?

I saw a hint of light in the eastern sky, so it must have been approaching dawn. A crow was perched on the edge of the roof. It ruffled its feathers then flapped its wings, took a few steps, lifted off, and flew east toward the glow on the horizon. I watched until it disappeared.

The sky was brightening but Venus and a few stars still were visible. I felt a warm, enveloping sadness. I missed my father, although I had never met him. I wanted to talk to him, to know him, but he had drifted away in his little boat, in his blood-stained shirt.

I walked to the very edge of the roof, as Ben had done one night and, like Ben, my toes hung just over the edge. I wasn't scared.

The sky was brightening by the minute. A few birds, welcoming the new day, flew overhead. I saw the first orange sliver of sun edge above the mountains east of Los Angeles. As it rose, I started to feel its warmth on my face and hands. I wanted to feel it all over me, unfiltered, so I slipped off my shorts and stood naked on the roof edge.

I watched the sun until it became too bright to look at directly, then I closed my eyes and extended my arms to the sky like the branches of a tree. I felt the sun's warmth on my fingertips, down my arms, and all over my body. I felt its radiant light and reflected it back into the world.

I stood motionless until it became so warm, I started to sweat, the little beads rolling down my chest and tickling my stomach. I put my shorts on and went back downstairs, quietly crawled into bed next to Jennifer, and immediately fell fast asleep.

A knock on the door woke me up.

It's seven o'clock, time for school, wake up, Renata said through the door. Do you by any chance know where Jennifer might be? she added.

You can come in, I said, and pulled the covers over Jennifer's naked body.

Renata opened the door. Yeah, this is where I thought I might find her, she said.

I need to tell you what's going on, Renata. We need to talk.

I think I'm old enough to figure out what's going on . . .

No, not this. I mean what's going on with me, I said. I started to sob.

Renata's demeanor changed and she suddenly looked concerned. Shall we call in sick? she said.

Oh, God, yes, please, I said, and Renata backed out of the room and closed the door.

I was pretty sure what had happened on the roof had been a dream, but not my dream. It felt like I was being dreamt. That's the only way I could describe it.

When Jennifer woke up, the first thing she said was, Where were you in the middle of the night? I woke up around four o'clock and you were gone.

I looked at the bottoms of my feet; they were covered in soot, as if from a fire.

I guess I was on the roof, I said.

Shit, Moon, you can't get stoned every time you're stressed out.

I didn't, I said. I wasn't stoned. I swear. I don't know what I was, Jen. I think I was insane up there. But I feel better now.

I hugged her tightly. We fell back asleep, and woke up at noon.

A letter from Ben arrived that day. He'd identified a national forest in Idaho that bordered Canada. He and two other draft dodgers were going to try and cross there under cover of darkness, hitchhike to Boise, and catch a bus to California. He asked me not to tell Renata until he had made it safely to Ojai.

Ben was coming home—unless he got apprehended on the way and thrown in jail—and Jennifer and I would join him on the commune. Then Ben and I would go to Iowa and confront that black hole in his life, so it wouldn't be able to suck the light out of him anymore.

Renata's Hodgkin's was in remission, and Shirley's new crusade was to keep me out of Vietnam. Or whatever goddamned imperialistic war we're going to be in when you turn eighteen, she said.

Of course, Moon Morrison was not a real person, and Charlie

Bruno had disappeared at age thirteen, so I had inadvertently come up with the best way yet to avoid the draft.

I didn't point this out to Shirley, and I appreciated her concern for me. I remembered how at first Shirley didn't want Renata to take me in. She must have thought I was damaged goods—which I was—but now she was fighting to make sure I wasn't taken away and sent off to war.

You've been through enough wars in your life, she said to me. I'll torch the damn induction office myself if they come after you.

If love is action . . . well, Shirley was nothing if not action.

And Jennifer, the first girl who didn't think I was boring, ugly, and stupid, the girl who loved me despite the fact that I was, literally, a lying bastard—was the girl who relieved me of my virginity.

What an odd assemblage of misfits: Two lesbians, a draft dodger, a girl fleeing her torment, and me, a runaway with identity issues. This was my personal five-star constellation in the night sky, my Pleiades. They were the people I loved. The family I chose and who chose me. Maybe they were also my sun.

But I was entangled with another assemblage of misfits: A deceased adventurer father whose dying wish was to be with me, a broken-hearted alcoholic mother who had conceived me in love, a half-brother who carried me in from the cold the night Sirius died, who was killed in a jungle in Vietnam at age nineteen. And that kid named Charlie I had tried to kill off, but who had somehow refused to die.

These stars weren't beautifully aligned in a constellation; they were scattered haphazardly across the night sky, emanating only the weakest of starlight. My family?

I still could erase them once and for all from my life, I thought.

My mom didn't know how or where to find me—other than that I lived in greater Los Angeles, along with seven million other people.

I could try again to kill off Charlie. But his resurrection had allowed me to learn who my real father was. And I wasn't confident that I ever could kill off Charlie for good. He wanted to know more about his father and only his mother could tell him that. He likely would keep pestering me.

I was straddling another fault line: On one side was Moon, on the other was Charlie. That alone would have been a stark and simple choice, one I already had made two years before. But here was the dilemma: Moon and Charlie shared the same heart and the same mind, and if Moon kept trying to expel Charlie from the heart and mind they shared, Charlie would sulk and throw old memories at Moon.

And Charlie had new information at his disposal: Information that made him stronger and more confident, for he now knew that he was conceived in love, that he'd had a father who'd wanted to be with him, and a crazy mother who cherished him. Moon didn't have either of those things. Deep down, Moon knew he'd been created by Charlie, or really by the empty shell that Charlie had thought he was.

Moon wouldn't be able to monopolize heart and mind. He would have to share with Charlie. What do you do when two people share the same heart and mind? I suppose that can work only if those two people learn to love each other and to remember that if a man hadn't been murdered in Mexico, they could have been one person all along.

But there was a third character, too.

Me, the one who thought about all this stuff, the one who looked at the reflection in the mirror, the one who briefly, blissfully, was a disembodied nameless thought in the middle of the infinite ocean, the one who would have to make a decision on behalf of Moon and Charlie.

If an earthquake had occurred along this fault line, its epicenter would have been the Motor Hotel on Century Boulevard. That's where I was as Moon and Charlie tussled inside my head and a steady rain fell on top of it. I stood outside for a long time, until I was thoroughly soaked and my long, wet hair was plastered to my face. People walking past with umbrellas looked quizzically at the teenage boy who apparently didn't have enough sense to get in out of the rain.

I climbed the stairs to the second floor and squished down the corridor to Room 206. I knew my mom still would be there, that she would not have left.

On this side of the door was Moon's constellation of stars, a constellation of love. On the other side was Charlie's constellation, a cluster mostly of hurt and sorrow and loss—but a loss that had once held love.

I didn't know what would happen if I knocked on that door, what cycle of action and reaction it would trigger, or what unforeseen consequences would result, or what dangers lay in ambush. I wanted someone to tell me what to do, but the decision was mine alone.

Moon and Charlie had stopped their fight in my head and were waiting for me to act. I placed my hand against the door. It was cold and uncaring. It offered no answers. I still could flee. If there was anything that I was good at, it was fleeing.

I could turn around and never look back. I could choose to be Moon forever, and damn Charlie to hell. I looked at the red Exit sign at the end of the corridor, a sign that teased me with promises of an escape from memories, from sorrow, from the past. It lured me like a siren, but I no longer trusted its promise.

I closed my eyes and held my hand against that door for an eternal moment, a moment frozen forever in time. And then I knocked.

NOW

Celeste showed up on a scorching summer day. I was pruning the lemon tree next to the house, and was about to go inside to get out of the hundred-degree heat, when she drove up in a dusty little red car with Arizona plates. Carla and I didn't get many visitors and didn't know anyone in Arizona, so I wiped my brow and prepared to give the lost driver directions to town or wherever she was going.

She got out of the car and stood next to it, looking around, taking in the scene. She locked the car door, not something someone asking for directions would do, and walked slowly toward me.

She was petite and had thick dark hair with gray streaks. She looked to be in her mid-forties. She wore tight jeans, a denim jacket over a white top—far too hot for a jacket, I thought—sunglasses and cowboy boots. They were stylish boots, not ones a real cowboy would wear.

I waited for her to approach. Can I help you? I said.

She stopped about five feet in front of me. You look like your picture, she said. An older version, but recognizable.

She took off her jacket and folded it over her arm. I looked at her closely, but nothing sparked.

Do I know you? I said.

You did, briefly, she said. You even held me briefly—or that's what Jennifer said. But it's been a long time. Forty-nine years.

223

You'd think there would be a trial period with sex, so your first time doesn't count towards reproduction. Like the exhibition games that professional sports teams play before the real season starts. You should get a few freebies to work out the kinks, learn your moves, get the rhythm down, and figure out the starting lineup without worrying about getting pregnant. But it doesn't work that way.

Celeste was conceived in Ben's bed in Renata's apartment, that night before I went up to the roof and experienced my . . . I still don't know what to call them: Visions? Hallucinations? Journeys to the other side, as Federico called them? Or psychotic breaks, as my psychiatrists labeled them? They then would write me the appropriate prescriptions, which I sampled a few times but never ingested with therapeutic consistency. I flushed more down the toilet than I ever swallowed.

Maybe it's no surprise that Jennifer and I scored bingo the first time we did it: I was on the edge that night—the edge of sanity, the edge of the roof, the edge of life—and maybe my body sensed that if I was going to procreate in this lifetime, it had better be right away, even if I was only fifteen. Those sperm cells believed they were on a serious mission to preserve my lineage, for what it was worth.

Jennifer's pregnancy was nine months of anguish followed by heartbreak. Her mother disowned her, which was a good thing because it meant she could still live with Renata and me. Her father disowned her, which was a good thing because it meant she didn't have to see him anymore. But those were the only good things.

She dropped out of school. She wanted to have the baby and she wanted us to get married. She wanted to move away from Los Angeles to start a new life—that part sounded familiar to me. She was sick throughout and had to spend the last six weeks on full bed rest.

I was on tremulous ground. Soon after learning I was fatherless, I learned I was going to be a father—an idea I couldn't get my head around until I actually held that crying, writhing, pinkish, barely-human-looking baby and realized that, other than sketchbooks filled with drawings, she was the only thing I ever had created. But I knew that being raised by two teenagers—especially us particular two teenagers—would virtually guarantee that baby a life of misery and despair.

I knew the only meaningful thing I ever had created would have to be handed over to other people to care for, to love, to nurture. My tears fell on her little pink face and mixed with hers.

Jennifer furiously resisted giving our baby up for adoption, but really had no choice. She and I were not married, she was a minor, she had no support, having been disowned by both her parents. Of Jennifer's three wishes—to keep her baby, to marry me, and to leave Los Angeles—only the last one came true.

I begged her to stay with me and told her that I wanted to marry her one day—and that's how I felt—but she stormed out of Renata's apartment, angry and resentful, one chilly February morning in 1971.

I sunk into a guilt-wracked depression, made deeper by the fact that I actually had held my child and looked into her eyes. Two months later, Jennifer sent Renata a postcard from Eugene, Oregon. That was the last I knew of Jennifer's whereabouts, until Celeste materialized on that hot summer day in a dusty red car and cowboy boots, and told me how she'd tracked down her birth mother and met her in a coffee shop in Denver.

Jennifer is surviving, Celeste answered when I asked about her mother. She's had more downs than ups in life, but she seems at peace. I really don't want to say more.

Jennifer told Celeste that she assumed I still was in California, and gave her my name, or at least the last of my names that she knew, but it proved enough information for Celeste to track me down with some creative sleuthing.

When I'd turned eighteen, I legally changed my name to Charles Moon Abrams-Anderson. I had reconciled with my being Charlie at that point, even more so after my mom told me I'd been named after Simon's grandfather—who had anglicized Chaim, my Jewish heritage. She assured me that Larry Bruno had nothing to do with my naming.

Abrams was my father's last name, Anderson was Renata's name, so voila: The final version of me, the one I have kept ever since.

My postpartum, post-Jennifer depression came close to pushing me over the edge again, closer than I ever had been. Several times I stood on the roof, swaying as I looked down, ultimately saved by cowardice.

Cowardice and one other thing: The prospect of Ben's return. He waited until early summer of 1971 to cross the border, to reduce his chances of freezing to death in the Idaho wilderness. For nearly two weeks he was *incommunicado*, which was good if it meant he had not been caught and arrested, but bad if it meant he had been eaten by bears.

I lived in a state of simmering anxiety until he called from his new safe house, near Ojai. Ben and I had kept Renata in the dark about his plans to protect her sanity and health, and when she heard his voice she was so happy she grabbed me and her keys and ran to the car still in her house slippers. Two hours and one speeding ticket later, our patchwork little family was together again.

Ben had to lay low and avoid contact with authorities of any type. He worked odd jobs, mastered the guitar, and ventured down to Venice now and then to see those among his old friends who he trusted. But it was too risky for him to come to the apartment, so we couldn't renew our nightly visits to our sacred roof space.

He and I spent a lot of time together after I finished high school—well, after I passed my GED, which I did in what would have been my junior year, so I could be paroled early from the educational system. We worked together for a landscaping company in Ojai—mowing lawns, digging French drains, trimming trees and hedges, laying sod, all of which we did stoned and happy.

Ben and I were by her side when Renata died in 1972 after her sleeping cancer awoke, angry and aggressive. It was the first loss of my life that I was able to fully share with another person, and Ben and I became one in our grief.

Two months later we drove to a modest Des Moines suburb to confront Ben's father. I was scared. Not scared of the pending confrontation, but scared over Ben's state of mind. He had just buried his mother and now was going to confront the father he had never known, the black hole in his heart. Those were two powerful emotional supernovas in a short span of time.

We parked across the street from his father's house, a midwestern rambler with a nicely manicured front lawn that draft dodgers might have mowed and an American flag proudly flying at the door. A teenage girl, perhaps sixteen or seventeen, came down the sidewalk with a gaggle of friends. They stood in front of the house talking and laughing, and then the friends parted and the girl—Ben's half-sister—went inside. About thirty minutes later, a car pulled into the driveway. A woman and teenage boy—Ben's half-brother—got out, each cradling a grocery bag.

It was all so perfect, a scene replicated millions of times every day, a scene that everyone wants to believe is the norm. But it was never my norm, or Ben's norm.

A red Corvette pulled up to the curb as the sun sank. Ben's father—we had seen his picture among Renata's effects—climbed out; he was wearing a suit, carrying a briefcase, still in sunglasses despite the failing light. Unlike his son, he was chubby, most likely the result of a sedentary life and business lunches. He walked slowly into the house as if enjoying the last few minutes of personal time before family life took over.

I looked at Ben for guidance, but he sat motionless as it got darker.

Well, I finally said gently, are you ready?

No, he said after a few minutes. I'm not.

He started the car and turned on the headlights, but remained parked.

I'm going to the door with you, Ben. I'm here for you, like I promised.

Why should I fuck up his life? Ben said. For what purpose? It's done, Moon. The damage is done. And I can't undo it. I can only cause more damage to more people. I'm not part of his story and never will be. He doesn't want me to be part of it. I can't force myself into it. This was a fucked-up idea. What was I thinking? What did I think it would change?

We sat in the car for another hour, engine running. Ben never took his eyes off the house. Lights came on indoors, and we could see figures moving about, probably getting ready for dinner, until we saw Ben's father close the curtains. Then Ben slowly drove off.

It took us eight days to get back to California. Ben meandered aimlessly but generally westward, taking state roads and county roads through small towns in Wyoming and Montana and Idaho. I never questioned his route; it obviously was what he needed to do.

We stayed in dumpy little motels with gravel parking lots and grizzled front desk clerks. There were long stretches of silence—comfortable silence, the kind of silence two people can share only when they are sure of each other's love—and long nights talking in the dark and drinking the cheapest liquor we could find.

Ben was struggling to accept things about his past and about who he was. I was struggling with my certainty that Jennifer had been the only girl who ever would love me, and that my little baby girl now belonged to someone else. We struggled together and comforted each other together. That's all I'll say about those eight days.

Ben moved to San Francisco soon after we got back to California. He waited tables by night and wrote music by day, and before long was performing at several coffee houses in the Castro.

I lived in Ojai with Renata's old friends, now my new friends, working odd jobs and hitchhiking thirty miles several times a week to Santa Barbara City College for studio art classes—and to my own surprise, I actually earned an AA degree.

I made some casual friends but, as always, never felt a compelling need for a wide social circle. Dating never crossed my mind. Ben and I visited each other every few months and talked on the phone so much that long distance bills were my biggest monthly expense.

One night we were each so stoned, we both fell asleep and I awoke four hours later to hear Ben snoring on the other end of the line; that was a notably expensive call. We celebrated together in San Francisco when Jimmy Carter pardoned draft dodgers in 1977.

I last saw Ben several days before he died in 1982. He had been sounding exhausted and had a dry hacking cough for several weeks that grew worse every time we talked. He always said he was fine, just working too hard; he discouraged me from visiting. And then his roommate called one night and said I had better come to San Francisco right away.

No one really knew what the Gay Cancer was at that time, but the sense of terror in San Francisco was palpable. Ben was on oxygen and could speak only in a whisper. He was resigned, almost cavalier in the face of death. He was ready; maybe he was even happy it was over. After Ben slipped into a coma, I left. I couldn't bear the thought of seeing his lifeless body. I sobbed so hard on the bus on the way back that no one sat near me, and the driver pulled off the road to come back and ask if I needed assistance.

I got off at the bus depot in Santa Barbara and made my way to the ocean, sat in the sand where the waves could break over me, and contemplated the fact that millions of years ago, sea creatures had ventured onto dry land and, over the millennia, had evolved into us, into humans, and one of those creatures ultimately had evolved into Ben, and now that particular chain of life was over, and for the life of me I couldn't figure out what it all was about.

It got dark and cold and by morning I was hypothermic and unconscious. I remember little of the next week except, upon discharge from the hospital's wacko ward, I was well armed with pill bottles, all of which I tossed. I didn't want to chemically tame my grief or quiet all the voices. If my grief drove me to insanity, then that's where I wanted to be, where I needed to be. I hitched back to Ojai and into the caring arms of my latest family, some of whom had known Ben when he was a toddler, living with Renata on the commune. In their presence I was free to be insane.

I inherited about a dozen cassette tapes of Ben's music, songs he had written and played in coffee houses, always after auditioning them first with me when I would visit. I still play them from time to time, always on his birthday or whenever I miss the sound of his voice.

When my mother answered the door of Room 206 that morning, I knew that nothing ever would be the same again. But then nothing ever has been the same and never will be. That phrase—nothing will be the same again—is a self-evident truth not worthy of its status as a maxim.

I promised my mother I would stay in touch, but I refused to give her an address or telephone number where she could reach me. I still needed a barrier against my past, at least initially, so contact would be one-way, and on my terms. I wrote her letters without a return address and called her from pay phones. But, as my eighteenth birthday and legal adulthood approached, I allowed our contacts to be two-way.

She was an open book: I learned a lot about my father and how things had happened the way they did. She told me about her electroshock treatments—that's why she sometimes would disappear—and the heavy-duty medications she had been prescribed. I knew she wanted my understanding and even my forgiveness, yet she never put me on the spot by asking for it. She has it though.

She told me that my father had been murdered in the Mexican state of Jalisco, in a little town called Villa Guerrero, and she sent me the postcards he'd sent her from there in the months before his death. He wrote of his friendship with a Wixaritari Indian shaman named Federico, who clearly was a very important person in my father's life. It was after spending several nights camping in the mountains around the village, with Federico as his spiritual guide, that my father made the decision to go back to my mother and me, and start a new life in California.

He wrote that in the last postcard he sent my mother.

In 1983, I bought a plane ticket to Guadalajara, where I paid more money to rent a rattletrap old car than it probably would have cost to buy it, and headed to Villa Guerrero. I drove into town as night fell, and found a place to stay just off the plaza; it was dirt cheap and everything was covered with dust, but the clerk was friendly and there was a little open-air bar out front where old men sat sipping tequila.

I ordered a drink and tried to ask if anyone knew of a shaman named Federico. But my Spanish was virtually nonexistent, so all I could say was, Federico . . . shaman? *Usted* know him? He was *amigo* with *mi padre*?

They all shook their heads and a few chuckled. I feared that Federico might have died or moved away. But I was still glad I had come, so I could at least walk the streets where my father had spent his last days.

The next morning, after a fitful night spent swatting mosquitos and rolling around on dirty sheets made damp by my sweat, I went to the bar in search of coffee. An old man was sitting alone at a table. We nodded to each other. The bartender handed me a cup of strong lukewarm coffee and a corn tortilla. I sat down at a table on the sidewalk and watched the passersby. I planned to spend the day going door to door asking if anyone knew Federico the shaman.

You Simon's boy?

I hadn't noticed the old man rise, but he now was standing next to my table looking down at me through narrow moist eyes. He was brown and wrinkled with skin like leather. His white hair was tied in a ponytail. His jaw quivered slightly and there didn't appear to be a single tooth in his head.

Yes, I said. Yes, I am.

I am the one you seek, said Federico.

I stayed in Villa Guerrero for a week. Like many Wixaritari Indians, Federico had spent his early life in the desert to the west, the ancestral home of his people. He had moved from town to town, wherever work opportunities took him, and eventually settled in Villa Guerrero, but he never married. He lived in a small house that he shared with his grandniece, Carla, who'd attended college in Guadalajara and taught English in a local school; she served as our interpreter.

231

Federico insisted that I stay with him and Carla, which meant sleeping on the concrete floor in the small kitchen. We stayed up late into the night talking, and after Federico went to bed on a cot in the main room, Carla and I would drink tequila and smoke cigarettes and keep talking until dawn, just as Ben and I had done so often.

She was beautiful and funny and tender and smart. It was my first glimpse of happiness since Ben's death.

I took copious notes of what Federico said, as translated by Carla: Your father was always questioning, always exploring, he said. Sometimes he seemed deeply sad, and sometimes as joyful as a child, especially when he was learning something new or seeing the world in a new way. And he loved the ladies—he loved loving. We spent much time together talking, like father and son, and spent many nights together in the mountains.

He was growing, he was becoming a strong person on the inside. He was learning to listen to the world and to the spirits. I was with him when he learned about you. He cried when he held the photos your mother sent him. I remember how he gently rubbed your picture with his finger, like he was caressing you. At first, he didn't know what to do, and I didn't tell him what to do. I let him find his path.

Right before he died everything became clear in his mind: He wanted to be with you and your mother. He realized that his real journey in life was to be there for your life journey. He was ready.

I asked Federico about my father's death.

Simon was walking near the plaza late one night, Federico said. He loved to take walks at night, I don't think he ever slept. He heard a girl screaming from a side street. She was young, a teenager, maybe younger. She was being bothered by a bunch of drunks. Simon ran to her, and it led to a fight. He was outnumbered, but he did enough that the girl was able to get away. When she came back with her brothers, your father was lying in the street. I don't even know how many times he'd been stabbed. I think maybe one of those guys had a grudge with him, probably over a woman.

Tears rolled down Federico's craggy face as he recounted this.

I wondered what eight-year-old Charlie Bruno was doing at the very moment that his father was dying. Had I been outside, looking at the stars? Was I curled up in bed with Sirius? Was I sitting at the kitchen table drawing pictures for my mom? Did something deep inside me register that moment in a way I didn't even notice at the time? Did I feel a tinge of sadness or loss, or a chill running up my spine?

I couldn't have known it then, but my life was about to spiral downward because a man I never knew was murdered on a mean street in a Mexican town I'd never heard of.

And I never knew how close my life had come to being different: What if my father had not been walking that night in the plaza? What if he had come home and saved me and Mom instead of saving that girl? What if I had moved to California when I was eight with Mom and Simon, instead of when I was thirteen with nothing but a rucksack and a few dollars?

We would have lived on a farm; that was Simon's plan. And no kids would have bullied me, because my father was an adventurer who had been all over the world, and no one would dare bully the kid of an adventurer. Oh no, the other kids would be in awe of me and would come to the farm to hear my father's stories about Africa and India and Mexico. And who knows? Maybe I still would have met Ben and Renata and Jennifer. At least there's a remote chance we might have met. My life would have been beyond anything I ever dreamed possible.

I had experienced enough in life by then to no longer believe in a lost Eden or ethereal fantasies. My father liked the ladies, Federico said. Who knows how our little family of three would have worked out? Who knows what would have gone wrong? At least I would have known who I was.

And then Federico told me this: My people believe that spirits of the dead visit their loved ones again five years after their death. Simon died in 1963, and in 1968 I started to see him in my internal journeys, the ones I take alone in the mountains. I talked to his spirit in my dreams and in my daytime visions, when he would appear to me in the form of a *cuervo*. Simon's spirit was very concerned about you, Federico said. His spirit feared you would die before your life's journey even started, before you had lived fully in this temporary realm of existence. His spirit was trying to reach you, to help you, to save you.

I left home in 1968, five years after my father died.

I returned to Villa Guerrero the next year, was married to Carla by a village magistrate—Carla and I had written to each other weekly—and lived with her and Federico for about six months. Federico taught me many of the things he had taught my father, although he was too old and frail now to hike up into the mountains. He told me about *peyote* but he wouldn't let me try it—it's powerful, he said, it's not for getting high, as you *gringos* want to do with it. You have to be very prepared.

And Federico taught me this: In the Wixaritari religion, one of the most powerful deities is Father Sun.

I had run away to California to find my sun, my father.

One day, out of the blue, Federico said to me: Take Carla to America; she is a smart girl, she will have a better life there.

Carla didn't want to leave Federico alone, but she craved the chance to emigrate; and as much as I loved the scenery and the pace of life, I didn't speak Spanish well enough to do any kind of work. I did spend many days happily drawing the wild cacti and exploring the mountains and, for the first time in my life, not reading (because there were no books in English), not absorbing information but simply experiencing being alive.

Federico had another grandniece in a nearby hamlet who agreed to take him in, and he would even have his own room in her house. After a tearful farewell—Carla and I knew we never would see Federico again—I took Carla back home with me.

We eventually saved up enough to buy a piece of land just outside of Ojai, and then saved some more and put down a double-wide. We had twin boys in 1987—Simon and Ben—who now are well into their own life journeys. I was in awe of them the day they were born and remain so today. But I was a needlessly overprotective parent who wanted nothing bad to befall them, no unhappiness ever to cross their paths. What a stressful delusion that was. I was downright terrified as they approached age thirteen, but they navigated those teenage years well, thanks mostly to Carla.

I teach art and astronomy classes at local private schools and adult education centers, and Carla works for the town of Ojai. I sunk more money than I should have into a telescope, and spend many nights looking at the stars and planets from the little observatory I built, complete with a retractable roof. I am on my third and most powerful telescope now. It has a camera adapter, so I have branched into celestial photography and have even had local galleries show my work. I sent my mother a framed photo I took of the Pleiades, but I never explained to her what that star cluster represented to me. I now am trying to photograph as many of Saturn's dozens of moons, around fifty at last count, as my telescope can pick up. There's something about me and moons.

Several times every year, I drive down to Venice alone and walk for hours. It has changed so much; it no longer is the Slum by the Sea. As I walk, I brush up against ghosts, smell memories as they flit by, and hear echoes. I always end the day on the beach, waiting for the sun to set, watching the waves roll in and wash over my feet. I can feel the presence of thirteen-year-old me standing in the wet sand by my side, as if time warped and I am here now and he is here then, and we are both here together, and finally I can love him. It's so real, it's as if I can reach out to him and take him in my arms and comfort him and tell him it will all be okay. Venice Beach will make it all okay.

My psychotic breaks—let's go with that term—have subsided. They most likely were the result of stress, the psychiatrists told me. Unlike my psychiatrists, I never saw them as a problem. I actually miss them. I learned the most about myself and everything was most clear to me when outwardly I was most crazy.

And that man on the boat, my father, whose fingers I briefly touched in my psychotic break on the roof of Renata's apartment building— he appeared in later psychotic breaks and still appears in my dreams, always young, as if he were frozen in time, which I guess he was.

I never had the ocean dream again after that last time on the roof in Venice, the time when it ended with me merging into the vast ocean, blissful. I suppose the dream had served its purpose and retired.

Celeste had planned on a quick drop-in visit—she didn't know what to expect or how I would react to seeing her—but she stayed for three days, primarily because of Carla who is by nature a welcoming and nurturing soul. Carla and I always have grown much of our food, and she gets immense pleasure out of feeding people. For me, it's my soul she feeds. Carla is my antidote, my human EpiPen.

Celeste and I took long walks in the orchards and fields of the Ojai Valley with my dog, Leonard, named after Leonard Cohen, a mutt with maybe a dash of wolf thrown in for flavor. That's when I told her my story, all of it, and she told me hers, or at least the parts she wanted to share with me.

I learned that I had grandchildren and she learned that she had a grandmother in Ohio who was pushing ninety, whom I visited every year, and who had come to California annually after the twins were born, but now was too fragile to travel.

I told Celeste I had thought about her often over the years and periodically dreamed about those few minutes I had held her, which I had assumed were the only minutes we ever would have together. I told her that she had a better life for having been adopted, and she agreed. I saw lots of Jennifer in Celeste, mainly her attitude.

We took a rest on our last walk and sat in an arroyo filled with wildflowers. Leonard lapped up water out of my cupped hands. When he was done, I wiped my hands on my pants, took Celeste's hand in both of mine and told her she had been conceived in the deepest of love on the most vital night of my life, a night when the air was filled with spirits and ghosts, when magical things were happening, the most magical of which was her creation.

May I give you a hug? Celeste asked a few hours later as she prepared to get in her car and drive back to Arizona.

You don't have to ask permission for that, I said, and we embraced. You've grown a tad since I last held you, I said.

She laughed and patted my back.

I know that I will see her again.

Acknowledgments

N O CREATION IS THE WORK of just one person. If I were to thank everyone in my life who has shaped my mind, my soul, and my writing, these acknowledgments would be longer than the book. So, I will limit myself to thanking, in alphabetical order, those whose influence was most direct and most pronounced, and whose support was unwavering (they deserve undying gratitude for their help, but no blame for my inadequacies): Sebastian Barajas, for his honest, heartfelt plot critiques; Wendy Mills, who supported my work, lifted my spirits, and offered sharp editorial suggestions; Kevin Popp, who helped me explore the interiority of things; and Carole Sargent, who believed in this book from the get-go and never failed to encourage me.

The late Robert J. Stegner, my writing teacher when I was a fifteen-year-old high school student in Alabama, first taught me the power of words when written clearly and well. He was the only formal writing instructor I ever had, and I still critique my writing through his eyes.

The authors who have influenced me are too many to name, but Padgett Powell's wonderful *Edisto* showed me the rich potential of a coming-of-age story if you treat your young protagonists seriously and allow them to express their conflicted inner voices.

Stephen McArthur and Rickey Gard Diamond, co-publishers of Rootstock Publishing, were willing to sign an author who was debuting well beyond his youth. Rickey also skillfully edited the manuscript, and Rootstock's entire team, especially Samantha Kolber, guided *Venice Beach* to publication with professionalism.

Finally, neither this book nor anything else good in my life would be possible without the support and love of my wife, Wendy Mills, and our son, Noah Habeeb. Wendy has always been an empathic sounding board, editor, and adviser, and—as Moon says about Carla—my antidote to the things that pull me down. As I was writing this book (an eleven year-long process) Noah was himself transitioning from youth to man, honing his fierce intelligence and broadening his horizons while retaining his zany sense of humor. Together, they form the planet around which I orbit.

Book Group Discussion Questions

- Read the epigraph at the front of the book. Why do you believe the author selected this passage? How does it reflect the theme of the book?

- Moon describes his former self, Charlie, as if he were a completely different person. And yet, Moon and Charlie inhabit the same body and share the same mind. Have you ever thought about a past incarnation of yourself as a different person? How do we reconcile with our past selves–especially if we did not like them? How did Moon/Charlie succeed in reconciling?

- Would you say that Moon is "confused" about his sexuality, or simply accepting of whatever sexual feelings he has? Why do you think he is relatively non-judgmental about homosexuality, despite the fact that at the time the book takes place (1968-1970) being gay was socially unacceptable (if not illegal)?

- Objects in the material world can often be "characters" in a novel. How would you describe the role of the following objects in the storyline of *Venice Beach*: The moon; the ocean; the Mariana Trench and its inhabitants; the rooftop of Allison's apartment building; marijuana.

- Why does Moon's late friend Jimmy Hollingsworth–or rather, Moon's memory and images of him–appear at several critical points in the book? What does Jimmy symbolize to Moon? Why does Moon seem to feel guilt over Jimmy's death by suicide?

- Moon has a recurring dream about the ocean that transforms as the story progresses. What do you believe is the changing meaning of this dream?

- At certain critical moments in the story, Moon sees a crow. Coincidence, or significant?

- Moon faced several pivotal moments in his coming-of-age journey: deciding to leave home; deciding to flee the shelter instead of being fostered; choosing to make the pot delivery to Ben; returning to the motor hotel to see his mother again. Why do you believe he made the decisions he did in these situations? How might his life have been different had he chosen differently in any of these situations?

- At the end of the story–in the "Now" epilogue section–Moon says that he never saw things so clearly as when he outwardly was insane. What do you think of this observation? Can emotional episodes that are labeled "mental illness" in fact offer valuable insights?

- Speaking of the "Now" section, how do you believe Moon's life has turned out? Did Venice Beach "make everything okay," as he says to his 13-year-old self while standing on the beach?

About the Author

WILLIAM MARK HABEEB WAS BORN and raised in Alabama, the son of a Lebanese immigrant father and a Cuban-American mother. He earned degrees in international relations at Georgetown and Johns Hopkins Universities, read literature and philosophy at the University of Sussex and studied psychoanalytic theory with the Washington Center for Psychoanalysis. He teaches in Georgetown University's School of Foreign Service and lives in Virginia. He is a member of the board of Virginia Humanities, the state's humanities council. Habeeb has published over a dozen non-fiction books for scholarly, general public and young adult audiences. His short fiction has appeared in the *Berkeley Fiction Review* and *Broken Pencil*. *Venice Beach* is his first novel.

Artist's Statement

VENICE BEACH 50 YEARS AGO—
A Postscript from the cover artist, Robert L. Huffstutter:

THERE IS SO MUCH MORE to say about the Venice Beach of 50 years ago than I can describe in words or designs. It was a little community by the sea where America began and ended. Today, it is a circus with concrete condos and freak shows. Sure, it is amusing, but the spirit died long ago when the clapboard cottages were killed by wrecking balls, when the people from another era began disappearing RIP. Yes, RIP, Venice by the sea of the 1960s.

—Robert L. Huffstutter, April 12, 2012

Also Available from Rootstock Publishing:

The Atomic Bomb on My Back
Taniguchi Sumiteru

Blue Desert
Celia Jeffries

*China in Another
Time: A Personal Story*
Claire Malcolm Lintilhac

An Everyday Cult
Gerette Buglion

*Fly with A Murder of Crows:
A Memoir*
Tuvia Feldman

The Inland Sea: A Mystery
Sam Clark

Junkyard at No Town
J.C. Myers

*The Language of Liberty:
A Citizen's Vocabulary*
Edwin C. Hagenstein

A Lawyer's Life to Live
Kimberly B. Cheney

Lifting Stones: Poems
Doug Stanfield

The Lost Grip: Poems
Eva Zimet

Lucy Dancer
Story and Illustrations by Eva Zimet

Nobody Hitchhikes Anymore
Ed Griffin-Nolan

*Preaching Happiness:
Creating a Just and Joyful World*
Ginny Sassaman

*Red Scare in the Green Mountains:
Vermont in the McCarthy Era
1946–1960*
Rick Winston

Safe as Lightning: Poems
Scudder H. Parker

Street of Storytellers
Doug Wilhelm

*Tales of Bialystok:
A Jewish Journey from
Czarist Russia to America*
Charles Zachariah Goldberg

*To the Man in the Red Suit:
Poems*
Christina Fulton

*Uncivil Liberties:
A Novel*
Bernie Lambek

The Violin Family
Melissa Perley;
Illustrated by Fiona Lee Maclean

Walking Home: Trail Stories
Celia Ryker

Wave of the Day: Collected Poems
Mary Elizabeth Winn

*Whole Worlds Could Pass Away:
Collected Stories*
Rickey Gard Diamond

*You Have a Hammer:
Building Grant Proposals for
Social Justice*
Barbara Floersch

CPSIA information can be obtained
at www.ICGtesting.com
Printed in the USA
BVHW081154110821
614085BV00007B/503

9 781578 690619